Charity   e

Once by a neighbor boy on a farm when she'd been sixteen.

The second time, she'd been twenty-three and the man had proposed marriage, making it clear to her that he was probably her last chance. She'd found the experience revolting and been happy to have her last chance pass by.

But she had never been kissed like this, as though she were something precious, as though there was time for it, as though it was something for her rather than something for the man who bestowed it. . . .

Jack lifted his head to draw in a desperate breath, aware of a fever in his blood running out of all proportion to that chaste little kiss. His mind and his body were already racing ahead to imagine the kiss prolonged and deepened and carried to an inevitable conclusion. At least he could stop saying no to himself. After one simple kiss he knew that was an answer he'd never accept.

Dear Reader,

This month brings another exciting first from Harlequin Historicals. A time-travel story. But *Across Time,* by author Nina Beaumont, is not an ordinary time-travel. It is the story of a young woman catapulted through time into the body of her ancestor, the evil Isabella di Montefiore. Don't miss this passionate tale of treachery and desire.

And just in time for the new year comes another daring love story from DeLoras Scott, *Spitfire.* When the headstrong daughter of a wealthy rancher runs away to find her *bandido* lover, gunslinger Lang Cooper is sent out to bring her back.

For those of you who enjoyed *Beloved Deceiver,* we have a new book from Laurie Grant, *The Raven and the Swan.* Awarded a former abbey for his loyalty to the Tudor crown, Miles Raven is shocked to find himself the protector of an innocent young orphan who seems determined to wreak havoc on his well-ordered life.

Readers of contemporary romance will surely recognize the name Muriel Jensen. In *Trust,* the author's first historical romance, the sparks fly between a woman with a notorious past and an ambitious businessman in turn-of-the-century Oregon.

Keep a lookout for next month's titles wherever Harlequin Historicals are sold.

Sincerely,

Tracy Farrell
Senior Editor

Please address questions and book requests to:
Reader Service
U.S.: P.O. Box 1325, Buffalo, NY 14269
Canadian: P.O. Box 1050, Niagara Falls, Ont. L2E 7G7

TRUST

MURIEL JENSEN

Harlequin Books

TORONTO • NEW YORK • LONDON
AMSTERDAM • PARIS • SYDNEY • HAMBURG
STOCKHOLM • ATHENS • TOKYO • MILAN
MADRID • WARSAW • BUDAPEST • AUCKLAND

ISBN 0-373-28806-9

TRUST

Copyright © 1994 by Muriel Jensen.

This edition published by arrangement with Harlequin Enterprises B. V.

® and TM are trademarks of the publisher. Trademarks indicated with
® are registered in the United States Patent and Trademark Office, the
Canadian Trade Marks Office and in other countries.

Printed in U.S.A.

Books by Muriel Jensen

Harlequin American Romance

MURIEL JENSEN

started writing in the sixth grade...and just never stopped. Marrying a journalist taught Muriel the art of discipline and the playful art of arguing whether it's easier to get the "who, when, where and why" in the first paragraph or to take 100,000 words in which to do it. Muriel lives in Astoria, Oregon, with her husband, two cats and a golden retriever. She also has three grown children.

In loving memory of Vera Gault, who knew all there was to know about old Astoria.

Chapter One

Astoria, Oregon—1900

So this was Swill Town. Charity Ross surveyed the waterfront teeming with loud, bawdy life and found that she was more fascinated than offended. An elegant carriage pulled by beautiful black horses rolled past between delivery wagons loaded with goods from nearby shops and factories. The sound they made on the wooden planks built over the Columbia River tidal flats competed with the music of a tinkling piano and loud laughter drifting out from the many saloons that shared space on this curious wharf. Drunks wove by her, some of them on the arms of painted ladies wearing silk and feathers. An occasional woman's scream, followed by high-pitched laughter, also came from the saloons, and Charity had to force herself to stay away from the doors for a closer look. She paused to shake her head in wonder. The strange surroundings made the prairies of Dawson, Kansas, where she grew up, seem as remote as the sands of Arabia.

She shouldn't be here. Respectable Astorians stayed away from Swill Town, according to the gentleman behind the desk at the Parker House, where she was staying. It was a hotbed of liquor, prostitution and political corruption that was an embarrassment to the entire state. Even the governor had called upon the citizens to clean up their waterfront. She thought with satisfaction that it seemed ideal for her purposes. A little seamstress's shop and anonymity were all she wanted out of life.

Charity followed a smaller utility dock that jutted out at a right angle into the river. There was nothing here but coiled ropes and sea gulls sitting on the pilings. Beyond, small boats with strange sails resembling bat's wings drifted against the backdrop of the tranquil green hills of Washington.

This was the western edge of Oregon, where the great Columbia River swept into the Pacific Ocean. She'd learned as a child in school that Lewis and Clark had explored an inland waterway to the ocean, and she now stood at the very place of their journey's end. Excitement swelled in her, and the worries that had plagued her all morning fled. What did it matter that she hadn't found permanent lodgings, or a shop she could afford in which to open her business? She was here! The rest would come if she was patient and logical.

How often had her mother said that? A brief stab of grief marred her excitement as she heard her mother's weary voice, "Patience, Charity. Patience. And *think* before you *do*."

Unfortunately, her impulsive, impatient nature often made it difficult for Charity to recall the advice in time. She was usually petticoat deep in some problem or other before it occurred to her that she should have listened to her mother. She used to shake her head over Charity's misadventures with the grim admonition, "You've some of your father in you, child. Try to remember, Charity, what it got him—and us.''

Charity drew a deep breath, swallowing the sadness. As of three months ago, there was no one left to admonish her. Her mother had died quietly of despair.

But now, there was no one to answer to or consult. Charity considered herself an independent woman and was comfortable with that status, at least for now. After a lifetime of social alienation, her mother's depression and the drudgery of supporting herself and her mother, the freedom was intoxicating.

''Hi!''

Charity turned at the sound of a childish voice, wondering where it could have come from. She saw no one.

''Down here!'' the voice called again.

Charity leaned cautiously over the edge of the railing to the stretch of sand below. It was low tide, and a small boy of eight or nine stood on a log amid a sandy carpet of flotsam and stranded fish. The stench was nauseating, but the boy was beautiful. He was small and sturdily built, with bright red hair and a broad smile. He hitched up his brown woolen pants as he waved at her.

''Hello!'' Charity called. ''Are you supposed to be down there?''

''No,'' he admitted candidly. ''I'm supposed to be going home, but I wanted to talk to my uncle Jack. He owns the box shop.'' He pointed to a factory on the wharf that ran parallel to the dock on which she stood. ''What's your name?''

''Charity,'' she replied. ''What's your name?''

''I'm Red Roughian, the peril of the seas! I'm sailing away on a pirate ship.''

The boy jumped off the log and assumed a fencing stance, as though he held off a boarding party with his cutlass.

Charity looked up the wharf, hoping someone would materialize to claim the child. She had to continue her search for a place to house her shop, but she hated to leave the boy alone. It was one thing for her to be fascinated by the life she saw in Swill Town, but it was another to leave a small child unattended in the middle of it.

"Will you show me where your uncle Jack is?" she asked.

He squinted at her, absently fending off an invisible enemy with creative hand and footwork. "Not now, my ship is in danger!"

Charity had a feeling his little bottom would be in danger if his mother knew where he was. Advancing on his invisible enemy, he disappeared under the wharf. Gathering her skirts about her, Charity started down the slimy ladder apparently used by the owners of the small boats that tied up there.

"If I help you repel the enemy," she asked, "will you show me where your uncle is?"

"Aye, matey!" the boy replied, dancing backward. "We've got to gut this black-hearted scum or they'll steal our booty and our women!"

Walking across the mucky sand toward the boy, Charity reflected that this would be just the type of incident over which her mother would have shaken her head. But she was charmed by the boy, intrigued with her surroundings and reluctant to leave him alone. And it had been far too long since she had played.

Charity aligned herself with him. "You may have the women, Captain Roughian," she said, aiming her parasol at an imaginary foe. "I claim a share of the booty."

"It will be yours for your loyalty, Charity," the boy said grandly. Then gesturing behind him as though he commanded a bloodthirsty army, he made a broad beckoning gesture. A sweep of his hand indicated the darkness under the wharf. "Drive them back to the caves!"

"Take that, you scurvy lot!" With a form more musketeer-like than that of a pirate, Charity lunged with her parasol, following Red Roughian into the rank underside of the wharf.

When the enemy roared back at them, Charity and the boy stood still. She had imagined that, Charity thought. Some conveyance had passed overhead and... The growl came again, a deep, angry bellow that raised gooseflesh on every inch of her body. She reached out for the boy's arm and stepped back, her heart beginning to pound.

"It's a bear, Charity," the boy said in a small voice.

"We're in town," Charity said reasonably, trying to dispel her fear as she continued to back away. "It can't be a bear."

"Uncle J-Jack," the boy stammered, "says—says bears come down here fishing when the tide's out. I thought he was kidding."

Uncle Jack had not been kidding. That became apparent to Charity as a large black bear stepped out of the darkness under the wharf. It was also obvious, judging by his continuous growls and his displeased attitude, that the fishing was not going well. His dark eyes gleamed angrily, and he bared pink gums and long, sharp incisors.

For an instant Charity felt as though every function in her body had stopped. She had no breath, no heartbeat, no coherent thought. Even terror seemed frozen in a mist of unreality. Then fear came to life, rippling up her spine, propelling her limbs and forcing her brain to work.

"Mother's going to be mad at me," the boy said feebly. He was fiercely holding Charity's hand.

Continuing to back away, she sent up a hasty prayer that he would survive to take his scolding. "Listen to me, Captain Roughian," Charity said as she began to push the boy slightly away from her toward the river. "I'm going to make the bear follow me, and I want you to get around him, get up the ladder and go for help."

"What if he eats you?" the boy asked practically.

Charity suppressed a hysterical temptation to laugh. "Then tell whoever comes to help that you're sorry you bothered them. Go on, now. Move very slowly."

The boy obeyed her orders with creditable calm. Noting the shift in movement, the bear growled low in his throat. Charity stepped on something and glanced down as she strove to regain her balance. A stranded salmon looked up at her accusingly. She reached down and tossed it at the bear. He batted it away with his paw. Beyond him, the boy scrambled up the ladder like a monkey.

Certain her mother was looking down from heaven and shaking her head, Charity tried to be logical. It was too late for her to resist impulse, but there had to be a way out of this. If she could only think!

She stumbled again, this time over a sturdy tree branch. A weapon! She picked it up and used it to shield herself.

"Listen, bear," she said, her voice quaking. "I believe in letting everyone and every*thing* do what it feels it must in life." She tried to swallow and found that she couldn't. "I'll let you fish if you'll let me get back up that ladder."

The bear growled and swiped in her direction with a gigantic clawed paw. His teeth clicked together in a sound that made her blood run cold.

"Well, I ask you to reconsider," she said, talking to maintain her sanity and control. The sound of her own voice reminded her that she wasn't dead yet. "Charity Butler is not to be trifled with." The fact that she remembered the false name she'd chosen to use in her new life gave her courage. She stopped and held her ground. "So just get on your way," she finished firmly.

Unaffected by her logic, the bear growled again and lumbered toward her, eating up the small space that separated them. Unable to hold back a scream, Charity closed her eyes tightly and swung.

Jack McCarren skidded to a halt at the edge of the wharf, unable to believe his eyes. In the middle of the flats, a woman dressed in yellow, complete with a strange little hat with a bird in it and a string bag dangling from her wrist, held a bear at bay with a length of branch and conversation.

"I'll let you fish," he heard her say, "if you'll let me get back up that ladder."

"My God!" Rolf Kauppi, who'd followed him out of his office when Jon had come in screaming for help, stared at the scene before them in disbelief.

Though Jack had run ahead, leaving Jon in his dust, he'd felt sure the child's description of a beautiful young woman at the mercy of a bear would turn out to be another of his imaginative exaggerations. It definitely was not.

Jack climbed nimbly down several rungs of the ladder, then leapt the remaining distance to the sand, spewing wood debris and dank seaweed as he landed in the small space between the woman and the bear. The bear growled and the woman screamed. Jack shouted at the bear and waved his arms.

As though it was a language it understood, the bear replied in precisely the same way, only more fiercely: it issued a deep, primitive growl from its powerful chest, opened its mouth wide enough to swallow a large dog and flailed a paw that could flatten a man with a single swipe.

Rolf landed beside Jack, also shouting loudly and waving his arms. The bear dropped to all fours and growled again.

Without looking away, Jack shouted to the woman, "Get out of here!"

She didn't move. After a moment's hesitation, she asked from right behind him, "Is he leaving?"

Unable to believe his ears, Jack exchanged a confused look with Rolf. They pushed the bear farther back with more shouts and windmill-like movements of their arms.

"I certainly hope so," Jack replied breathlessly, unwilling to look away from the bear. He moved between it and the ladder that led up to the wharf. "Go now!"

"Not until he's gone," the small voice said firmly. "I won't leave the two of you to be eaten."

The bear stopped to consider the stranded salmon, and Jack spun on the woman impatiently. His busy schedule today had not included fighting a bear or arguing with the woman he was trying to save from it.

"That's considerate," he said as he looked into stubborn brown eyes, "but eating you won't keep him busy for ten seconds before he lunches on us, so feel free to deprive him of his appetizer. Go now," he ordered, "or I will feed you to him to cover *our* retreat."

She gave one blink of long silky lashes that nearly hit the brim of her straw hat and picked up her skirts. She sidled to the ladder, and Jack kept pace with her, staying between her and the bear. The shiny black head turned to watch her, a low growl in its throat, then it turned back to the salmon.

"We'll help you, miss," someone called from atop the pier, and two pairs of arms reached down to pull her up the ladder. Jack saw that a crowd had appeared on the wharf to watch the action.

As he moved back to join Rolf, the bear made one more threatening move in their direction, then picked up his fish and turned away. He lumbered down the flats, moving parallel to the wharf, his coarse black coat, which covered the insulating fat collected over his winter's hibernation, rippling in the sunshine.

There were cheers and applause from the audience overhead.

Rolf put a hand to his heart and sagged against a pier piling. "God," he said breathlessly. "All I wanted to do was ask you if I could leave early this evening to check out the new chanteuse at the Riverboat. And here I am—" he looked about himself in wonder "—standing in the river screaming at a bear. I haven't had my beer yet, have I?"

Jack laughed thinly, catching his breath as he put an arm around Rolf's shoulder. "Come on." He led him toward the ladder. "You were very heroic. And it would be cruel of me to make you stay late tonight when you have such a story to tell the chanteuse."

Jacob and Enos Peterson, two of Jack's employees, reached down to haul Rolf and Jack up the ladder. "We followed you when we saw Jonny Donovan running after the two of you. Are you all right?"

"Yes." Jack looked around for Jon. "Where is he?"

"Here, Uncle Jack." Jonathan, freckles standing out on his beaming face, pulled the woman in yellow toward his uncle. "This is Charity. She helped me repel the scurvy sons of the Barbary brotherhood." His face sobered for a moment, then he added with obvious admiration, "And she was very good with the bear, too."

Jack looked from one to the other and asked sternly, "How did you happen to be down there?" Around them, the crowd began to disperse.

"I told you," Jon replied. "We were playing pirates."

Jack looked skeptically from the boy to the woman. "Both of you?" he asked.

Without the distraction of an angry bear, Jack was able to survey the young woman. He knew everyone in Astoria, but he'd never seen her before. He'd have remembered. She was average in height, slender and very pretty, though pale at the moment. The hem of her dress was soaked and sandy, and her hat was slightly askew. Her dignity, however, was very much in place.

Her brown eyes reflected momentary embarrassment, then looked at him evenly. "Both of us," she replied. "We had an agreement. Red Roughian got the women, and I got the booty."

Jack resisted being charmed. "And which of you got the bear?"

She put a protective arm around the boy's shoulders, apparently resenting Jack's suggestion that she'd been less than wise in encouraging the boy's play under the wharf. "We really hadn't time to discuss it, but I imagine we'd have placed his skin on the hearth in our island hideaway."

Jack folded his arms. "Considering the state of the bear's temper when I found you, you'd have had some trouble doing that."

Charity wasn't sure she liked Uncle Jack, though it was difficult to find fault with a man who'd just saved her life.

To give him his due, he was certainly handsome, with thick, rich black hair and eyes almost as dark. The lines of his face were strong and angular. Little surprise he considered himself an authority on just where a woman and a child should be.

She resented that. When she left Kansas, she'd resolved that no one would ever tell her where she could go or what she could do again.

He was coatless, she noticed, the sleeves of his white shirt rolled above his elbows. He'd apparently run right out of the factory at the boy's call for help.

She felt her stance soften despite herself.

She cleared her throat. "Yes, well. We almost had him talked into surrendering. Thank you, by the way." She squared her shoulders and nodded politely, letting her dignity slip just a little. "We appreciate your coming to our rescue." Her eyes moved to Rolf and she smiled. "And you. Thank you."

"My pleasure, Charity." Rolf bowed. "I have an unhealthy habit of following Jack into trouble."

Her smile widened. "I've an annoying attraction to it, myself. Well . . ." She tried to free her hand from Jon's clasp, but he held fast. "I'd best be on my way."

"Where?" Jack asked.

When a lift of her eyebrow suggested it was none of his concern, he explained patiently, "This is Swill Town. It isn't safe for ladies to wander around here on their own. You're new here?"

"Yes."

"Visiting?"

"No." She put a hand to her waist, a small frown pleating her brow as though she had a pain. "I moved her three days ago. I intend to settle. I'm looking for a shop to rent."

Rolf frowned. "In Swill Town?"

Charity looked at the unpretentious surroundings. "Everything downtown is too expensive. I might be able to afford a place here—something small where I can have my seamstress shop in the front and a room for myself in the back."

Rolf frowned and shook his head. "A Swill Town address won't be good at all for your business."

"Where is your family?" Jack asked.

"I'm here alone."

"You're alone on the wharf, or alone in Astoria?"

"I'm alone in life." Charity clarified the matter once and for all.

Jack looked over her pale face and small body and considered that a sad circumstance—not to mention a dangerous one. The Astoria waterfront was no place for a well-bred single lady, and he couldn't leave her there.

"Where are you staying?" he asked. "Jon and I will walk you back."

Charity heard the question, but she was suddenly having difficulty formulating an answer. Her nostrils were filled with the stench of the tidal flats, her stomach felt hollow because she'd eaten only one meal a day for the last few days to stretch her meager funds, and her mind was suddenly registering the fact that she'd stood toe-to-toe with a large, smelly black bear who'd seriously considered having her for lunch. She wished the man would stop asking her questions and let her return to her hotel room to lie down. Things were beginning to spin.

Jack watched her put a trembling hand to her forehead. "Are you ill?" he asked, reaching out to tilt her chin up.

She drew in an unsteady breath. "No, I . . . I . . ."

"She's going to faint," Rolf predicted.

Charity focused on him. "Nonsense," she denied, then promptly did just that.

Jack caught her and lifted her into his arms.

"I'll get the freight wagon," Rolf said over his shoulder, already loping along the wharf.

"What's the matter with her?" Jon asked worriedly, running to keep up with Jack as he carried his light burden.

"Just scared, probably," Jack replied.

"But she was very brave."

"Being brave doesn't mean you aren't scared."

"*I* was scared," Jon admitted. "Where are we gonna take her? She didn't tell us where she lives."

"We'll take her to your mother's." Rolf and a team of bays intercepted Jack at the corner of the street and the wharf. Jon leapt into the back of the carriage and helped his uncle support Charity. They propped her up against the seat and then, leaned her dead weight against Jack, who sat beside her. Jon climbed into the front beside Rolf.

"Where to?" Rolf asked. "Where do you suppose she's staying?"

"Take us to Letty's," Jack instructed. "She's been looking for a boarder for months now."

Rolf looked at him over his shoulder, his expression doubtful. "Letty's address won't be any better for her business than a Swill Town address. You know that."

Charity moaned in his arms and Jack removed her hat. He spared Rolf a glance. "Just drive, please."

Rolf muttered something under his breath, slapped the reins, and the big bays started up the hill to the rows of homes rising in degree of elegance as the grade steepened.

He wasn't getting involved, Jack told himself. She needed a place to stay and a friend, and he knew a woman who could fill both needs. That was all.

Charity moaned again, and he looked down at the pretty face propped against his shoulder. The cheeks were pale, the eyelashes long and dark, the lips pink and parted ever so slightly. His eyes stopped there, missing the firm little point of her chin. A complex tenderness coupled with simple lust fisted inside him.

No, he told himself firmly. He had plans, and they did not include a newly arrived seamstress, no matter how inviting her mouth or how dire her circumstances. His life was on schedule. He wanted to keep it that way.

Chapter Two

Charity opened her eyes to the sight of a gray brocade vest and the gold loops of a watch chain disappearing into a pocket. She felt something warm and solid under her cheek. Momentarily disoriented, she was aware of a sense of comfort and security that had been absent in her life for some time. She knew those feelings to be inappropriate to her circumstances, though she couldn't remember why. Then she was jounced as the wagon hit a hole, and she raised her head as she came fully awake. Ah, yes. The wharf. The bear. The man.

Familiar dark eyes looked into hers. She put a hand to her woozy head and said, before she could stop herself, "Uncle Jack."

He laughed, steadying her as she straightened on the seat. "You can just call me Jack. How do you feel?"

She frowned, trying to decide. "A little dizzy," she replied finally, "but all right. What happened?"

"You fainted."

"No," she denied, then, remembering that she'd awakened in his arms, she was forced to accept the truth. "I did, didn't I? I apologize for being a nuisance. First the bear, and now this." She sighed, and, finding her hat on the floor, dusted it off and placed it on her head. She located only one pin in it, but secured it as best she could. There, that was better.

"Mama's going to take care of you," Jon said, turning in his seat to smile at her.

"Oh, please," Charity said to Jack. "Don't inconvenience anyone. I'm fine. If you'll just take me to the Parker House, I—"

"Here we are," Rolf announced, pulling the team to a stop in front of the most beautiful house Charity had ever seen. It was white with red shutters, in the Queen Anne style that was going up all over the country, according to the paper she'd read on the train west. It had gables that looked out on a breathtaking view of the river and the unusual boats with their winglike sails. A deep porch wrapped all around, and wild roses grew on an arched trellis that appeared to lead into a garden.

"You live here?" she asked Jon in astonishment.

"Yes!" he replied proudly, leaping to the grass. He stood on tiptoe to tug on Charity's arm. "Come on."

"Slow down, Jon," Jack said, stepping over Charity to jump down beside the boy. "She might still be a little wobbly." He reached up to lift Charity down.

Charity leaned over to put her hands on his shoulders. The movement made her head spin, and she gasped in dismay as she felt herself falling. But strong hands braced her waist and a sturdy shoulder caught her weight.

When the action stopped, she had both arms around Jack's neck. He had her firmly around the waist, and one of his hands cupped her bottom and held her intimately against him. Her feet dangled clear of the ground. There was no breath in her lungs.

Jack's chin rested on a soft, round breast. Under one hand, he felt the stiffness of corset. Under the other was a delicious, warm softness... He lowered Charity to the ground instantly and took a step back, his usual control seriously upset. As Charity made a production of straightening her clothes, he collided with something and turned in surprise to look into Letitia Donovan's amused gray eyes.

"Well, Jack." She looked over his coatless, casual appearance, smiled interestedly at Charity, then frowned scoldingly at her son. "I presume this call has something to do with why Jonathan is over an hour late coming home?" She glanced at the man at the reins. "Hello, Rolf."

"Letitia." Rolf nodded.

"Well, Jon?" she demanded.

Jon inched behind Jack. "You tell her, Uncle Jack."

Letty tended to be volatile, and Jack wasn't sure how to tell her her pride and joy had just gone several rounds with a bear. He'd have to be at the top of his form to do that, and he wasn't quite himself at the moment. So he ignored the issue temporarily. "We'll get to that. Letty, this is a friend Jon met downtown. Letitia Donovan, may I present Charity, ah . . ."

"Charity Butler." She extended her hand. "I just arrived from Kansas a few days ago and Jonathan befriended me."

Charity looked into large gray eyes the same color as a stormy sky. They were placed in a beautiful, pink-cheeked face along with a small, straight nose and a smiling mouth. The features were framed by bright golden hair smoothed back into an intricate chignon. Charity liked the woman instantly. And she could see the concern in Letitia's eyes over how her son had met a strange woman, and how Jack had brought her home without even knowing her last name.

"Has your husband taken a job here?" Letitia asked.

Charity shook her head. "I'm not married. I've come alone. I want to open my own shop here."

Letitia raised an eyebrow. "That's very brave, or very foolish."

Charity shrugged. "The first twenty-five years of my life were very conventional and very unremarkable. I was looking for something else."

Letitia nodded slowly, apparently finding that easy to understand.

"She fainted!" Jon announced as though it had been a laudable accomplishment.

Letty studied her in concern. "My goodness. Are you all right?"

"Oh, fine, thank you," Charity assured her. "I've never fainted before. It must have been . . ." She stopped herself, catching Jack's cautioning eyes and remembering his careful avoidance of the incident on the flats. For Jon's sake, she sidestepped it, too. "I can't imagine what happened."

Jon, however, had no such finesse. "Uncle Jack thinks it's 'cause you were scared," Jon said.

"Scared?" Letty asked.

"'Cause of the b—"

Jack clamped a hand over Jon's mouth and smiled blandly at Letty. "May we come inside?"

Letitia looked suspiciously at the small group gathered on her front lawn, then picked up her skirts and turned to the house, replying doubtfully, "Of course. Kristine was just serving tea and Finnish biscuit."

Rolf leaned down and asked Jack quietly, "Want me to stay for moral support?"

Jack sighed. "What I'm going to need here is artillery support," he said wryly. "You go on back and make sure the cannery order gets out. I'll be back in time for you to leave early.''

As the strong bays pulled away, Jack turned to find Jon waiting for him and the two women chatting amiably as they went into the house.

''Mama's going to be mad,'' Jon said, taking Jack's hand.

''You fought a bear, Jonny,'' Jack said, towing him toward the house. ''Ladies get upset about things like that.''

Finnish biscuit, Charity discovered, was not a biscuit at all, but a braided sweet bread redolent of nutmeg and cardamom. Between the delicious bread and the intimidating elegance of glossy woodwork, sparkling chandeliers, colorful fabrics and blue carpet, Charity was completely distracted from the conversation. Until Letitia exclaimed, ''A bear? A bear!''

Letty, looking up in horror as Jack tried to relate calmly what had happened, poured tea onto Charity's plate rather than into her cup. ''Damnation!'' she cried, setting the pot down and trading Charity's plate with Jack's, as though certain he'd been somehow responsible and should be the one to suffer. Then she repeated, apparently still incredulous, ''A bear?''

''He was fishing like Uncle Jack said they do when the tide's out and the fish get stuck.'' Jon, trying to talk his way out of trouble, carried on without a breath, pausing only to pucker his lips and cross his eyes in a creditable imitation of a beached salmon. ''I was fighting pirates and Charity came down to help me, then the bear came out from under the pier and Charity told me to go up the ladder and get help, so I ran to get Uncle Jack, and he and Mr. Kauppi ran down with me and jumped off the pier to save Charity, only the bear didn't want to leave, so they—"

"I sent you," Letty interrupted quietly, "to Mrs. Fulton's house to tell her about the meeting on Friday. Mrs. Fulton's house is nowhere near the waterfront."

"Well . . ." Jonathan gravitated toward Jack's chair, knotting and unknotting his fingers. "I needed to see Uncle Jack."

"I didn't send you to see Uncle Jack," Letty said implacably. "I sent you to Mrs. Fulton's."

Jonathan sat on the arm of Jack's chair. "I went to Mrs. Fulton's and gave her the message. She said to tell you she'll bring apple cake to the meeting. Then I was gonna come home, but I saw one of Papa's ships leaving and I got . . . lonesome." The boy's voice changed in quality, and Charity saw both adults react to it.

Letty's mouth softened then saddened, and Jack put a hand on the boy's back, rubbing gently.

"When I get lonesome," the boy went on, shuffling a foot, "I go see Uncle Jack."

For a moment everyone was silent, then Letty said reasonably, "But you weren't at Uncle Jack's, you were playing on the flats. If Charity hadn't been there, and if Uncle Jack had been away from the factory, you . . . you might have . . ."

"The river attracted me, too," Charity said, trying to distract her hostess from consideration of what might have been. "I can see how it happened to Jon. It's so beautiful that you can't help but be drawn into all the wonder it suggests—like pirates and faraway places."

Letty sighed, apparently feeling her firm stand wilting.

"Perhaps if you apologize for worrying your mother," Jack said to Jon, "and promise not to go running off without telling her where you're going, she'll understand that you're sorry.''

Jon looked up at his mother with large, dark blue eyes. "I'm sorry, Mama. I promise.''

"Very well.'' Letty sighed gustily. "Take your biscuit and cocoa upstairs and tell Kristine to run you a bath. You smell like a fish. You're going to attract every hungry cat in the neighborhood.''

Looking much relieved, Jon hugged Jack, then crossed the room to hug his mother. She sent him on his way with a halfhearted swat.

The moment he was out of earshot, she looked at Jack with genuine concern. "That boy's going to be the death of me.''

Jack smiled, apparently not sharing her fears. "Because he's just like you. Headstrong and impulsive.''

Letty closed her eyes and shook her head. "What am I going to do with him?''

"Send for his father,'' Jack replied quietly.

She opened her eyes and leveled them on him, their expression rife with indignation. "His father knows where we are. He needs no one to send for him.''

"When a man is sent away,'' Jack said, "he's probably reluctant to come back uninvited.''

"I did not send Connor away.''

"You didn't try to stop him.''

Letty gave him one last disgusted look, then smiled apologetically at Charity. "I'm sorry. Old family linen. Jack and my husband grew up together. Jack always takes his side.'' She turned to Jack. "I think the only reason you're not upset about today's little incident, is that saving a woman and a child from a bear is bound to help your campaign.''

"Campaign?'' Charity asked.

"Jack's running for mayor," Letty said, spreading creamy butter on a slice of biscuit. She smiled at him. "He probably hired the bear."

Jack held a bite of bread, making a production of letting the tea drip off it. "Letty, you're lucky you married Connor and not me," he said. "I'd sooner drown you than leave you."

Unimpressed, Letty turned to Charity. "What's this about a shop?"

"I'm a good seamstress," Charity explained, palming her teacup. "I want to open a shop here if I can find a proper location."

"What would you need?"

"Two rooms," Charity replied. "They wouldn't have to be very large, just big enough for my sewing machine and several shelves and cupboards. I'd live in the other to keep costs down."

Letty turned to Jack with a fond smile, her acerbic manner toward him softening. "You've brought me the boarder I've been searching for, and here I've gone and maligned you."

Jack pretended hurt feelings. "Don't think about it. I'll just eat my soggy biscuit without complaint."

"Boarder?" Charity asked.

Letty turned to her, putting her teacup on the table. "I've had a lovely room to let for several months. It adjoins another room I use just to store Connor's things. I can easily find another place for those." She cast a dry glance at Jack.

Charity couldn't believe her ears. Then she glanced nervously at the mahogany furnishings, the fancy sideboard filled with crystal, the piano, and doubted that she could afford one room of such elegance, much less two.

"Letty, I appreciate the offer, but I'm afraid..."

Apparently reading her mind, Letitia waved away her objections and stood. "I'm sure we'll reach agreement. Come along. I'll show you."

Charity could not believe the rent Letty proposed. It was less than she'd expected to pay in Swill Town.

The room Letty had been trying to rent had a Hudson's Bay bed, a dresser and a marble-topped washbasin. In front of the window was a writing desk and an armchair rooker with a leather seat for reading or looking out over the garden. At the foot of the bed was a trunk with extra blankets.

The second room was wallpapered in stripes of pale pink roses. It contained an empty bookshelf she could use for supplies and a deep closet for safe storage of fabric and garments. It also had a private entrance that led onto the porch, then to a stone walk to the street. It was perfect. More than perfect.

"The bedroom is ready to move into," Letty said, "but this second room will need a little cleaning and decorating."

Charity tried to look firm. "Letty, it's far more comfortable and elegant than anything I'd hoped to find, but the rent you suggest is...is..."

"I'll lower it," Letty said hopefully.

"No, no!" Charity protested. "It's far too low already. What I mean is—"

"Listen to me." Letty pulled her down beside her on the edge of the bed and drew a deep breath. "I have to tell you something about myself."

"Letty..." Charity tried to ward off any confessions about which she could not care less. She liked Letty, and she had secrets in her own past she wouldn't share with anyone.

"No, let me speak," Letty insisted. "This might affect your business. I must be honest."

"Very well." Charity waited, expecting her to divulge some scandal in her past that had driven away her husband.

"I'm a suffragist," Letty said.

That declaration hung in the air between them as Letty paused for effect, then sighed heavily. "It's made me a social pariah. In this nest of old-world men, seafarers and loggers with inflated egos, it's worse than having the plague. I give rallies, distribute literature, hold fundraising events and generally make a nuisance of myself. It isn't that I want to force my beliefs on everyone, it's just that I think every opinion has a right to be heard. I won't force mine on you, but the struggle for women's rights is a part of my life and it'll probably disturb yours a little if you take the rooms. It drove my husband away."

There was none of the glibness she showed Jack when she talked about Connor, Charity noted, but a deep and real pain. Then she smiled, her elegant face softening. "Then, of course, there's Jonathan. He's nosy and not very quiet and he seems to like you. He'll probably pester you to death. So what do you think? You might not get any business when people discover your shop is in my home. I'm not very popular, except with the women in my Ladies for the Vote organization."

Naive prejudice existed everywhere, Charity knew. She'd been a victim of it herself. Though she was aware of the women's struggle for the right to vote, she'd been too busy trying to keep food on the table and a roof over her head to become involved.

All she wanted from her new start in Astoria was anonymity and a chance to prove that she was a skilled and creative seamstress. Prejudice often took a back seat when fine work and a fair price were involved. She felt sure fate was placing a golden opportunity in her hands.

"Oh, Letty, these rooms are precisely what I need," Charity said. "But my conscience won't let me pay so little."

"On the days when I have my meetings," Letty bargained, placing a hand over hers, "it would help if you could keep an eye on Jon. That would be worth far more to me than extra rent. If the ladies in Paris begin sending for you to design their dresses and you make so much money you have to stuff your corsets with it, then you can pay more."

Charity couldn't help but laugh at that image. "Then I'll take the rooms. Thank you."

Letty hugged her excitedly, took her hand and led her to the sitting room where Jack waited. "She's taking the rooms," she said as Jack looked up from the *Astorian Daily Budget* and got to his feet. "Can you have her things moved here?"

"Oh, no," Charity protested, looking from one to the other, then stopping on Jack's vaguely amused face. "I appreciate your help, but I'm sure you must be anxious to get back to your place of business. I'm sure I can hire a cab and find someone to help me transport my things."

"Jack will do it," Letty said confidently.

Charity looked at Jack in mute dismay, helpless against her hostess's determination.

Jack smiled wryly. "Letty has decreed that I help you," he said, "and it wouldn't be safe for me to do otherwise. Is everything in your room?"

Charity dug in her lace pouch for her room key and handed it to him, finding something curiously debauched in the gesture. "Yes. My own bags aren't very heavy, but my bolts of fabric and boxes of notions are awkward to handle, I'm afraid.'' She compounded the strange feeling by asking, ''Shouldn't I come and help you?''

She got a sudden mental image of the two of them in her hotel room and blushed. ''I mean, you . . . you won't know what to take.'' What was wrong with her?

''I'll manage,'' Jack said. He studied her high color and grinned. ''If I miss anything, it's a short trip back.''

''Thank you,'' Letty said, planting both hands on Jack's face and pulling him down to kiss his cheek. ''For not letting that bear eat my son.''

''I prevented the bear from eating Charity,'' he said, his grin widening as he winked at Charity over Letty's head. ''She's the one who saved your son.''

Jack wandered slowly down the hill toward the factory that had consumed all his energy for the past eight years. On his mind at the moment, however, was a dark-haired woman who'd held a bear off with a length of cedar, and who smelled of roses. And who blushed furiously when she handed him her hotel room key. He didn't want to think about her; he just didn't seem able to stop himself.

He'd been right in bringing her to Letty, of course. He'd made a promise to Connor that he'd watch over his family, send regular reports through the mail and stop to see him in Portland whenever he went upriver on business. He suspected Charity would be much-needed company for Letty.

Finding a place of business for Charity was a service to the community, a small boost to its economy. Injecting new life into Astoria's commerce was one of the points on his platform in the race for mayor.

So, in effect, helping Charity Butler had been a means of keeping his promise to Connor while upholding his promise to the community. Suddenly, he felt better about the whole thing. He wasn't falling for a woman. He was simply being a good friend and a reliable politician.

Letty smiled at Charity as they occupied opposite ends of the sofa and finished their tea. "Well, that's nice," Letty said softly, almost to herself. "That's very nice."

"What is?" Charity asked.

Letty considered her a moment, then put a hand over hers. "Why, having you here, of course."

Charity felt certain that hadn't been the source of Letty's enigmatic little smile, but her hostess went on, "I love being heroic for the cause. It suits my theatrical nature. But I hate being lonely." A frown appeared on Letty's brow. Charity suspected she was talking about loneliness on more than one level. Then she rubbed her forehead and looked up, smiling again. "We have Jack, of course, but I try very hard not to cling to him. He needs a life of his own—a family of his own."

Charity sipped her tea. "Things must be very different here. In Kansas, a handsome man of means is easy prey for eligible young women. A man like Jack wouldn't be single very long."

Letty smiled fondly. "Jack isn't prey for anyone. He thinks most young women frivolous, and he's so determined to make a secure place for himself in the community that he allows himself no time for frivolous things."

Charity frowned. "Every life needs a little frivolity."

Letty put her empty cup on the table and stood, taking Charity's hand. "I think you should tell him that. Come on. I'll introduce you to Kristine and Ming. Oh, it's going to be so nice to have another woman to have meals with and sit with in the garden on a sunny evening."

Charity was touched by her admission and more than willing to leave the old loneliness behind. "I've been very much alone since my mother died three months ago. I feel so lucky to have found you." She laughed. "Even if it did take a bear to do it."

Kristine was short and thickly built with a mass of glossy blond hair caught at the back of her head in a knot that defied its pins. Shiny tendrils fell around a plump face, which was porcelain white with two round spots of color on her broad cheeks. Her eyelashes were so blond they disappeared around her bright blue eyes.

She wiped dimpled floury hands on her apron as Letty stretched an arm around her and turned her to Charity. The woman's width made two of Letty's slender frame. "Charity, this is Kristine Rautio, the finest cook in all of Clatsop County." Kristine smiled shyly, but raised her chin as though convinced that what was said about her was true. "Kristine, this is our new boarder, Charity Butler. She's a seamstress, and she's going to open a shop in the east end of the house."

"Welcome, Miss Butler," Kristine said in a gentle singsong voice. Charity guessed her age at about thirty.

"Ming!" Letty called out as a shadow went past the kitchen's open door. "Come and meet Miss Butler."

The shadow came to the doorway and materialized. The young woman held a bottle and a rag that smelled of lemon oil.

Letty held an arm out to her, and she walked into it, barely reaching her employer's shoulder. She was tiny and fragile, her Chinese ancestry beautifully defined in a porcelain doll face. She kept her eyes down.

"Ming, this is Charity Butler," Letty said. "She's going to be living with us and opening a sewing shop. Charity, this is Ming. She keeps the house presentable."

Ming bowed deeply, gave her one quick smiling glance, then looked nervously at Kristine. Kristine nodded reassuringly, and Ming smiled again. They were friends, Charity decided, not just co-workers.

"I'm happy to meet both of you," Charity said. She felt very comfortable, suddenly, in this little bastion of women. "I'll try hard not to make any extra work for you." She smiled apologetically at Kristine. "Though I do like to eat. I'm afraid your Finnish biscuit has already spoiled me."

"Yes!" Kristine said with an emphatic nod. "Good. I love to cook."

"Ming, we'll need you to help us clean the storage room where I have Mr. Donovan's things. Mr. McCarren has gone back to the hotel for Miss Butler's bags. I'm sure he won't be more than an hour. We have a lot to do in the meantime."

Within an hour, Charity was feeling a certain sympathy for the gentleman whose possessions her presence had displaced. She'd helped Letty pack away her husband's stored clothes. They suggested a tall, large man. His cuff links and stickpins and other pieces of jewelry confirmed the wealth the house implied, and his books and fishing gear and a well-used banjo made Charity wish for the opportunity to meet him.

Letty, she noted, worked with a feverish speed as she folded everything into a trunk. Charity wondered if it was because Letty expected Jack to arrive at any moment, or because she found it hard to remain detached as she handled her husband's things.

Charity, wearing an apron to cover her traveling dress, pulled a pillowcase of miscellaneous things out of the bottom of a closet. She reached in and removed a bowl-shaped object on a stick. It was made of metal and appeared slightly larger than a teacup, but without the handle. She looked into it with a frown, then holding the stick, turned the cup in one hand.

"What is this?" she asked Letty.

Letty looked up from stuffing a pair of boots into the trunk. She looked both chagrined and amused as she brushed a wayward tendril of hair away with the back of her wrist.

"Something for which I should have demanded my money back," she said. She closed the trunk and sat on it, drawing a deep breath. "Whew! Let's stop for a minute. Ming. Ming!"

The young woman turned from waxing the now-empty bookcase. "Yes, Missy?"

"Stop. Sit down and rest." Letty pointed her to a chair. Ming looked at it uncertainly. Letty pointed again. "Sit. Sit."

Ming sat, her short legs sticking straight out in front of her. She appeared uncomfortable, as though not sure what to do when she wasn't working.

Letty patted the spot beside her on the trunk for Charity. She took the device from her and considered it with distaste.

"This," she explained, "was described in the Sears and Roebuck catalog as the Princess Developer."

Charity still didn't understand. "To develop what?"

Letty looked at her with mild impatience. "Does the shape suggest nothing to your imagination?"

Charity studied the open, globe-shaped device with its tapering tip and said finally, "Oh, my goodness. A bosom developer?"

"Exactly." With a dry glance at her two companions, Letty placed it over her right breast, much smaller than the enveloping bowl of the appliance, and admitted, "It didn't work."

Ming put a hand over her mouth to cover a giggle. Charity laughed aloud. "Letty, did you think it would?"

Letty nodded, studying the bowl on a stick as though still wondering why it hadn't. "I'm a trusting soul. The advertisement said that if I used it with the Princess Bust Food, a preparation developed by a French chemist that would feed the starved skin and wasted tissues with vegetable oils it would compel a free circulation of the blood through the flabby tissue and the...er...undeveloped parts would fill out and become...round."

They all broke out in laughter. Letty passed the device to Charity as though it was a scepter. "You may have it."

Jack stood on the threshold of the room with a box in his arms that must have contained an anvil and couldn't help but take a moment to enjoy the sight before him.

Letty, whom he'd known for years as a warm, amusing woman, had grown increasingly grim since her work with the Ladies for the Vote had alienated her from Astoria society, and even more so since Connor had left. He'd suspected having another woman in the house would be good for her, but he hadn't expected the change to be apparent so quickly.

Laughing hysterically beside her on the trunk was Charity, who wielded some strange wand as though it had magic powers. In the chair across from them, the little

Chinese maid, whom he'd never known to express emotion of any kind except nervousness, was doubled over in a paroxysm of laughter.

"Ah...boss," Rolf said from behind him. "I happen to be balancing half a dozen masts on my shoulder, and I'd like to put them *down*."

Jack moved into the room, grumbling at his friend over his shoulder. "My, God, Kauppi. They're only bolts of fabric. The way you've been complaining—"

"If you would think of them as masts with the sails still attached," Rolf said, following him into the room, "you'd understand how heavy they are."

The women wiped away tears of delight in an effort to regain composure, and rose to help.

"Tell me the truth," Jack said breathlessly to Charity as he leaned on the crate he'd just lowered, "you're really a blacksmith, aren't you?"

She laughed and shook her head. "This is my sewing machine. Thank you so much for moving my things." She became serious suddenly as Rolf, Letty and Ming carried the thick, paper-wrapped bolts of fabric across the room. She lowered her voice. "And thank you for bringing me here. Letty's wonderful."

"She is," he agreed. "You seem to be fast friends already." He pointed to the wand device she'd left on the trunk. "What is that?"

She glanced in the direction of his pointing finger and color flooded her face to her hairline. "It's a...a flowerpot." She picked it up to demonstrate. "For plants that must be protected." She glanced up at the sudden interest of the other occupants of the room. "The stick goes into the ground," she said, holding it so that the stick pointed downward. She placed a fist into the cup. "The plant goes in here."

Her expression seemed to dare him to refute her explanation.

She turned to Letty. "Isn't that so, Letty?"

"Oh, yes," Letty returned, the carefully set lines of her grave expression looking as though they might dissolve into laughter at any moment. "A flowerpot."

Jack took another look at the tapering globe shape, then into Charity's brown eyes, his own glowing with humor.

He had no idea what the thing was really for, but he could safely guess just what might fit into the cup. Though he understood her reluctance to be honest, he couldn't resist the temptation to tease.

"A flower," he said softly, his smiling gaze significant, "that would require special handling." He turned to Rolf. "Come on, Kauppi. Two more loads from the wagon and you can leave for the Star Saloon and your chanteuse."

As Charity lay in her comfortable bed that night and said her prayers, she thanked God for the long list of blessings the day had brought. Several new friends, comfortable lodgings and an elegant little shop. She sighed in contentment as she felt the distance lengthen between herself and Kansas.

The new life she'd come in search of was actually taking shape. She tried not to think about the man in it, but his face took shape behind her closed eyes despite her efforts. She blamed long years of spinsterhood for this very new and silly infatuation. She rolled onto her stomach and turned her thoughts to designing a dress for Letty as a thank-you for her kindness.

Chapter Three

"Your first commission, Charity," Letty said as they stood in the middle of the sewing room and surveyed the results of two days spent cleaning and organizing, "is to make nine sashes for Ladies for the Vote. Something shiny that will get everyone's attention."

Charity reached for a bolt of gold taffeta for which she'd sent for all the way from New York. "This?"

Letty fingered it. "This would be perfect. The ladies are coming over this afternoon. I won't involve you in our meeting, but I'd like to introduce you. It could mean business for you."

Charity replaced the bolt. "I'd like that, Letty. Then I'll take Jon to town with me to keep him out of the way. I need a few yards of lace and some buttons."

The doorbell peeled and Letty squeezed her hand. "Here are my ladies."

Charity found Letty's little army of suffragists an interesting study of women. There were all body types and personalities. Ingrid Rasmussen was tall and beautiful and filled with youthful fervor as she dandled a baby on her knee. Carlotta Wayman was small and plump and seemed almost unsure about being there. There was a pair of sweet-faced spinster sisters, Harriet and Henrietta

Clune, very average and angular in appearance, but unfailingly polite and positive in their attitudes. Their father had been a preacher, Charity learned.

Genevieve Winston was middle-aged and elegant and knew all the latest gossip. Louisa Ellison and Amanda Parks were sisters-in-law who had defied their husbands to come to the meeting. Amanda appeared nervous, Louisa defiant.

Then there was Agnes Butterfield, an avid bird-watcher, as fluttery and cheerful as the subjects of her many long hours of study.

Charity wasn't sure what she'd expected of Letty's friends, but they certainly weren't the fire-spewing dragons they were made out to be in all the stories she'd heard and read about the movement.

Letty introduced Charity and explained about her recent move from Kansas and her new business. "She has many patterns and the most sumptuous fabrics you've ever seen," Letty enthused. "And she'll be doing alterations, as well. Please be sure to tell your friends."

Genevieve laughed wryly. "What friends? When we befriended you, Letty, we lost all our other ones."

There was good-natured laughter.

"Then tell your enemies," Letty retorted, laughing herself. "A beautiful, reasonably priced dress is something every woman, suffragist or not, wants."

As the meeting was called to order, Charity went looking for Jon and found him in the kitchen, charming cookies from Kristine.

Kristine looked doubtfully out the window at the pewter sky. "Bring your umbrella, Miss Charity," she suggested. "Storm coming."

Charity held it up to show she was already prepared. "We shouldn't be long enough to get wet," Charity promised. After the two days spent preparing her shop, she was anxious to get into the fresh air and to take in the wonderful view of the river.

Jon explained the ships to her as they trudged hand in hand down the hill. "That's a fore-and-aft-rigged schooner," he said, pointing to a three-masted ship heading upriver toward Portland. "And that's a square-rigged bark, probably taking on supplies." He indicated another large ship at the docks, sails furled against the background of Washington across the river.

"What are those funny sails?" Charity asked, pointing to the large collection of curious bat wing sails she'd noticed the day she'd been exploring Swill Town.

"The Finns use them on their fishing boats," Jon replied: "Papa says they're very good fishermen. Kristine's husband is a fisherman, and Rolf's father was, too." He squinted at her. "There's a funny joke about the river. Want to hear it?"

"Yes."

"Why is the Columbia River like a fish?"

"Why?" she asked dutifully.

"Because it has Finns on both sides!" He laughed uproariously. "See, because Finnish people live in Washington, too. So it has—"

Laughing, Charity hugged him. "I understand, Jon. It's a wonderful joke. Oh, there's the rain."

Two drops plopped on Charity's face before she got the umbrella up. She pulled Jon close to her side, trying to protect him from the quickening rain. She leaned down as they hurried the last block to town. The afternoon darkened and the wind blew, making a mockery of spring.

Their hurrying footsteps made hollow sounds as they turned onto the pier. A man holding an umbrella, a pipe in his mouth, sat in front of a shop and fished through a space between the planks.

"Can we go see Uncle Jack?" Jon asked, trying to pull her in the direction of the box factory.

Charity pulled him back. "Jon, we musn't bother him. He has work to do, and so do we. If you'll help me find the shop that sells buttons, I'll buy you a cinnamon stick."

Charity knew where the shop was. In the two days she'd spent looking for a place to rent, she'd learned the location of most of the downtown merchants. But she knew also that Jon had a one-track mind and that, unless diverted, he wouldn't let her rest until they visited the box factory. And she didn't want to.

Jack McCarren was constantly on her mind, and that was beginning to bother her. She'd come to Astoria to begin a new life and a new business, not to take up with a man. Not that he'd suggested taking up with her. He'd never implied anything of the kind. She'd just looked into his eyes and read things, things that probably weren't really there. Things that were just the result of an old maid's imagination.

Anyway, the less she had to do with him, the better. He appeared at Letty's usually once a day, she'd noticed, to check on her and Jon and to give them some tidbit of news about people or things with which Charity was still unfamiliar. She hid in her room every time he came.

The last time she'd spoken to him he'd made the remark about the flowerpot. She still blushed when she thought of it.

No man had never spoken to her like that before. Actually, men had hardly spoken to her at all. She knew she wasn't exceptionally pretty or vivacious. Her mother had often told her that unexceptional looks and a propensity for trouble were not an appealing combination in a woman. So far, her mother had been right.

Jack McCarren *had* saved her from the bear, but he'd been impatient with her for putting herself in a position to require his rescue. No. She sighed acceptingly. She would not be happy with a man in her life. He would have expectations of her and place restrictions on her. She'd put all those little tyrannies aside when she'd left Kansas and the past behind.

But... She let herself think of the picture Jack McCarren had made when he'd seemed to leap out of the sky and place himself between her and the bear—broad-backed, lean-hipped, dark and handsome and excitingly competent. She sighed. If only she could find a man like that who'd let her do as she pleased.

She laughed aloud at her own dream as she recalled the men she'd known in her life—her father, his friends, their neighbors—all eager to command, but unavailable when help was needed. The dream simply did not exist.

The woman in the dry-goods shop was friendly and courteous when Charity introduced herself.

"I'm going to be dressmaking and doing alterations," Charity said, looking through a bin of buttons. She pulled Jon's questing fingers from a dress form. "I'll need jet dress buttons and plain white buttons for a man's shirt. Oh, and I'd like to look at lace trims."

"Well, how nice," the woman said. "I'm Augusta Coley, and this—" she pointed down the counter where a man arranged bolts of red, white and blue bunting "—is my husband, Ezra." Ezra looked up and smiled.

Augusta brought out button stock that had just arrived and wasn't yet unpacked and let Charity pick through it while she waited on another customer.

Jon exclaimed excitedly over a set of buttons with anchors on them, so Charity put them with her purchases, determined to make him a sailor jacket. His eyes widened at her growing pile of items. "What are those white buttons for?"

"I'm going to make a shirt for Uncle Jack," she said, studying a length of lace. "As a thank-you for saving us from the bear."

"We heard about that," Augusta said, her husband now occupied with the customer. "That certainly was exciting. So that was you?"

Charity nodded reluctantly. "I'd just arrived two days before. It was quite an introduction to Astoria."

The woman's eyes took on a different quality. Charity couldn't quite define it, but she sensed a lessening in the woman's enthusiasm. Ezra and the customer had turned in their direction.

"Where," August asked, "did you say your shop is located?"

"I'm in Letitia Donovan's home," Charity said with a smile. "On Grand Street."

The gasp in the little shop was audible. She felt Jon tense beside her and she finally understood. She remembered Letty's insistence that she'd become a social pariah, and the little joke her ladies had made just this afternoon about losing their friends.

First she felt sick. Then she became angry.

Augusta lowered her eyes to the things Charity had intended to purchase and spread them out on the counter.

"Well, now, most of these things haven't been checked in yet and I'm not sure I should let them go after all."

Charity stared at the top of her head, but the woman refused to look up.

"And these other things—" she moved buttons around with bony fingers "—have gone up in price, but we haven't had time to change the sign."

As the woman fussed nervously with them, the anchor buttons slid along the counter. Charity caught them by slapping her hand on them. The thump was loud in the small shop.

"How much *should* they be?" she asked quietly.

"Well..." Augusta began.

Ezra came to take a supportive stance beside his wife. "Five dollars a half dozen."

Charity looked into his face. It was a scholarly, handsome face made ugly at the moment by a sneer.

"In the New York catalogs," Charity said, struggling against a straining temper, "they're five cents a piece."

"Then you should buy them in New York," Ezra said.

The customer, an older woman in an expensive coat, laughed.

"I'm living," Charity replied, "in Astoria."

Ezra snickered. "With the Oregon equivalent of Mrs. Satan. I'm afraid you won't find many things in this town at a price you can afford."

Charity didn't know much about the women's movement, but Victoria Woodhull Martin, known as Mrs. Satan, had been written about in every newspaper from Boston to Seattle—and apparently in Astoria.

"Letitia Donovan," Charity said, her voice vibrating with the strength of her anger, "is a kind, intelligent woman who is trying to educate those around her to a new idea. I would think *Satan,*" she went on, "would be a title more applicable to someone who would charge one hundred times the fair price for a card of buttons."

The Coleys stared at her and she stared back. Ezra finally lowered his eyes. Augusta did not.

Charity picked up six anchor buttons and the white shirt buttons and handed over a ten-dollar bill. It was the principle of the matter.

"I've promised the boy the anchor buttons, and I need the shirt buttons," she said, "but from now on I'll advise all my customers to purchase their notions from the New York catalog where the prices and the service are more reasonable."

"You won't have any customers as long as you live with Letty Donovan," Augusta prophesied. "First she shut the door on her husband, then she took up with Jack McCarren, and we all know where *he* was spawned."

Charity saw a haze of red over everything, and before she could stop herself, she raised her closed umbrella. Both Coleys took a horrified step back. For a moment she saw the couple as two of Jon's imaginary black-hearted Barbary brotherhood, and she'd have run them through without a second thought. But that reminded her that an impressionable little boy stood beside her, so she simply worked the opening and closing slide so that the umbrella swelled and folded like a great, black bird, spewing raindrops all over them. They backed away, raising their arms and shouting as though she was pelting them with something lethal.

She dropped the buttons into her bag and slammed out of the shop. She opened the umbrella over Jon, giving him the handle to hold.

"But you'll get wet," he protested.

"I need to get wet," she told him as the rain, now falling heavily, sluiced over her taffeta and velvetta hat and onto her coat, drenching her in minutes. She didn't care. She was surprised steam didn't radiate from her where the rain hit.

Jon said worriedly, "Let's go see Uncle Jack."

Jack. She remembered Augusta Coley's ugly remark, and though she didn't understand it, she'd have gladly run her through a second time to avenge Jack's honor.

She'd lived in Letty's house only three days, but she felt she could stake her life on the fact that Letty's and Jack's friendship, though warm and affectionate, was nothing more. And wherever he'd been "spawned," she knew she'd be hard put to find a kinder man anywhere.

"We're going to buy your cinnamon stick," Charity said, taking Jon's hand and pulling him along after her, "and then we're going home."

"You're going to get a sniffle," Jon warned.

"I have a handkerchief," she said. "Where is the candy shop?"

Jon pointed. "Hoeflers is right there."

Charity gave Jon a coin and sent him inside while she waited in front. The pheasant feather on her hat now hung in her eyes, and she was so wet she knew she must look like something on which one would find barnacles. She didn't care. She was still fuming.

"Charity, what are you doing with your umbrella folded when it's pouring rain?" Jack demanded.

Again, he'd seemed to materialize out of nowhere, wearing the same disgusted expression he'd worn that day on the tidal flats. He wore a long, yellow oilskin coat and a sou'wester. Rain dripped from its brim.

Impotent anger always brought her to tears, but she fought them off, unwilling to explain to him what had happened.

"Good afternoon, Mr. McCarren," she said politely. "Jon and I are shopping. How are you?"

He folded his arms, becoming a wall between her and the hurrying passersby. "Mr. McCarren?" he asked, exaggerating her formality. "Three days ago I was Uncle Jack."

"Three days ago I fainted," she said, having to hold her feather aside to see his face. "Today I'm well aware of my surroundings."

Jack heard the odd grimness in her voice. "What happened?" he asked.

"Nothing," she replied, looking him in the eye, daring him not to challenge her.

There was obviously something wrong, but he wasn't sure how to get to the source. So he turned to what he could understand. "Put your umbrella up," he said, "before you drown."

She gave him one quick, impatient glance. "I do not work for you at the box factory, Mr. McCarren," she said. "And Connor Donovan has not asked you to watch out for *me*. I'm not your responsibility."

His eyebrow went up at her sharp reply. But before he could comment, Jon flew out of the candy shop, his lips red from a cinnamon stick.

"Hi, Uncle Jack!" he said. "We're shopping."

Jack decided to change his approach. "Jon, would you ask Charity to open her umbrella before she catches pneumonia?"

Jon shook his head. "She needs to get wet."

"Why?" Jack asked.

"Jon…" Charity cautioned, trying to pull him along, but he refused to budge. Jack McCarren was like a magnet to him.

"She's angry," Jon explained. "Mr. Coley made her pay ten dollars for a few buttons."

Jack frowned. "Why?"

Jon studied his candy and sighed. "I think because she lives with Mama and me."

Charity held her breath, afraid Jon might go on with what else the Coleys had said. But he stopped.

That was all Jack had to hear, however. Charity saw his eyes ignite. He turned in the direction of the dry-goods store, but Charity caught the slick sleeve of his coat and held fast.

"No!" she said firmly.

When he spun on her, anger in every line of his face, she added more quietly, "I'm sure it would do neither Letty nor my business any good if you made a fuss."

"I've no intention of making a fuss." He repeated her feminine word with emphasis for its lack of scope. "I intend to break a nose—"

"Please," she said, tightening her grip on his coat, looking deeply into his eyes. "That wouldn't be a good example for Jon."

"And Mrs. Coley wouldn't give you Charity's money back," Jon said, "'cause she doesn't like you, either."

Jack did not seem surprised, though he did appear interested.

Once more Charity tried to pull Jon along with her. "Come on, Jon."

Jack stopped her with a hand on her arm. "What did she say?"

Jon shrugged. "I didn't understand it. Something about you visiting Mama. And she said that everybody knew where you were..." He frowned and shrugged again. "I forget the word."

Jack studied the boy a moment, and Charity saw something change in his eyes. Curiously, it was something she recognized without understanding it, because it was something she'd often felt. Something he'd thought he'd left behind him had slapped him in the face. The anger suddenly left her with the downward sweep of the rain, and she felt only tired and depressed.

Jack turned to her. "Do you remember the word?"

She shook her head. "I wasn't paying much attention. After all, I'd just paid ten dollars for twelve buttons."

Jack's lips parted, as though he intended to insist that she tell him, then he glanced at Jon, who was all eyes and ears, and changed his mind.

He shook his head at Charity. "Take off your coat," he said.

"What?" she asked, resisting as he took her bag and umbrella from her and handed them to Jon.

"Take off your coat," he repeated, beginning to unbutton his. When she opened her mouth to protest, he said loudly, "Do it!"

She did. He swung his large yellow coat over her and buttoned it. It was warm from his body and cozily lined with wool. It dragged on the ground.

"Oh, being seen in this is going to gain me so *many* customers." She held the sides out and did a turn. "I must look like the cover of the *Parisienne*. I—oops!" She stepped on the trailing hem and fell forward. Jack steadied her, already drenched himself.

"Do try to behave with a little decorum," he said, his good humor returning. "We are downtown, and I am a candidate for mayor. My carriage is at the other end of the block. Wait here and I'll take you home."

He took the umbrella from Jon, opened it and placed it in her hands. Jon pushed her purse at her, anxious to be rid of it.

Jack loped down the street and was back in a moment in a small covered carriage that took them swiftly to Letty's.

"We'll use my private entrance," Charity said before Jon started toward the front door. "Your mama's guests are still here and we don't want to disturb the meeting." She turned to Jack, whose jacket and pants were soaked through, and said briskly, "Come inside. I'm sure there must be something of Mr. Donovan's we can find for you to change into."

"Ah..." Jack helped her down, looking uncertainly in the direction of the front window through which he could see a few members of Letty's group peering out at them. "I'm not sure it's a good idea for you to be seen bringing a man into your rooms."

Charity followed his gaze to the two Clune sisters watching them through the window. "Don't be silly," she said. "Their father was a preacher. I'm sure they're above leaping to conclusions."

"No one," he said, "is above leaping to conclusions."

"Jack, I'm in no mood to be argued with." She looked at him sternly. "Now, come with me."

Jack followed Charity as she made her way carefully up the path and the porch steps to the side door, his coat held up high to allow her safety of movement. He held the umbrella over her and Jon while she dug in the little mesh bag for her key, produced it and opened the door.

He found himself standing in the middle of the room that only two days ago had been a pile of boxes and a log raft of bolts of fabric. Now it was a tidy little room with a sewing machine, shelves filled with the various gewgaws with which women decorated their clothes, and bolts of fabric lined along one wall in a cheerful tableau of color and texture. She'd accomplished a lot in a short amount of time. He studied her neat, straight back as she removed his coat and hung it on an oak rack in a corner of the room and wondered, not for the first time, what had brought her all this way from Kansas—alone.

She turned to him with a faintly uncomfortable smile and handed him a blanket. "Excuse us for a few moments. I'll get Jon dried off and ask Kristine to put on some tea. You can take your wet things off in my room." She pointed through the open door. "And I'll be back in a moment with something for you to put on."

Jack did as she said, walking into her bedroom and closing the door. A hundred thoughts crowded his mind at the sight of the wide tester bed and the warm-looking quilt. He shook his head at his own vulnerability and began to peel off his wet clothes.

No, he told himself for the twentieth time since he'd met her. Getting entangled with a woman would not be good for his career at this point.

And, anyway, she'd probably gotten an earful from Mrs. Coley. He felt sure Charity was now telling herself that *he* would not be good for *her*. That was all right. He'd live. He always managed to survive. Now he was doing better than just surviving. He was achieving, acquiring, aspiring. He just had to accept that while hard work and determination could get him material things, they couldn't get him the soft, seductive, accommodating, loving woman every man dreamed of. She was out of reach for him. Trouble was, he'd had difficulty his whole life accepting the limits society tried to place on him.

He was down to the buff when there was a light rap on the door and it opened a few inches, admitting a small hand holding two folded garments.

When Jack took them with a thank-you, the hand disappeared then reappeared with a pair of alligator slippers.

"Pass your wet things out," Charity's voice directed. "Kristine will dry them near the stove."

As she'd made it clear she was in no mood to argue, Jack complied.

He was sitting on the chair that faced Charity's sewing machine, dressed in a pair of Connor's old gray worsted pants and a blue wool roll-necked sweater, when she returned with a tray laden with a teapot, cups and a plate of cookies.

He stood up, took the tray from her and carried it to a small table across the room near the window. Two rocking chairs faced it. She gestured for him to take one and she took the other.

"You're a woman of remarkable industry," he said, leaning back as she poured tea. He had to drag his eyes away from her graceful hands when she handed his cup across. "The room looks ready for business."

"It is," she replied with a smile. She seemed to have shed the grim mood of earlier and was quietly cheerful. Or it might have been a trick of the stormy afternoon light coming through the lace curtains. She seemed to glow, like the sun trapped in a cloudy sky. Studying her peaches-and-cream skin, remembering her fury when he'd first run into her today and the reason for it, he was beginning to forget all the reasons he didn't need a woman in his life.

"Letty's provided me with my first job," she said, offering him the plate of cookies. "I'm making sashes for her ladies."

He smiled, selecting a cookie filled with plump raisins, feeling very content to be in this alien, feminine environment. "I hope the job requires buttons, considering what you paid for those you purchased today."

"I'd promised some of the buttons to Jon," she said, replacing the plate and putting one of the cookies on her saucer. "He liked them because they had anchors on them. I thought I'd make him a jacket."

"But he said you bought twelve buttons."

She glanced at him as she carefully broke her cookie in two. "The others were for you."

He felt the pleasure of surprise. "Oh?"

She nodded, stirring sugar into her tea. "I wanted to make you a shirt as a thank-you for... for all the kindness you've shown me."

The mental image of her slender fingers working on something that would touch his skin sent a ripple of sensation along his spine. The thoughtfulness of the gesture sent the ripple deep.

"You've already thanked me," he demurred politely.

She nodded, then bit her cookie, chewed and swallowed. "But I thought saving my life merited something that showed a little more effort. I'm afraid needlework is all I have to offer."

That wasn't true, he thought. That wasn't true at all. "I'd be honored," he said, "to be the first man in Astoria with a shirt made by..." He hesitated. "Have you decided on a business name?"

"Charity Butler's Sewing and Alterations," she said. She looked at him with amusement over the rim of her teacup. "Unimaginative but accurate."

He nodded approval. "That's important." Out of the corner of his eye he noticed the hat she'd removed when she'd walked into the room. He reached for it, holding it up to examine its drooping bow and sopping feather. He put it down again and turned to Charity.

"I'd like to know what Mrs. Coley told you," he said quietly, placing his cup on the table.

"Jack, it doesn't matter." She began to fuss, filling his cup, avoiding his eyes. "I didn't understand it anyway."

"If you told me," he insisted, taking the pot out of her hands and putting it aside, causing her to look at him, "I could explain it to you."

"It's none of my business."

"Perhaps I would like it to be."

Charity was surprised and momentarily speechless. His inky gaze did things to her she'd never experienced before. He seemed always to affect her on two levels. She felt a comfortable kinship with him she'd never experienced with another man, and yet always underlying that peaceful rapport was a vaguely dangerous excitement. Without words, he seemed to promise things she'd never even imagined before. She wasn't sure she'd ever have the courage to explore them, but she was sure how she felt about their friendship.

"I consider you a friend," she said. "I need no explanations."

He smiled at her stubbornness. "Tell me."

She sighed, resigned to the inevitable. She had little difficulty remembering the exact words. "She said that Letty had tossed her husband out then taken up with you, and that everyone knew where you'd been..." She stumbled over the word.

"Go on," he prodded.

"Spawned," she said with angry disgust.

He took that with silence, his expression unchanging.

"Do you?" he asked.

"What?"

"Know where I was spawned."

She expelled an impatient breath. "People aren't spawned, they're born," she replied, "and I can't see what difference it makes."

"It makes a lot of difference to a lot of people. You should know," he said, pausing, lowering his voice, "what you're getting into."

She looked at him uncertainly, her pulse quickening. "I thought I was simply opening a shop and making new friends."

He accepted that with a wry smile. "Friendships grow and change, like everything else. Ask Letty and Connor."

"They're living a hundred miles apart," she pointed out, her eyes widening with interest and amusement. "Are you suggesting we're about to quarrel and you're going to move to Portland?"

He looked heavenward in exasperation, then at her angelically innocent expression. "No, I am not." His voice held a note of gentle scolding. "May I conduct this conversation?"

She nodded. "Of course. Although conversations are usually two-sided. Anything else is oratory. But do go on."

He decided to skirt for the moment the delicate suggestion that something was developing between them and proceed to the heart of the matter.

"My mother was one of the Astor Street girls," he said baldly, leaning back in his chair, squaring one foot on the knee of the other leg. "I'm sure you saw some of them when you toured Swill Town."

She nodded, trying not to betray her surprise. He seemed so completely the gentleman.

"She was very popular," he went on, "primarily because she was softhearted and kind and looked for good in everyone. Other children teased me, but I had Con's friendship, my mother's love, and I was well fed and sheltered. She died when I was eleven."

"How did you survive?" Charity asked in a whisper, trying to imagine this strong, competent man as a helpless child.

"My mother's friends saw that I had food every day," he said with a reminiscent smile, "and I knew every shop and warehouse that could be gotten into for shelter after dark. When Connor's parents found out how I was living, they took me in. I worked summers at the box factory. Later, they sent me to Princeton with Connor."

Charity's sympathy turned to respect. She shook her head. "And now you own the box factory. How satisfying that must be, to know how far you've come."

He nodded, a frown forming. "Because some people were kind. What I find difficult to accept is that I can't put the past behind me. That is, I can, but there are people who can't."

"I don't see why you should have to put it behind you at all. It's part of you. It happened to you. I understand that you wouldn't want it discussed over dinner all the time, but you can't expect to erase it." She tried to speak with authority, all the time thinking what a fraud she was. She'd moved eighteen hundred miles across the country to get away from Kansas for the very same reason, but he didn't have to know that. "People's ignorance will always be a part of life, so you have to learn to live with it."

He studied her so long she shifted uncomfortably, wondering if he'd sensed her lies.

"And this opinion you have," he said, "will hold up when you accompany me to the Fisher Opera House on Saturday night and some of Astoria society turn their noses up at us?"

Her heart thudded against her ribs. A hundred cautions came to mind. She didn't need a distraction now.

Generally, she didn't believe men to have staying power when life became difficult. Though Jack seemed unique, she really knew very little about him. And if her friendship with Letty made the Coleys charge her ten dollars for a dozen buttons, what would a romance with Jack McCarren cost her?

Somehow, none of that seemed to matter. The moment she'd stepped on the train in Dawson, her life had ceased to be about caution. It occurred to her that she should honor his honesty by being truthful about her own past, but he hadn't asked, and she functioned best when she put it out of her mind.

"Only some noses?" she asked.

He shrugged a shoulder. "Ignorance isn't an all-pervading ailment. Astoria society has a very healthy side." He grinned. "Some people like me simply for the charming gentleman that I am."

"Then I would like to accompany you."

He studied her a long moment, his eyes going over her face feature by feature before settling on her mouth. He looked at it so long she felt the breath leave her lungs so that she had to part her lips to draw a shallow breath.

He stood and reached a hand across the table to help her to her feet. He tugged her gently to his side and took both her hands, looking into her pink, expectant face.

"You'll be asking for trouble," he warned.

Charity knew he wasn't talking about society trouble.

She felt the warmth and energy from him, and that hint of tantalizing danger she was almost beginning to welcome.

"Trouble seems to find me," she said softly, ensnared by his eyes, "even when I deliberately try to evade it. I'm beginning to believe I could be fated for trouble. Perhaps *you* should think twice."

He shook his head and she felt herself drowning in his eyes. "Instinct has served me well," he said, "and it tells me you are fated for *me*.

Jack moved one hand to the back of her waist, and the fingers of his other hand threaded into her upswept hair. Before she could protest his intentions they were deed.

He kissed her gently but lengthily, his mouth warm and mobile and coaxingly artful. He smelled of the rain and bay rum cologne.

Charity had been kissed twice before. Once by a neighbor boy on a farm when she'd been sixteen. He'd been fumbly and unsure. The second time had been after her life had turned upside down. She'd been twenty-three and the man had been thirty and had proposed marriage, making it clear to her that he was probably her last chance. He'd been forceful and hurtful, and she'd found the experience revolting. She'd been happy to let her last chance pass by.

She had never been kissed like this, as though she was something precious, as though there was time for it, as though it was something for her rather than something for the man who bestowed it.

He held her with a firmness that was gentle and kissed her with an ardor that was tender, opening his mouth on hers, yet simply nipping at her lips, leaving her to wonder what deeper intimacies he withheld.

Charity's heart fluttered, and there was a curious little palpitation deep inside, at the heart of her womanhood.

Jack lifted his head to draw in a desperate breath, aware of a fever in his blood running out of all proportion to that chaste little kiss. His mind and his body were already racing ahead to imagine the kiss prolonged and deepened and carried to an inevitable conclusion. God! He had to bring himself to reality with considerable effort. At least he could now stop saying no to himself. After one simple kiss he knew that was an answer he'd never accept.

He looked into the startled velvet of her eyes.

"I think," he said, unable to withhold a smile, "that we're both fated for trouble."

Chapter Four

Charity raised the needle arm on her sewing machine and eased the gray oxford skirt out from under it. Then she turned in her chair and shook out the yards of fabric, running a critical and experienced eye over the three black satin bands trimming the bottom.

"Perfect!" Letty praised, breezing into the room in a crisp white silk waist and a skirt of blue and black crepon. She lifted an armful of figured brilliantine from the chair near Charity and fell into it with a dramatic sigh, placing the mound of fabric in her lap. "Can the illustrious Miss Butler put everything aside for a moment and join me for tea? I swear, in a week's time you've become the busiest seamstress in Astoria. You're turning out to be rather dull company. Work, work, work!"

Charity stood and draped the skirt over a rack behind her. She turned to Letty with a grin. "And whose fault is that? You must have coerced every one of your Ladies for the Vote to order something. With three dresses for yourself, shirts and pants for Jon and new aprons for Kristine and Ming, I'll be busy until Christmas."

"I didn't have to coerce anyone," Letty insisted. "Everyone noticed your smart little waists and skirts in pretty colors, and they want to look just like you." With a little laugh she indicated the plain skirt Charity had just finished and draped over the rack. "Except for Harriet and Henrietta, of course. Their preacher father must have taught them that color was sinful. They're just as plain on the outside as they are beautiful on the inside."

Charity took the fabric from Letty's lap and placed it on the chair she'd just vacated. "I'm trying to nudge them in a more fashionable direction. I had Harriet almost interested in this brilliantine, but when Henrietta looked uncertain, she changed her mind."

Letty led the way to the parlor. "I hope you can do it before the big rally in the fall."

"What rally?"

"I just received a letter in this morning's mail. Judith Vineyard and Coleen Hensley, chairmen of the northwest district of Ladies for the Vote, are coming *here* and have asked me to organize a three-day rally. I'm so excited!" In the sitting room, Letty took one end of a beautifully inlaid divan with a red and gold velvet cushion and gestured Charity to the other. Kristine was already setting out the teapot and a plate of scones.

"I have to step up marches and rallies in the meantime," Letty said, pouring, "so that we can involve more women in the cause and show Judith and Coleen that we're finally revitalizing the movement in the northwest and doing our part toward securing a state referendum for suffrage."

Charity nodded with forced enthusiasm, privately convinced Letty was imagining more of a following than she had. She accepted a cup of steaming tea. "Where will this take place?"

"At Carnahan's Hall," Letty replied, giving Charity a wry tilt of her eyebrow over the rim of her cup. "Presuming they'll allow me to rent it. Avarice usually prevails, but where suffragists are concerned, you can never be certain. Anyway..." Letty's gray eyes took on an anticipatory gleam. "I will have to write a brilliant speech, and my Ladies for the Vote will have to look wonderful."

"You always do."

Letty shrugged in dismissal of Charity's praise. "I mean competent, intelligent, strong...so that men, and other women, too, will look at us and see women worthy of responsibility and trust."

Charity smiled ingenuously. "I could dress you like Mr. Roosevelt and put padding in your shoulders. The mustache you must handle on your own."

Letty dissolved into a fit of laughter. Charity poured her more tea and put the cup into her hand as she fought for breath. "Maybe I should let you write my speech, as well," Letty said finally. "Of course, you have things to think about other than women's struggle for the vote. Things of a more...personal nature."

Letty's tone was speculative, suggestive. Charity stiffened, instinctively suspicious. Her heart gave an uncomfortable lurch. Did she know? Had someone found out already?

"What do you mean?" she asked, hearing the high, nervous note in her voice.

Letty blinked, her teasing smile slowly dissolving as she studied the sudden tension in Charity's face. "I meant Jack, Charity," she said quietly. "He's taking you to the opera house tonight, and despite your busy work schedule, you have a glow about you. What else would I have meant?"

Charity's lungs filled with air once again and her heart slowed its frantic beating. She busied herself with buttering a scone to avoid Letty's eyes. "I thought you were suggesting that I had bears to battle, or that I'd do better spending my time with the Princess Developer."

Letty laughed, distracted. "We may just have to settle for our paltry endowments. What will you wear tonight?"

Charity relaxed further as the conversation took a safer channel. "I had noble intentions of making myself something wonderful, but thanks to your efforts on my behalf, I've hardly had time to breathe." She frowned in resignation. "I'll have to wear my old green satin and hope that no one notices it's four years old."

"Come with me." Without waiting for her compliance, Letty took hold of her arm and pulled her into the bedroom. She knelt before a large trunk. The scent of vanilla wafted up as she opened it.

Letty's slender hands swept through a colorful array of expensive dresses and gowns. "I've a dark pink silk that should be perfect for you. Ah, here it is." She pulled out a gown in a beautiful shade of raspberry with lace at the sleeves and a décolleté neckline. She shook it out and handed it to Charity.

Charity held it up against her, unable to resist the temptation to twist and turn in front of the mirror, trying to imagine herself in the sumptuous gown. The color was flattering to her fair skin and dark features, and the exquisite trim made her feel as though she twirled in front of the mirror of a Parisian couturiere.

Charity glanced at Letty in the mirror, torn between wanting very much to wear the dress and fearing that something might happen to it while she did. "Letty, I couldn't. What if I tore it or soiled it?"

Apparently lost in thought, Letty required a moment to answer. She finally sighed and closed the trunk. "Then I have dozens more. Let me see if I can find the shoes."

She rummaged in a small closet. "Here they are!" She handed out a pair of satin slippers the same shade as the dress.

"What if it rains tonight?" Charity argued halfheartedly. She'd never slipped her feet into a pair of shoes so elegant and obviously expensive. "If I got mud on these, Letty, I'd never forgive myself."

Letty dismissed that problem with a wave of her hand and got to her feet, making a production of brushing off her skirt. "Connor bought the dress and shoes for me in a little shop in Portland. I haven't worn them since he left, and I don't intend to ever again."

"Too many memories?" Charity asked gently.

Letty sank onto the edge of her bed, hooked an arm around the post and leaned her head against it. A little spasm of pain crossed her face, and Charity knew for certain that Letty Donovan was still very much in love with her husband.

"We went to Portland for our anniversary," she said in a weary voice. "We left Jonathan with Jack and spent an entire week on our own." A small dreamy smile appeared on her lips. "We went to the theater every night, slept late every morning..." Her voice caught and her brow furrowed. "It was a wonderful time for us. He'd completely put aside all thoughts of shipping schedules and cargoes, and I had no one to think about but Connor and me."

As Letty concentrated on the past, her wide gray eyes unfocused, a tear slid down her cheek.

Charity sat beside her and put a comforting hand to her back. "Would it help to tell me what happened to change all that?"

Letty put a hand to her eyes, drew a deep breath and sniffed. Charity delved into a pocket and handed her a lace-trimmed hanky.

"Thank you. I'm afraid we're beyond any kind of help," Letty said, dabbing at her eyes. "It was all so silly, so inconsequential, but it's gone too far." She straightened and squared her shoulders, folding her arms. Her eyes took on a new militant light. "He's stubborn and hardheaded and he thinks he can handle his home just as he does one of his ships. Well, I'm not an itinerant sailor, and I won't have terms dictated to me."

"What happened, Letty?"

Letty sighed again, working the handkerchief in her fingers. "It was silly, really. It was a Sunday morning, and I had a meeting with my ladies scheduled for after lunch. He didn't necessarily approve of my work, but he'd been tolerant of it so far. But that morning, a group of his friends arrived unexpectedly on the steamer from Portland, and he wanted me to stay home and help entertain them."

Letty stood and stalked across the room to the window. "Had he made it a request rather than an order, I might have conceded. As it was, I told him he was selfishly concerned with nothing but his own affairs and didn't care about the important work I was doing." She turned away from the window and paced toward Charity.

"He said that I cared more about a bunch of spoiled, dissatisfied women than I did about him." She stopped at the foot of the bed, caught the post in both hands and leaned her forehead against it. "The unfortunate thing was that we had this argument on the steps of Grace Episcopal Church after morning service. His friends were watching, and so were mine."

"So neither of you could back down," Charity guessed.

"Precisely. I went to the rally, and he and his friends returned to Portland that afternoon, and he hasn't been home since."

Charity stood and put an arm around Letty's shoulders. "Don't you think you should do something about this? You obviously miss him, and so does Jonathan."

Letty shook her head adamantly. "No. If he wants to come home, he knows where home is. And I have every intention of continuing my work. This is a perfect example of how women have been manipulated throughout history to serve the needs of men and ignore their own talents and purposes. They tolerate us as long as we continue to provide their every comfort, but the moment our needs interfere with theirs, they issue orders and edicts. Well, I lecture my ladies against being slaves to anyone's ambitions but their own, and I certainly can't live contrary to my own words."

Letty was composed now, dry-eyed and her old wryly acerbic self. Charity studied her in concern.

"There's usually a middle ground, Letty. I imagine that with a little effort, you and Connor could find it."

Letty shook her head, her expression mildly pitying. "You've never been in love, have you, Charity? There is no middle ground where love is concerned. You must have everything—complete love, full trust, total faith in who and what you are. We've lost that."

"How do you know?"

Letty's eyes were grimly resigned. "Because he's stayed away a year while Jon and I have missed him and pined for him. He couldn't stay away if he felt anything for us."

"Letty," Charity said reasonably, "*you* claim to love and miss *him,* yet you've done nothing to repair the breach. He's done nothing more than be as prideful as you are.''

Letty raised an eyebrow and asked calmly, ''Would you like me to raise your rent? Or would you prefer that we drop this subject, resume our tea, then find you a cape to wear over the pink dress?''

Charity laughed softly and pushed Letty toward the sitting room. ''A lopsided choice, I must say. I'll take the tea, thank you.''

A rose. No, something more exotic yet somehow comfortable. Honeysuckle. Charity, in her dark pink gown, reminded Jack of a clutch of perfumed honeysuckle. Her hair, piled in a dark, glossy, complicated tangle of curls, gave her an air of royalty.

As he settled her beside him in the opera house and helped her slip the plush white cape off her shoulders, he felt his heart pause between beats. His first glimpse of the ivory flesh of her shoulders and the barest suggestion of the swell beneath the rounded neck of her dress made him forget everything. His eyes followed the well-defined roundness of her bosom before he could stop himself.

''The dress belongs to Letty,'' Charity said, her voice quiet and faintly strangled.

He tore his gaze away from its fascinated perusal and found her cheeks pinker than her dress. He'd embarrassed her.

''The dress is beautiful,'' he said quietly, lowering his voice as people filled the seats around them. ''But I was admiring you.''

''Jack, behave yourself,'' she whispered, but he noticed that she couldn't quite withhold a smile.

"I'm not *Uncle* Jack tonight," he warned. "I'm just a man who's waited a lonely lifetime for the right woman."

Charity smiled sweetly. "Then please don't behave like the wrong man," she said. "Your eyes are seeing more of me than is visible."

He loved that about her, he thought, as he watched her eyes scan the elegant men and beautiful women taking their seats. She was real and disarmingly honest. She would not pretend that she couldn't read what she saw in his eyes.

After the brief kiss in her little shop the other afternoon, he'd been haunted with images of her. He'd imagined her in his office at the factory and in his bedroom every sleepless night. He'd told himself she couldn't be as beautiful, as appealing to him as he remembered. It was simply a bachelor's fantasy, the dreams of a lonely man.

But he'd been wrong.

Her cheeks were as pink, her eyes as sparkling and filled with humor and interest, her hands as small, her hair as gleaming as a crisp winter night. What he felt for her after one brief week alarmed him. He had to move slowly, he reminded himself. He had to take care.

"Good evening, Jack."

Jack looked up to find Walter Johnson, the incumbent mayor, looking down at him, offering his hand over the back of the padded seats. Certain his opponent's good manners could only be attributed to the presence of an *Astorian Daily Budget* reporter nearby, Jack stood with a smile, happy to play out the charade. For the past few months, Johnson had done his best to vilify Jack in private and in the press.

"Mayor Johnson. How are you this evening?" He shook hands with him, then turned to the stout, handsome woman at his side. "Mrs. Johnson. You look..." He hesitated, gazing at the woman's monstrosity of a dress in funereal colors, "Very nice. Have you met Charity Butler? She's new in Astoria. Charity, this is Walter Johnson, my illustrious opponent in the race for mayor. And Eleanor Johnson, his wife."

Charity offered her hand. Johnson kissed it, looking into her eyes like a hungry wolf, as though she were some meaty little prey.

"Ah, yes," he said smoothly. "The young lady who tangled with the bear under the wharf." He turned to Jack with a venomous smile. "You're quite the hero." He let the praise hang between them for a moment, then he added with obvious relish, "At least among the people of Swill Town and the *ladies* who claim to have witnessed the entire incident."

"Really," Jack said with interest. "And how did you happen to be among them to discuss my heroism?"

Johnson flushed angrily. Mrs. Johnson's formidable features stiffened and she studied Jack with indignation.

"The story was related to me," Johnson replied through gritted teeth.

"I see."

There was a flurry of activity as a couple took their seats next to those occupied by the Johnsons. It was the Coleys.

Charity's heart sank, but her shoulders stiffened.

"Miss Butler, I believe you already know our dear friends, the Coleys." Walter Johnson's smiling introduction must have appeared gracious to anyone watching. One had to be close to see that the move had been calculated to embarrass her.

Everyone within sight of them in the large room had doubtless heard the story of the bear and knew that

Charity was living at Letty's. And Augusta Coley had probably not made a secret of their exchange over the buttons. The little social tableau was being watched with avid interest. Charity thought with dismay that she was losing her grip on the quiet anonymity for which she'd come to the western end of the continent.

But she couldn't start over with cowardice. She smiled politely at the Coleys. "We are acquainted. How nice to see you again." To Mrs. Johnson she added affably, "The Coleys and I shared a highway robbery experience together."

Jack coughed, Walter Johnson became even more purple, and Mrs. Johnson stared at Charity openmouthed. The Coleys turned to one another in disbelief.

Mercifully, the theater lights went down, and a hush fell over the audience as the curtain rose. Jack sat, easing Charity down beside him.

"Well done," he praised in a whisper. "I suppose I shouldn't be surprised that your wit is as sharp and skillful as your needle."

He took her hand as he spoke. She had a little difficulty concentrating on a reply.

"I've a finely honed sense of self-preservation," she finally whispered.

He looked into her eyes, his frown apparent, even in the darkness. "Why?" he asked.

Charity vowed to keep a more level head about her when he touched her. She'd almost slipped.

She put a finger to her lips and pointed to the stage where the first act of *The Real Widow Brown* was beginning. Though he continued to watch her, she concentrated on the stage. He finally laced her fingers with his, drew their linked hands to his knee and rested them there as he turned his attention to the stage.

Charity tried to imagine that it was a table and not his knee. But she could feel the warmth of his solid thigh through the fabric of his pants. She felt as though Jack's strength flowed into her, up the length of her arm and into her chest where her heart beat with steady strength. It surprised and alarmed her. It was because they were allied in their social disfavor, she thought. They'd banded together against their mutual enemy—the narrow-minded and the bigoted. That was all it was.

Soon the weight of his hand around hers became comfortable and she forgot the unpleasant introductions. The play was cheerful and witty, and she found it easy to lose herself in the hilarious antics of the players as the story unfolded.

By the time the lights went up, she had a sparkle in her eye and laughter on her lips.

Jack was pleased to see it. He was also pleased to see the polite, relaxed smile she held in place while the people surrounding them in the exodus from the opera house stared, making little effort to conceal their avid curiosity and their whispers.

Out on the planked sidewalk where a cool drizzle had begun, a short round gentleman approached and slapped Jack heartily on the back. "Jack!" he said in a booming voice. "Heard about the bear. Expected you'd come to see me for stitches." He tipped his hat to Charity. "Ma'am."

"Emmett." Jack rubbed his shoulder with a grin. "I escaped harm at the hands of the bear," he said. "But now I may have to have my shoulder set thanks to my ham-handed physician. Charity Butler, I'd like you to meet Dr. Emmett Parson. Emmett, Charity Butler, a friend of Letty's."

Dr. Parson removed his hat and bowed. "Miss Butler." When he raised his head again, his eyes held a gleam of humor. "Another rabble-rousing suffragist?"

"Emmett," Jack cautioned quietly but firmly. "Behave yourself."

Charity smiled sweetly. "I hope you're not the only physician in Astoria, Dr. Parson."

He shook his head, perplexed. "No. My good friend Bethenia Owens-Adair still practices."

Her smile took on a suggestion of a threat. "You will need her if you malign Letitia Donovan to me."

The doctor studied her in startled surprise for a moment, then guffawed. Those gathered on the opera house steps looked at one another and shook their heads.

"Oh, please," Dr. Parson said. "Give me the pleasure of taking the two of you home in my cab. I have to become better acquainted with this young lady, and it's beginning to rain on us."

Jack turned to Charity with a grin. "You will promise not to harm him?"

"If he promises not to call Letty names."

Emmett Parson took Charity's arm and led her to a carriage drawn by two black horses, their coats glossy and sleek in the glow of the electric streetlight. She settled into the once elegant but now worn gray velvet interior. Jack sat beside her, making more room in the small space by putting his arm behind her on the back of the seat.

The doctor, sitting across from them, smiled at Charity. "Rabble-rousing suffragist?" he repeated in considering tones. "To which term do you object? She is a suffragist. It's a term the ladies apply to themselves."

Charity nodded. "True. But it does the objects of her efforts a disservice to call them rabble. They're women,

Dr. Parson.'' She thought of the ladies who gathered regularly in Letty's parlor and felt real indignation on their behalf.

He laughed softly. ''Actually, young lady, you've threatened one of your own number. I believe women should be free of the ignorance and slavery enforced on them by polite society. I think they should be free of cumbersome clothing.''

''Altogether?'' Jack asked in apparent innocence.

The doctor seemed to know him better than to believe the pose and sent him a quelling look.

Charity scolded him with a soft, ''Jack!''

''Free of cumbersome clothing,'' the doctor repeated, ''and free of confining corsets that deform their spines and interfere with the duties of their lungs.''

Charity put a hand to her waist where she could feel the steel bones of the corset—one of the first things she put on in the morning and the last she removed at night. Be free of it? She couldn't imagine it.

''Attended a medical conference in Denver recently,'' Dr. Parson went on, his brow furrowed, his eyes intent. ''A colleague of mine reported on the lives that have been ruined by corsets and pounds of petticoats. The statistics are shocking. I believe women should be free of barbaric torture in the name of fashion.''

''Oh, dear,'' Charity said.

The doctor raised an eyebrow.

''Charity's a seamstress,'' Jack explained, dropping his arm from the seat to her shoulders, steadying her as the coach began the climb up the hill. ''She's just opened a shop in her rooms at Letty's. You continue to talk of eliminating fashion and she'll do you an injury yet.''

The doctor, on the uphill side of the carriage, was forced to brace his foot on the seat near Jack to stop himself from falling over on them.

"Well, not all fashion," Parson amended. "And, anyway, there's a challenge for you, young lady. If you want to serve the cause of freedom for women, design something comfortable for them to wear." He pointed a disparaging hand in the vicinity of her tightly confined torso. "You can't be comfortable trussed up like a turkey."

"Emmett!" Jack couldn't help a smile. "Good God. You spend too much time alone with your medical journals. You're losing the knack of cultured conversation."

Unoffended, Parson pushed the door open as the carriage pulled up in front of Letty's. He stepped down and grinned at Jack as he alighted. "I apologize. I forget that speaking one's mind makes politicians uncomfortable."

Jack shook his head at him, reaching into the coach to help Charity down. "Sometimes, Emmett," he said, "you'd make God Himself uncomfortable. But thank you for the ride home."

"Shall I wait for you?"

"No, thank you. I'll see Charity inside, then I'm just a block away. I'll walk."

Parson tipped his hat to Charity. "A pleasure, Miss Butler. I hope I haven't offended you with my ravings. I have strong opinions and I never seem to mind who knows them."

Charity shook her head. "Not at all, doctor. It was a pleasure and an experience meeting you." She added the last with an ingenuous smile. Jack saw his crusty friend melt. "If you truly are a supporter of suffragists, perhaps I could suggest that Letty find a duty for you."

The doctor looked at Jack, obviously startled. Then he nodded. "Perhaps. Something small. I'm a very busy man."

"Of course."

As the cab pulled away, Jack and Charity ambled up her private walk to her rooms. A light had been left on in her shop window.

"I had a lovely evening, Jack," Charity said, turning at her door to give him a smiling glance as she delved in her drawstring purse for her key.

He took the purse from her and placed it on the window frame. Then he trapped her against the door with a hand on it on either side of her head. "I'd like to make it lovelier," he said, his eyes bright and deep in the shadows. His voice seemed to flow over her and soothe her like a length of velvet. Still, she recognized the danger.

She flattened a hand against his chest. It was like pushing against a stone wall.

"Jack," she said breathlessly, "I insist you behave like a gentleman."

"Oh, I will." He came even closer, her restraining hand nothing more than an adornment on his chest. "Like a gentleman with very strong feelings for a lady."

"One does not develop strong feelings," she said hastily and falsely, "in a matter of days."

"Let me show you," he said, lowering his head, his lips hovering just above hers, "how wrong you are."

"Then—then . . ." she stammered, struggling to maintain a grip on her good sense. But every other sense was under assault and soon to be overpowered. "I . . . would no longer *be* a lady."

"Nonsense," he said, and his lips closed the fractional space that separated him from her.

It amazed her that she could be sharply aware of herself and still very much aware of every little move he made.

She inhaled the subtle, masculine scent of him—the clean night air clinging to his clothing, the soap he'd used, his faintly rum-scented cologne. Even her own spicy rose fragrance had attached itself to him.

His warm, dry mouth nibbled at hers, kissed it, then nibbled again, working gently to pry her lips apart. She felt his arms come around her and pull her away from the door. She felt them lift her off her feet and settle her against him, his tongue invading her mouth as she gasped in surprise.

And then she lost awareness of everything but the kiss. Her tongue parried with his of its own accord; she found herself tasting him as he tasted her. Everything spun and shook, and there was a loud clamor in her ears, a fast-moving chaos in her body. Blood rushed, her heart pounded, and her lungs strained for air.

He finally freed her mouth and she dropped her face against his shoulder, gasping for breath, unable, unwilling to let him go.

They stood silently in the shadows for a long moment, she hanging from his neck like some bewitching amulet. Then he leaned down slowly and put her on her feet. He released her and reached to the window frame for her purse.

She tottered dangerously. He tucked her into his shoulder, laughing softly while fumbling with the small bag to find her key.

Successful at last, he felt for the lock and inserted the key. A loud click followed and he pushed the door open, standing with her still in his arm on the threshhold. The light in the window cast a small glow in the doorway. Her eyes looked into his, languid, impassioned, confused.

"Oh, Jack," she whispered simply. The sound reflected everything he saw in her eyes, but he heard something else he didn't like... A faint regret?

He kissed her again, hotly, quickly, to dissolve the sound. He didn't want to hear that she wasn't as completely taken with him as he was with her.

To his surprise, she kissed him back as ardently, then gave him one sweet, punctuating kiss. "I must go inside," she said. The sound had left her voice, but the look was now in her eyes.

He leaned in the doorway when she tried to close the door. "And I must have a new coat."

She shook her head at him, barely restraining a smile. "Jack, you're the best-dressed man in Astoria."

"But I'm running for mayor. I have to look superb. And there's a picnic on the Fourth of July. I need something to wear."

She tossed her purse inside and folded her arms. "Something red, white and blue. Something subtle with a flag across the back?" She giggled. "Or perhaps I could simply wrap you in Letty's bunting."

At that point, he'd have let her wrap him in barbed wire. "When shall I return for a fitting?"

She straightened and tried to push the door closed. "I'll use one of Connor's jackets for a pattern."

Jack held the door. "I'm bigger in the shoulders. And taller."

Her glance disputed that as she tugged off a glove. "His clothes fit you perfectly the day we were caught in the rain."

"I've grown since."

She stopped in the act of unbuttoning the second glove, laughing softly over his outrageous claim. "Between the ears, perhaps?"

A glint in his eye noted the sharp, though teasing barb. "Young lady," he said, leaning over her with half-hearted menace, "one day your wit will earn you dire retribution."

Her eyes widened in pretended dismay. "I don't imagine it would be wise for the mayoral candidate to be seen chastising Astoria's newest merchant."

"Then don't," he said quietly, "provoke him." He leaned to kiss her quickly once more. "I'll be here Wednesday with a cord of wood for Letty," he said, backing away. "In the afternoon. See that you fit me into your appointments."

That wouldn't be difficult, she thought. So far, except for Letty's ladies, she hadn't made one. "Two-thirty," she whispered loudly after him.

He nodded approval, then turned and headed for the street and home.

Charity closed the door behind her and leaned against it a moment, her eyes closed as she relived their kiss in every minute detail. Then she put a hand over her eyes as she recalled her strong, warm response to it. She'd hung inches off the ground for a long moment afterward, completely powerless to move or function.

Oh, God, she thought, walking worriedly to the window as she yanked off the second glove. There was danger where Jack McCarren was concerned. The devil of it was, the danger lay not with him, but with her.

Chapter Five

"Good morning, Miss Butler," Eleanor Johnson said when Charity opened the door. She looked over her shoulder and then back with a small smile, as though afraid her visit might be witnessed.

"Good morning, Mrs. Johnson," Charity replied, trying desperately not to betray surprise.

"I'd like to hire you." The woman didn't stammer or blink, but she clutched the handles of an embossed leather shopping bag. Had the bag been human, Charity thought, it would have died of asphyxiation.

Charity pushed her door open wider. "Won't you come inside, Mrs. Johnson?"

Eleanor Johnson sailed into the room, chin and formidable bosom held high.

Charity scooped the ever-present length of fabric, a simple cambric this time, off the room's overstuffed chair.

The woman sat on the very edge of the chair looking vaguely uncomfortable and embarrassed. Charity wasn't sure whether to be annoyed with her attitude or pleased that she'd come to what she must consider a den of suffragists.

Charity took the chair behind her sewing machine and turned to her guest with a smile of professional politeness. "How can I help you?"

Her guest seem to stiffen even further, still clutching the handles of her bag. "The other night at the opera house," she said, "you looked stunning." She sighed and ran a disparaging hand down the length of her own dress. "I, on the other hand, always look like a stevedore wearing a mourning dress."

Charity was taken aback by her self-deprecating candor. "Mrs. Johnson, that isn't . . ."

"True? Of course it is. I've always had these generous proportions and I've no idea how to dress them. One hears that brown and black are slimming, but they're also depressing. I would like to change my appearance."

That decision stated, she walked to the row of fabric bolts across the room. "I know it wouldn't suit me, but I admired that berry-colored dress you wore. Is there anything similar that would be appropriate for me?"

Charity thought it prudent not to tell Mrs. Johnson that she had borrowed the raspberry dress from Letty. And she thought she knew just what to do for her first customer outside of the Ladies for the Vote. She picked the current *Parisienne* off her sewing machine and went to stand beside Eleanor Johnson as she fingered fabrics.

"Fashion is taking a positive change for those of you blessed with bosoms and hips," Charity said diplomatically. She placed the magazine atop the bolts and pointed to an illustration of a dinner gown designed by Callot Soeurs.

"Blessed?" A stately eyebrow went up.

"Lines are straighter, simpler, more elegant," she explained. "With your posture, you would look almost royal in something like this."

Charity studied Eleanor Johnson's graying blond hair and pale blue eyes. She also noticed a subtle softening of her cool, controlled demeanor. She could like her, Charity thought.

"In a soft green or blue. The satin you're holding would be perfect."

"You're certain it isn't too...young?"

Charity pulled out the bolt and drew her to the mirror. She loosed a length of fabric and draped it around her.

The difference the soft blue made in Eleanor Johnson's complexion surprised a smile out of her.

"A short, loose sleeve," Charity said, creative excitement growing in her. "And a high neckline. What do you think?"

The woman frowned in the mirror. "You're certain?"

"Confidently so."

Charity made a sketch they agreed upon, took her measurements and accepted a deposit with false aplomb.

"If I'm as pleased as I believe I'll be," Eleanor Johnson said, "I'll come to you for an entirely new wardrobe when my husband is reelected."

The remark was intended to measure her reaction, Charity guessed. Unwilling to disappoint her, Charity smiled.

"And I was so hoping to be able to do more work for you."

Eleanor Johnson laughed softly as she pulled on her gloves. "Jack doesn't stand a chance, my dear."

"I suppose we'll see."

"I suppose we will."

Charity and her customer were discussing a time for her to return for a fitting when Letty burst in with a tea tray.

"Charity, I'm beginning to frighten myself with the prospect of hostessing Mrs. Vineyard and Mrs. Hensley at the convention. I swear I—" She stopped abruptly at the sight of Eleanor Johnson. She smiled with delighted surprise. "Hello, Nell. How nice to see you." She looked at the fabrics strewn around the small room and the paper on which Charity made notes. "You've come to have a dress made. How wonderful! Charity is far and away the best dressmaker this side of St. Louis."

"If she's able to make *me* look presentable," the woman said, her cool control back in place as she marched past Letty with her nose in the air, "she will be. Goodbye, Miss Butler." She did not say goodbye to Letty.

For an instant there was hurt in Letty's gray eyes, and a glimpse of the loneliness Charity sometimes saw there.

Charity walked Eleanor Johnson the few steps to the door and opened it for her. The frail camaraderie that had grown between them had disappeared.

Charity closed the door behind her very first customer outside Letty's circle of friends and felt a sense of acute depression. She rounded on Letty.

"How dare you let her make you feel uncomfortable in your own home," Charity scolded, taking the tea tray to the small table near the window and setting it down with a bang that made the crockery tinkle.

Letty, surprised by her vehemence, took the chair across the table and said, mildly defensive, "These two rooms are *your* home, not mine. And I shouldn't have burst in without—"

"Nonsense!" Charity interrupted. "You allow me free run of your end of the house. I assure you you're welcome in mine at any time, whether or not I have a customer."

"Polite ladies are not supposed to keep company with me. It's a fact, Charity."

Charity poured tea into the delicate china cups, then frowned at Letty as she held one out to her. "It's ridiculous."

Letty sipped her tea, then put her cup down and raised an eyebrow at Charity. "Now, now. There's no need to be upset. I deal with this all the time."

"It's absurd!"

"It's life."

Charity fell into the other chair and broke a piece of Finnish biscuit in half with a vicious twist of her fingers. "Well, you may deal with it in your end of the house, but in *my* end of the house, things will be different."

Letty reached across the table and patted her hand. "Charity, really. This does not call for apoplexy, it calls for compassion. Nell, for all her strength, is bound by convention and the demands of her husband's position."

"Do you know her very well?" Charity asked moodily.

"Well enough. We served on many church and civic committees until I fell into disgrace. She's a very competent woman."

"I thought I might like her, until she walked past you as though you weren't there."

"She has an intimidating presence, but it conceals a caring nature. Her husband's a pig, though. Astoria won't clean up as long as he's mayor."

"You mean he's corrupt?"

"I'm sure of it. So are Jack and Connor and anyone with a functioning brain. But Walter Johnson can be smooth, also. Last year he raised money loudly and publicly for a new school in Upper Town. So now no one notices that he looks the other way when men are shang-haied off the docks in Swill Town. It's even rumored that he's somehow allied with Ah Chun.''

Charity tore daintily at her biscuit and frowned. ''Who?''

''A work contractor in Chinatown,'' Letty replied, pushing a little bowl of butter Charity's way. ''The good contractors serve a purpose, I suppose, finding work for their countrymen when they come here.''

''Like an agency?''

Letty gave her a grim glance. ''In Ah Chun's case, it's not quite that civilized. He's one of the bad ones. He was somewhat of a thug in China and came here to escape retribution. In any case, he's in a position to exert a lot of control. He contracts workers for the canneries, ne-gotiates their wages, hours, work to be done. He some-times even provides their meals and lodgings.

''At the end of the season, the employer pays the con-tractor and he in turn pays the men. Whatever is left is his. In the meantime, he has most likely paid the work-ers' passage here, served as his banker and his landlord. The worker can be indebted to him for a lifetime.''

''It's difficult to believe anyone would want to be-come involved with him.''

''I'm sure the cannery workers believe they're coming to a better life than the poverty they knew at home, and some are simply at the mercy of circumstances—like Ming.''

Charity's eyes widened. ''Ming works for this man?''

Letty nodded. ''She had little choice. A ship's captain bought her from her father for three bags of rice and brought her over illegally on his ship. She was stranded here when his ship was wrecked coming over the bar. She had no money, and a reputation as a protitute because she had belonged to the captain. Ah Chun lent her money to buy clothes and found her a place to stay. Then he wanted her to repay him by working in his house of prostitution."

"No!"

"She refused, and came here instead. She'd become acquainted with Lum Quing, a man I buy my fruit and vegetables from. He knew I was looking for someone. Ah Chun allows it, as long as she turns in a share of her pay to him."

Charity put her cup down, indignant at the young woman's circumstances. "Are there no laws against such usury?"

"It's Chinatown," Letty replied quietly. "We don't understand them, and they don't understand us. They're usually left to take care of their own problems."

"Well, it sounds to me like a custom of avarice rather than a matter of culture."

"I agree. But that's the way it is. Getting back to Nell, I don't know if she has any idea what her husband is up to. I can't believe she'd stand for it if she did. She's always been very honest and forthright. On the other hand, he is her husband. If she does know, I imagine she feels she owes him a degree of loyalty."

Charity rocked gently back and forth. "She seems confident he'll be reelected."

Letty smiled affectionately. "Half the town considers Jack an upstart with ideas above his Astor Street background. The other half thinks he's imaginative and clever and filled with sound ideas for the city's future. It's hard to predict how the election will go."

She put her cup down and considered Charity. "You never did tell me how things went at the opera house the other night," she said.

Charity swallowed a bite of biscuit and pretended to misunderstand. "The play was delightful. I met Dr. Parson."

Letty gave her a severe look. "That isn't what I mean."

"Did you know that Dr. Parson believes women should have the vote?" Charity went on, ignoring Letty's pointed glare. "I told him you could find a duty for him. He asked that it be something small because he's a busy man."

"Thank you."

"I also met Nell Johnson. She saw me wearing *your* dress, and came here presuming I'd made it. I didn't enlighten her. By the way, your sashes are finished. Shall we try one on you?"

Charity went to the trunk where she had wrapped the sashes in paper for safekeeping.

Letty sighed. "You don't want to talk about Jack, do you?"

Charity shook her head apologetically. "Not at the moment. Perhaps when I better understand how I feel."

"Very well," Letty allowed with dramatic disappointment. "I suppose I can wait."

Letty came to stand beside her and Charity slipped the bright fabric over Letty's head so that it lay across her breast from shoulder to hip.

Letty studied herself in the mirror. "Perfect." She looked down to study the appliqué. "You do fine work, Charity. I can hardly see the stitches. Did you make one for yourself?" she teased, slipping it off. "We're beginning to think of you as one of our number, you know. Won't you join our parade on Tuesday? We're going to march through town to let everyone know about the rally next week."

Charity laughed lightly as she wrapped the sash. "I'm afraid not, Letty. I haven't the heart of a soldier." She certainly didn't need any additional attention. Living with Letty and attending the opera with Jack McCarren had already brought her more than she wanted. She'd had her first real customer this morning. Life in Astoria just might work out after all.

Letty picked up the tea tray and smiled at her. "I'm sure Napoleon would have been far less successful without his beautiful uniforms and the valiant little seamstresses who sewed them."

Charity bowed theatrically as Letty passed. "Thank you, Bonaparte."

"Letitia Donovan, you have the thickest head I've ever encountered on man or woman! What did you expect would happen when you marched into the Sunset Saloon?"

Charity looked up from the latest *Parisienne* and identified the angry male voice as Jack McCarren's. Surprise and curiosity drew her out of her rooms to the edge of the parlor. The last she knew, Letty had left with her ladies to march downtown. She hadn't mentioned a plan to stop at a saloon.

"I expected to be treated like a lady!" Letty shouted back. Charity couldn't see her, but her voice sounded high and a little shaken. Though the tone of the argument didn't encourage interference, concern brought Charity into the room.

Letty was sitting in the red and gold velvet chair that matched the divan. Jack knelt before her, touching his handkerchief to the corner of her mouth where there was a small trickle of blood.

"Letty!" Charity rushed forward as Kristine came from the kitchen with a bowl of water and a towel. Ming followed with the decanter of brandy and a glass.

"A lady would never have gone into a saloon!" Jack pointed out angrily, brushing her hand away when she tried to remove his.

"What happened?" Charity demanded. She took the towel from Kristine's arm, wet it in the bowl, then applied it to Letty's lip. Jack stepped out of the way. "What were you doing in a saloon?"

"Begging for trouble!" Jack replied. "It wasn't enough that she had to march her ladies through Swill Town. She had to go into the saloon!"

"Will you stop shouting at her!" Charity shouted at Jack. "She's been hurt."

"Well, that is no surprise, Charity," he said just as loudly, apparently oblivious to her request. "I am shouting because all my reasonably spoken opinions have been ignored. I told her going into the saloon was not a sound idea. But she wouldn't listen. She *had* to tell Spit Delaney that it was transparent and small of him to plan to give away free beer the day of her rally. She *had* to tell him that he was responsible for the enslavement of women."

Charity winced. Letty sighed. The plume on her hat fluttered as though still attached to the bird that had donated it. "By that time," Letty admitted quietly, a little regretfully, "I was beginning to lose my temper."

"Oh," Jack said in mock surprise. "That must be why you leapt onto the bar and kicked over all the beer lined up before the paying customers."

"Hardly all," she corrected stiffly. "You pulled me down before I was halfway along the bar."

"That's because Bo Englund was coming at you with a bottle! I'm sure he wasn't planning to offer you a drink."

"If you had left me on the bar I'd have never been hit!"

"If you had stayed outside after I dragged you down, you'd have never been hit!"

"You ducked on purpose!"

"I ducked because that's a strategy one follows when one is being swung at! I didn't know you had come back inside!" Jack had come around her chair now, and he stood over her. "You cannot walk into a saloon, accuse a man of every sin under the sun, and expect to escape unscathed. Now, you either promise me that you will abandon such grandstand measures or I'll send a telegram to Connor tonight."

Letty was out of the chair like a shot. "You do that and I will never speak to you again."

"At the moment," he replied calmly, glaring at her, "that fails miserably as a deterrent."

Letty stared at him one shaky moment, then her face crumpled and she ran from the room in tears. Kristine and Ming followed.

Charity turned to Jack, bristling. "Are you happy now?"

"Do I look happy?" he asked in the same tone. "She came this close..." He held up his thumb and forefinger, leaving a very small space between them. "This close to being seriously hurt. Not every man who spends time in a saloon is a degenerate or has abandoned his family or despoiled innocent women. Some are decent, honest men who need a quiet place to spend a little time and forget the duties and responsibilities that weigh on them. But there are a few who wouldn't think twice about eliminating anyone who interferes with that time—man or woman.''

Charity suddenly saw the deep-rooted concern in his eyes. ''Jack,'' she said gently. ''You must relax. Letty is all right.'' She pushed him gently toward the chair Letty had recently occupied. ''Sit down. I'll get you a brandy.''

He caught her hand and resisted her efforts to see him seated. ''I do not want a brandy. I want to know why you did nothing to stop her.''

Completely taken aback, Charity blinked. ''Stop her? Jack, I'm her tenant, not her mother or her nanny. Letty does what she believes to be right.''

''Right?'' he barked at Charity. ''Right? Is it right to put yourself in danger when you have an eight-year-old son and a husband who need you?''

''I'm sure it wasn't her intention to put herself in danger,'' Charity replied calmly. ''And if her husband needs her so much, I find it interesting that he remains invisible. If you're concerned about Letty's safety, why are you shouting at me rather than at the gentleman who attacked her with a bottle?''

''Because he's probably still unconscious where I left him,'' he returned. The he closed his eyes, drew a deep breath and shook his head. ''I apologize,'' he said, putting a hand to her shoulder. ''I didn't mean to shout at you. It just frightens me to think about what could have happened if Rolf hadn't been having lunch at the saloon and seen Letty march in. By the time I got there, all hell had broken loose and she was in danger of having her hair parted with a bottle of Rock and Rye. You ladies have got to think before you act.''

Charity was completely annoyed with his attitude and she removed his hand from her shoulder. ''If you are referring to me, you're right. I will have to think before I act. So far I've remained on the sidelines, neither for Letty's suffragists nor against them, too busy with starting my business to be concerned. But if you are referring to Letty, I assure you she has thought about the path she's chosen—every lonely afternoon and evening. I'm sure fighting for what she believes has left her with a lot of empty time to *think*."

Jack squared his shoulders, obviously as annoyed with her as she was with him. "There are civilized ways to go about proposing changes. Invading a saloon is not one of them."

Charity folded her arms. "Perhaps you could leave us a list of what is acceptable and what is not."

"Charity—"

"Or perhaps you would prefer to simply leave."

Jack studied her for one long moment, then snatched his hat from the low table and stalked to the door. He stopped to turn and glower at her. "I thought you'd be a good influence on Letty," he said. "Apparently I was mistaken."

She shrugged a careless shoulder. "I thought you a good friend. I see that I was wrong, as well."

He yanked the door open. "You weren't wrong, Charity," he said. "Simply misguided about the duties of a friend. I'll be by tomorrow for my fitting as scheduled."

She nodded. "My pins and I will be ready."

Jack walked down the hill to the factory and contemplated mayhem. He had a mind to put Letty in one of his big cannery boxes and ship her to Connor on the Portland steamer—C.O.D. Let him find a way to reason with her.

He would deal with the sassy Miss Butler himself. He suspected her sharp-tongued superiority could be softened if she was kept too busy to talk.

The whistle blew the end of shift when he was within a block of the factory. By the time he made his way along the pier, he was passing his men who were shrugging into jackets and calling their goodbyes.

"Get her home safe and sound, Mr. McCarren?" one of the men shouted at him. Everyone turned to hear his answer. He'd had quite an audience during the incident with Letty.

"I did," he replied with a wave.

"Put her in the kitchen where she belongs?"

"I'm afraid she isn't mine to put anywhere. Good night, men."

"My woman knows better than to try that on me."

Jack heard their grumbles as they streamed up the pier toward home.

"Mr. Donovan needs to get himself home and give her a little something to do," another man called out.

"A bored woman is an unhappy woman."

"My woman ain't bored, but she ain't happy, either."

"Well, she lives with *you*, Einer." There was back-slapping and good-natured guffaws.

Jack disappeared into the quiet of the factory and his office, thinking guiltily that he hadn't given time to his campaign in days. He was too busy thinking of Charity or saving Letty from assault.

He knew acting on Letty's behalf this afternoon hadn't helped his chances of becoming mayor. But he'd sworn to himself when he'd started this that he'd bow to no interests but his own. If keeping his promise to Connor to watch out for Letty resulted in his losing the election, then so be it. But he was intent on doing his damnedest to somehow manage her safety and his campaign at the same time. He could see clearly it wasn't going to be easy.

"You sending for Connor?" Rolf made himself comfortable on the corner of Jack's desk. He picked up a pencil and tapped it against his thigh.

"No," Jack replied, trying to restore order to his desk. "Did the mill's order get out?"

"Of course." Rolf watched Jack's hands sift through the paperwork, then asked quietly, "Charity's angry with you, too, isn't she?"

Jack looked at him, impatient but interested. "How did you know that?"

"Nothing ever rattles you except the pretty little lady from Kansas. Didn't like you cutting short the little warrior queen's battle against the enslavement of women, did she?"

Jack leaned back in his chair with an indignant sigh. "She was completely unreasonable."

Rolf didn't seem to understand why he was surprised. "She's a woman. They come that way."

Jack shook his head. "Not this one. She's usually calm and orderly and very sane. But when I suggested that she and Letty and her ladies think before they act, she turned on me like a summer storm."

Rolf rolled his eyes heavenward and laughed. "No wonder. How did you manage to live this long thinking you could criticize a woman's behavior?"

"I didn't criticize, I just suggested..."

"A woman takes suggestion as criticism."

"So what do you do? Let them execute every outrageous idea that crosses their minds and pray they don't get maimed or killed or worse?"

Rolf thought about that. "I think so. Either that or marry them. Marriage is supposed to give you the right to tell them what to do. But it doesn't always work. My uncle Olaf has a leg that isn't right to this day because he told my aunt Maia she should watch her tongue. She did. She clenched it between her teeth as she swung the shovel at him."

Jack was never sure if Rolf's endless stories about his eccentric relatives were true or not. But at the moment, he could identify with Olaf.

"Why don't you join me for dinner tonight? I don't imagine you were invited to Letty's."

"You're not seeing the chanteuse?"

"No. She has an offer of marriage from a fisherman from String Town."

"And you don't wish to counteroffer?"

Rolf leapt off the desk and reached to the rack for his hat. "No. She wants six children. I'm not sure I have the stamina."

Jack stood, laughing. "To produce them or to raise them?"

Rolf put his hat on at a rakish angle. "You know my prowess is legend. Raising them would be the problem. I have to be available to you sixteen hours every day to help you manage this place, to help you fight off bears, to counsel you on women . . ."

Jack put an arm around his shoulders and led him to the door. "Then I suppose dinner should be on me."

"This will be good." Kristine dabbed witch hazel on Letty's swollen lip. "Tomorrow it will not hurt, and by the next day, it will not be big anymore."

"Thank you, Kristine." The four women and Jon were crowded into the bathroom.

"Why don't you let me bring you supper in bed," Charity suggested.

"We'll have dinner at the table," Letty said firmly. She finally pulled Kristine's hand away, assuring her that she was fine. "It's just a small cut." Letty worked her jaw, then smiled. "There. I'm fine."

Ming, still holding the brandy and the twice filled glass, filled it a third time and held it out to Letty. Charity was a little surprised when she took it and downed it. The pain her friend was feeling at the moment was not in her jaw, Charity suspected. Letty had been defeated and embarrassed and shouted at. She needed a loving husband's comfort. But he was a hundred miles away.

Letty handed the glass to Ming, took Jon's hand and headed in a slightly irregular line for the dining room.

"Uncle Jack was very angry," Jon noted as he took his seat beside his mother. "You don't think he won't ever come back, do you?"

"I'm sure he'll be back," Letty said, shaking out her napkin and placing it on her lap. Kristine and Ming hurried into the kitchen. "In fact, I'm going to the factory first thing in the morning to apologize."

"What?" Charity sat on Letty's other side and glowered at her. "Why should you be the one to apologize? He has no right to shout at you and tell you how to behave."

"He was quite right about the saloon," Letty said, helping Jon with his napkin. "Going in was an impulse I regret. I'd had such hopes for the march. And then the saloon keeper came out and offered free beer to everyone standing on the street to divert their attention." She sighed wryly at Charity. "Men have so many tools to use against us. They can challenge our femininity, accuse us of neglecting our families, of being malcontents and sexless hooligans. They can dispense free beer. What can we do? Promise them intelligent, well-rounded, free-thinking women who will better their lives and enliven their homes? Somehow I think they'd fail to believe that. The frustration finally drove me to behave stupidly.''

"It wasn't stupid,'' Charity defended. "It was brave.''

Letty shook her head. "It was foolish. And Jack was only keeping his promise to Connor.''

At the sound of his father's name, Jon brightened. "Papa might come home to scold you, Mama,'' he said.

Letty smiled blandly at Charity. "Now, there's a delightful prospect.''

Chapter Six

Jack arrived at Letty's door with an armload of flowers before she'd finished breakfast.

"You're featherbrained," he said, placing them in her arms with a smile, "but I'm sorry I shouted at you."

Letty clutched the flowers to her chest and invited him inside. "Name-calling is such a lovely way to start the day. Will you join us for breakfast?"

"Please."

Letty led the way into the dining room, calling for Kristine to set another place and bring a vase.

As Jack sat down, Charity stood and picked up her plate.

"I suppose I've spoiled your appetite," he taunted after her as she went toward the kitchen.

"If not my entire day," she called back without turning around.

Jack frowned as Kristine put a napkin and utensils in front of him. "Your ladies are a difficult bunch, Letty," he said.

"She's not one of my ladies, Jack," Letty denied. "She's just my friend. Friends are loyal."

Jack closed his eyes in exasperation. When he opened them he found a plate filled with eggs, bacon and bread.

"Thank you, Kristine. I am your friend, Letty. But I've a certain ob—"

She forestalled him with a smile. "I know. Enjoy your breakfast. I assure you I will not be calling on saloons in the near future. You may rest easy."

He nodded to be agreeable and to reestablish their peaceful relationship. But with the advent of the growing campaign for women's suffrage and the arrival of Miss Charity Butler, he seriously doubted he'd ever rest easy again.

The door that connected the conservatory with Charity's shop was open. Jack rapped on it.

"Come in, Jack," Charity called from across the room where she stored a short section of French and English worsteds, cassimere, serge and vicuña.

Her manner was as formal as it had been when he'd left the house the night before, but she did deign to glance in his direction as she beckoned him to the fabric. He took that as a positive sign.

"I presume," she said, placing her hand at the top of a bolt and tilting it sideways so that she could finger an end of it and hold it out to him, "that you'll want something lightweight, probably white."

He didn't look at the fabric. He observed instead the way the morning sun through the window highlighted the gleaming, dark richness of her hair, which was gathered loosely atop her head. Little curls danced around her ears and the nape of her neck above her high lace-trimmed collar. The need to tug on one and watch it spring back was almost overwhelming.

Charity held the fabric a little higher, trying to divert his disturbing dark eyes from the slow perusal of her hair. She was finding it an effort to maintain yesterday's annoyance with him. He looked so crisp and fresh this morning. He seemed to take up all the space in her small workshop and, for some reason she couldn't understand, all the air surrounding her. She had to breathe deeply to fill her lungs.

His eyes left her hair to watch the lacy bodice of her waist rise and fall as she drew a breath. Then they rose to her eyes, alarmingly dark and knowing.

"It would help, Jack," she said, lowering her lashes and holding the fabric even higher, "if you would pay attention to the task at hand."

"But I am," he replied.

Her eyes glanced up to take issue with that. "You're staring at my... at me." She blushed.

"I am," he admitted. "Perhaps we have differing opinions on precisely what the task at hand is."

She tried to look businesslike despite the flush in her cheeks. "I thought you were here for a fitting."

"I am." With a quick movement she didn't see coming, he pushed the bolt of fabric into its slot against the wall, then pulled her into his arms.

A little squeak of surprise escaped her as she felt herself gently imprisoned against a beautifully cut gray wool jacket by the wonderfully large and tensile muscles it concealed. Strong arms closed around her until she felt her soft bosom flattened against the solid wall of his chest.

Slightly overbalanced, she clung to his shoulders, his knee between hers.

"There now," Jack said softly, a hand flattened between her shoulder blades, holding her still. "A perfect fit. You are clever at this, Charity."

She had to struggle to think. Her brain was overpowered with sensation. "We were to...select a fabric... for..."

"I like the white you showed me," he said, his eyes concentrating on the supple fullness of her bottom lip. As he watched, she pursed it.

"You didn't look at it," she said.

"If you like it," he said, slowly lowering his head, "I like it."

She should draw back, she told herself. She should push against him. But he held her so firmly, she was sure the struggle would be futile. And she knew she didn't want him to release her before he had kissed her.

She breathed his name in token protest.

He closed his mouth over hers and swallowed the whisper. He kissed her long and lingeringly, as though he had nothing more to do this sunny morning but drive her mindless with his artful lips.

He finally raised his head and smiled into her half-closed eyes. "Another perfect fit," he said, still holding her to him with one hand while the thumb of the other smoothed an involuntary tremble in her lower lip. "With no effort at all."

"Charity! I must tell you that Nell Johnson admired my dress at the Tea and Musicale on Sunday and she asked me where— Oh, dear!"

Harriet Clune's little speech had begun in the middle of the conservatory, long before she appeared in the doorway of Charity's shop. It stopped abruptly when she reached the middle of the room and spotted the object of her search in the arms of Jack McCarren.

Charity pushed herself out of Jack's embrace with a guilty start and turned to Harriet, her cheeks red with leftover ardor and sharp embarrassment.

Jack nodded at Harriet with a grin. "Good morning, Miss Clune. You're looking lovely this morning."

She blushed and giggled. "It's this dress Charity made for me." She did a swift and surprisingly graceful turn. She gave Charity a paradoxical smile that held both censure and approval. "I apologize for the interruption. I'll tell Letty all about it while we're having tea, and she can tell you about it when you're no longer...when you're free." With a parting wave for Jack, Harriet disappeared.

Charity smoothed the front of her blouse and unnecessarily tugged at her sleeves as she went back to the row of fabrics.

"So much for the professionalism I try so hard to put forth," she said with a glance at Jack that suggested the failure was his fault. "Now, can we get down to business?"

He leaned a hip on the edge of her sewing table and folded his arms. "We were conducting business," he said. "Serious business. But I imagine you're talking about fabric and buttons and not romance."

"That's right." She pulled the fabric out again, then held a mother-of-pearl button against it. "Double-breasted will be the new fashion in the fall," she said, returning his smiling gaze with one of gravity. "But if you would feel safer remaining conservative, single-breasted would still be appropriate."

Jack considered a moment. "I'm not sure that a mayor who looks like a page out of a Paris magazine would appeal to the voters of Astoria. I believe single-breasted would be the wiser choice," he said finally.

"Of course." She pushed the bolt in place. "I suppose your constituency in Swill Town would be appalled by liberal notions such as women's suffrage and fashion." She walked around him to drop the buttons on her sewing table and pick up her tape measure. She turned to face him. "Stand, please."

"Swill Town," he said quietly, straightening to his full height with a determined purpose that made her take a step backward, "has its seedy element. But it is also filled with hardworking men and women polite society considers unsuitable. You sought rooms there yourself a brief two weeks ago."

Her stance softened immediately. "I know that. I apologize. I'm not angry at them." An upward flick of her eyelashes told him precisely with whom she *was* angry.

"Ah, now we come to it," he said. "You're annoyed with me for daring to tell the heroic Letitia Donovan that she behaved badly. Well, I'm afraid young women who choose to be alone in life are sometimes in need of a man's guidance and protection to avoid disaster, whether they like it or not."

"Is that so? Remove your jacket, please."

"My dear Miss Butler," he said as he unfastened the three leather buttons, "every time you get me in this room, you proceed to undress me. Perhaps we should discuss your intentions."

"My intentions are simply to measure you, Mr. McCarren." She placed one end of her tape at the base of his collar. The other end she held carefully away from him to just below his hips, trying to ignore his broad back and immaculate white shirt. "Has it never occurred to you that women who choose to be alone in this world do so because they don't want the interference of a man in their lives?"

"Is that why you are alone?" He looked at her over his shoulder. The action turned his body slightly, causing his buttocks to bump against the hand in which she held the tape.

She yanked it away as though she'd been scalded and leaned over the table to write down the measurement. She straightened and turned him around, bending his arm at the elbow and measuring him from the middle of his back to the point of his elbow, then from his elbow to his wrist.

"Well?" he asked when she offered no answer.

"I'm alone," she said, noting the measurements, "because my mother passed away. I thought I'd explained that."

"Where is your father?"

"In Kansas." It wasn't precisely a lie, she rationalized. She lifted his arms up and away from his body, then leaned into him to wrap the tape around his chest. She caught that rum-soap scent again and felt everything inside her quiver at the breadth of him. His arms could close around her so easily and make her forget that she'd come here to start over—alone.

"A farmer?"

She noted the measurement, then lowered the tape to his waist. When she failed to answer, he took her face in his hands and lifted it to him. His eyes were curious and watchful. "A farmer?" he asked again.

"No." Despite her every effort, she felt it all rise inside her—the anguish, the embarrassment, the alienation. But she kept her expression carefully blank. "A sort of . . . miner."

He frowned, confused. "He allowed you to come out here alone?"

She shook her head. "We were never very fond of each other. I wouldn't have listened to him had he *tried* to stop me." That was true, if a little misleading. "Now, please." She removed his hands from her face and placed them out and away from his body while she took his waist measurement again. "It will be all your fault if your white jacket looks like Genghis Khan's tent."

He waited until she'd taken the measurement and written it down. Then he captured her chin between his thumb and forefinger and forced her to look into his eyes.

"Why are you afraid to discuss your family with me?"

She felt her heartbeat accelerate. Remain calm, she told herself forcefully. It's a perfectly logical question. She drew a deep breath and replied honestly. "Because the last few years of my life are not something I care to remember. I'm simply happy to have them behind me."

They weren't behind her. He could see the grief they'd caused her in her eyes. "All right." He dropped his hands and put them in his pockets, happy enough to dismiss the matter if that was what she wanted. "I just want to be sure you haven't abandoned a husband and a brood of children."

He saw the relief in her eyes. "I have, actually." She wound the tape measure around her fingers until she had a fat loop that she secured through the center with a pin. "I left an accountant in Boston with a set of twins, a cowboy in Texas with three little boys and my last, a railroad man in Topeka, with..." She dropped the tape into a cigar box on her table and stopped with a theatrical forefinger to her lips. "Let me think. Was it six or seven little girls? I can never recall, you see, because I never had the same number at supper."

"Well." Jack's dry glance acknowledged her evasive little game as he picked up his jacket. "I think it only fair to warn you that when I become husband number four, I won't allow you to run off on me."

Charity shook her head and went to take the jacket from him and hold it open. "Oh, after three husbands and a dozen children I've decided to live out my dotage quietly in Astoria. No more husbands for me."

He slipped into the jacket and turned to her, his gaze alarmingly direct despite a glint of humor. "I will be your one and only husband, Charity Butler," he said, shrugging his big shoulders to adjust the jacket before buttoning it. "And you will learn not to chafe at a little healthy guidance."

Charity followed him to her door. "I would have to be dead not to chafe at a little male guidance."

He stopped in the doorway to look at her. "You will not have to die. You will simply have to adjust to life in my arms." And, as though to remind her what that was like, he wrapped an arm around her and leaned over her to kiss her senseless. Then he walked out the door and left her standing in a square of morning sunshine, completely upset.

Charity watched him pause to send her a wink and a wave before going on his way. She waved back, plagued by a guilty conscience. She should have told him about her father rather than answer his questions with half-truths and outright lies.

She'd come to Astoria rather than accept a proposal of marriage because the only male example in her life, her father, represented every evil she prayed never to encounter again.

His drinking had taken every penny she'd tried to save from the day she began doing chores for the mayor's wife at nine years old. Protests had only earned her the back of his hand and a frightened warning from her mother to be quiet and let him be.

Her father would be gone for weeks at a time, then return with several friends, dirty and drunk, and make every day a misery until he was gone again.

Charity had watched her mother tiptoe nervously around him, afraid to complain or ask for even the most basic necessities. She'd averted her eyes from neighbors who'd turned their noses up at them and whispered about what her father did when he was away.

Charity closed her door and leaned against it, recalling what she'd told Jack about her father being a miner. It had been her touch of gallows humor. Though her father had never been gainfully employed as long as she could remember, he'd probably spent enough time on prison rock piles to give that a small measure of credence. She'd been ten before she realized her father was a notorious train robber.

Charity sat at her sewing machine and disconsolately fiddled with the length of brown wool lying across it. When she'd left Kansas, she'd sworn she'd never think about her father again and that no man would ever have a say in how she conducted her life.

She smoothed the wool between her fingers and drew a deep, unsettled breath. Of course, then she hadn't known men like Jack McCarren existed.

"But, missy..." Ming held the blue silk dress to her, her small bow-shaped mouth open in disbelief. "Not for Ming."

"Yes, it is," Charity insisted, coming around behind her to study her reflection in the mirror. It was impossible to tell over her standard dark quilted pants and worn jacket, but Charity felt sure the gown she'd made in the traditional Mandarin style would look beautiful on Ming.

"You did so much to help me get my shop ready that I wanted to thank you."

The concept of thanks seemed foreign to Ming as she looked at herself in the mirror again. Finally a smile dawned, then a small laugh erupted. Letty and Kristine, watching from the other side of her, burst into laughter.

"And this is for you, Kristine." Charity picked up pink and white dress from an overstuffed chair. "For Sundays and dances at Suomi Hall."

"Oh, Miss Charity." Kristine held the dress up by its ample shoulders and stared at it. "But why? Ming did all the work."

Charity came to give her a hug. "You bring me tea every morning and afternoon when I'm too busy to come to the kitchen for it."

"But that is my job."

"You aren't paid for the smiles that come with it, nor the witch hazel for my nicked fingers nor the massages for my sore back." She stepped back to smile fondly at the trio. "I count myself lucky to have come so far all alone and to have found such wonderful friends."

Letty placed an arm around her shoulders. "We feel fortunate, too, Charity. Thanks to you, we're the three best-dressed women in town." She looked at Charity's gray skirt, covered with thread and lint and chalk marks, and smiled wryly. "I certainly hope you've made something for yourself. Jack and Rolf are coming for dinner tonight. You look quite the ragamuffin at the moment."

Kristine and Ming hugged Charity in thanks, then left the room, talking excitedly and comparing their gifts.

Charity fought the stirring of excitement she felt at the prospect of seeing Jack. "You've invited the warden back?" she asked, trying to keep the pleasure out of her voice as she expressed surprise.

Letty laughed and idly surveyed the garments under production on the shelves in Charity's work closet. "You must understand something about Jack, and most men in general. They are born with the conviction that they alone know what is best for everyone, particularly those they love. The difficulty is…" She examined the skirt of a tea gown and glanced at Charity with a grin. "They have the muscle to execute their wishes." She fingered the delicate fabric, then let it drop and moved on to the skeletal construction of Jack's white jacket. "When we fight back in the same way, as frustration often drives us to do, we inevitably lose. So we have to be clever and resourceful. I forgot that. And it isn't fair to blame Jack for trying to protect me from the chaos that resulted in the saloon."

Letty's eyes lost their focus for a moment as she wandered away from the closet. Charity wondered if she was thinking that it was also not fair to blame Connor, either. Then she sighed and with a toss of her head Letty seemed to dismiss her thoughts. She turned to Charity with a knowing look. "And don't try to pretend that you won't be delighted to see him again. Despite the way you snipe at him when he visits, I know what's going on inside you, Charity Butler."

Charity began to tidy up the room, folding remnants of fabric and rolling up trims. "The only thing going on inside me is the plan to build my little business and make every woman in Astoria dress like a princess."

"Every princess," Letty said gently, "should have a prince."

Charity shook her head, placing folded fabric into her trunk. "Not this one."

Letty took a pile of folded fabric from the chair and took it to Charity. "Why not?"

Charity tucked it into a corner, covered the whole with paper, then lowered the lid and straightened.

"For the same reason, that you and Connor are living apart. I don't want a man directing my life any more than you want one telling you what to do."

Letty shook her head. "But Connor and I had a basic difference of opinion. Until that time, our marriage was lovely."

Now Charity was the one confused. "Then why don't you try to recapture that? If you were happy together once, certainly you can be happy together again?"

Letty considered a moment, then shook her head again. "I don't think so. We both went too far, said too much. But you..." She took Charity's arms and frowned into her dark eyes. "I don't understand what holds you back. Jack does tend to give orders, but I'm sure he would be a kind and attentive husband."

Despite their argument the other night, Charity had little doubt he would be a good husband. But even if they'd known each other long enough to consider such a thing, he was a man with a difficult past trying to fit into a very demanding society. Added to that, he was a candidate for mayor, carefully watched by everyone. And she was the notorious Calvin Ross's daughter.

A cold feeling settled in the pit of her stomach. She had moved eighteen hundred miles away, but she had not escaped the fact of her parentage, even though she'd changed her name.

Letty dipped her head to look into Charity's eyes. "Charity, what is it?" she asked quietly. "What did you leave behind in Kansas?"

Nothing, she realized sadly. She'd brought it with her. It would always be with her.

She forced a smile for Letty and a brisk tone that would make her stop questioning. "I told Jack I'd left behind a railroad husband and seven little girls."

Letty blinked. "Whatever for?"

Charity bustled around, continuing to tidy. "Because he'd asked me if I'd left a husband behind in Kansas."

Charity expected Letty to laugh. She didn't. She simply watched her clear off the surface of her worktable. "So he's seen that look, too," she said quietly. "Sometimes your eyes are haunted, Charity."

The simple statement struck Charity like a slap. Haunted was precisely the way she felt, when she had time to think about it.

To cover her surprise, Charity grinned at Letty as she dropped a colorful quilted cloth over her sewing machine. "The ghost of old debts," she said in a quavery voice.

"Very well, *don't* tell me," Letty said, feigning hurt feelings as she went to the door. "Keep it to yourself and let me imagine the worst. Perhaps you did abandon a husband and seven little girls."

"Oh, I did," Charity said. "Shall I name them for you? There was Alice, Belinda, Cornelia, Dorcas..."

Letty rolled her eyes and left the room.

Charity sank into the chair in front of her sewing machine, exhausted. It was difficult to pretend with Letty, and not much easier with Jack. Perhaps she could plead a headache tonight, and avoid dinner altogether.

Charity dismissed the idea as she walked into her bedroom. That would be cowardly. When she'd packed her bags for Oregon, she'd decided she had to face life as it was and make a place for herself in it. She couldn't do that by hiding in her room.

She lay back on the bed and stretched her arms over her head, letting her mind and her body relax so that she could prepare for the evening ahead.

Then, unbidden, an image of Jack beside her on the bed rose in her mind. She had little trouble conjuring his kisses now that she was becoming so familiar with them. As clearly as though it was happening, she felt his warm nakedness against her own, his muscled chest to her soft breasts, his angular leg against her own, his...

She sat up abruptly, breathing heavily, her mind and senses reeling. It couldn't be. It simply couldn't be. She went to her closet and selected her favorite dinner dress, white with a high pearl collar and a lace bodice with lace appliqués on the skirt. It was the prettiest dress she owned, and she chose it to prove to herself that she could do this.

She would present herself at the table and be charming to Letty's guests, but she would tolerate none of Jack's flirtations, nor his remarks about matrimony, because Charity Butler had plans of her own that did not include him. But mostly because, though he didn't know it, his plans could not include her.

Her resolve nearly disappeared the moment he walked into the room. Letty, lighting candles on the white lace cloth, shooed her to the door, insisting that Kristine couldn't leave the kitchen, and Ming was searching the cupboards for the gravy boat.

Jack, hat in hand as she held the door, opened his mouth as though to speak, then stopped, his eyes slowly tracing every inch of her. "Charity," he said finally. "You're a vision."

"Jack, please don't start," she cautioned him, secretly pleased with his reaction. "Come in. Good evening, Rolf."

"You *are* a vision," Rolf said, sweeping off his hat as she closed the door behind them. "We haven't walked through the pearly gates, have we?"

Jack laughed dryly. "I don't believe the pearly gates would admit us, Rolf."

He gave his hat to Charity, as did Rolf, and watched her reach up gracefully to place them on the oak rack. The ruching of her gown camouflaged her hips, but not their gentle sway as she moved. He stared, almost overcome.

"You're here for pot roast," Rolf whispered in his ear, "not to devour the young lady."

"I can't help it," Jack returned softly. "I've a desperate craving for the young lady."

Then Jonathan was upon them, and before long they were all seated in the middle of the living room floor assembling the cars of a tin train.

"Papa sent it on the *River Rose,*" Jonathan boasted, his face lit with pleasure.

Letty brought them wine in crystal goblets.

"None for me?" Jonathan asked.

"There'll be milk for you with dinner, Jonny. Now, don't pester your uncle. He's here to relax. I'll be right back as soon as we find the gravy boat."

"Perhaps it's moored on the river," Rolf suggested. Jonathan laughed and Jack and Letty groaned.

"He means because it's called a boat, it should be on the river. Like a real boat," Jonathan was quick to explain, anxious to help them understand the joke.

Jack nodded, ruffling the boy's hair. "Thank you, Jon."

Letty disappeared into the kitchen. Jon, on his knees, pushed the train across the rose-patterned carpet.

Jack rested a forearm on his raised knee and regarded his friend with a crooked eyebrow. "Perhaps its moored on the river? My God, Kauppi. You're beginning to frighten me. Humor is one thing—insanity is another."

Rolf, reclining on an elbow, examined a piece of metal track Jonathan had abandoned in search of new horizons. "I believe I'm influenced by the doubtful company I keep. You aren't—"

He stopped abruptly at a sudden chorus of high-pitched shrieks followed instantly by a reverberating crash.

Jack raced into the kitchen, Rolf right behind him. He saw Letty and Kristine kneeling over a confusing mound of blue-clad legs, white lace and what appeared to be bloomer ruffles.

"Oh, Jack!" Letty beckoned him closer. "Ming's fallen on Charity! Come and help us."

"What?" he asked, alarmed at the little moans and groans coming from the colorful, faintly stirring pile.

"She was standing on the counter looking for the gravy boat and she lost her footing. Charity tried to catch her when she went off balance, and she fell on top of her."

Letty spoke hurriedly and nervously as Jack lifted Ming off Charity and handed her up to Rolf. She appeared shaken and disoriented.

"Take her into the parlor and put her on the settee," Letty said, shooing Kristine to follow and check on her friend.

Jack ran his hands lightly over Charity's arms and legs. "I don't think anything's broken," he said, putting a hand to Charity's face as her eyelashes fluttered. "Charity? Does anything hurt?"

"My shoulder." She winced as she tried to prop herself up in a sitting position. Jack put a hand on her back to help her. "I don't think it's anything serious. I just hit the table on my way down. Is Ming all right?"

"I think so," Letty said.

Jack leaned her over his arm to inspect her shoulder. The soft skin was red and already bruising.

"Oh, Charity, your dress is ruined," Letty said, noticing a ragged tear in the lacey fabric.

"Letitia, for God's sake," Jack said impatiently. "The girl's nearly cracked her skull and you're worried about her dress?"

Letty raised an eyebrow at his tone, then rose to her feet in a flurry of taffeta skirt. "Put her on the divan. I'll get the witch hazel. I'm going to have to start buying it by the case."

As Letty disappeared, Jack braced Charity's back, then slipped a hand under her legs. She tried to push against him.

"I can walk, Jack," she said, but he wasn't listening. She was already several feet off the ground in a pair of sturdy male arms.

Jack gave the swinging door into the dining room a kick that swung it far enough to allow them through.

"Jack," Charity tried again, wriggling in his hold, "you can put me down. I'm perfectly capable of—"

"Of unnecessary speech at inappropriate times," he finished for her. "Yes, I know. This would be easier for both of us if you'd just be still."

They passed Ming lying on the settee with Rolf and Kristine hovering over her.

"Ming is well," Charity heard her say. "Miss Chatty very soft."

"Miss Chatty?" Jack repeated softly as he eased Charity onto the divan across the room. "Now, that's appropriate."

Charity made a face at him as he propped pillows behind her and positioned her to keep her bruise from making contact with the upholstery.

Jack sat on the edge of the divan beside her. He placed an arm on the carved wood of the back, trapping her. She felt the air around her whisk away, like fire up a chimney, and knew it had nothing to do with the fall.

His eyes were dark with concern as they moved over her face. "Are you certain you feel all right, apart from your shoulder?"

"Quite sure," she insisted. "Ming probably weighs less than Jonathan, and we didn't fall very far."

"What were you doing in the kitchen, anyway?" he asked.

The question had a slightly censorious tone, and she took advantage of it to plague him. It was so satisfying. "Why, flying in the face of danger, of course. We single women have an unsettling tendency to do that. I believe it's because we have no men in our lives to protect us from disaster and guide our steps in the—"

"That's enough," Jack said with a smile that wasn't entirely composed of amusement. "Thank you, Letty." Letty handed him the bottle of witch hazel and a cloth, then went to the settee to check on Ming.

His ministrations to her shoulder were gentle. When he caused her to wince, he placed a kiss on the gentle slope. "I'm sorry," he said softly. "Here. One more application and we're finished."

"Jack," she whispered in mortification, looking over her shoulder to see if anyone had noticed. But the others were busy steadying Ming on her feet and standing by as she walked a few steps.

"There." He ignored her concern and sat back to shake his head. "It is too bad about the dress."

Charity reached a hand to try to assess the damage. "If the tear isn't too large," she said, "I can repair it with a lace appliqué." Then she frowned at her dusty skirt. "Provided I haven't dirtied it beyond redemption. Kristine keeps a spotless kitchen, but we've all been tramping through it this evening trying to help."

"All on our account?" Jack asked.

"Yes," Charity replied candidly. "Letty does consider you her dearest friend."

Jack reciprocated that thought with an inclination of his head. Then his eyes pinned hers, alive with amusement and some emotion she was afraid to investigate too closely. "And what do you consider me, Charity?"

Charity looked into his handsome face, the challenge to her independence clearly written there, and replied with a little sigh. "A threat to my peace of mind."

Chapter Seven

"I will not hear of it!" Letty said firmly, putting Ming's coat around her shoulders. "Rolf will take you home at once, and you are not to come tomorrow if you don't feel well." She studied the angry bruise on the young woman's hand, a victim of the table that had bruised Charity.

"But Ming is fine." She tried to protest softly, clutching the paper-wrapped bundle of her new dress as she resisted Letty's efforts to push her toward the door.

"Come on, little one." Rolf reached a large hand out for her. "There's little point in arguing. Letty can talk longer than we can."

Ming studied the hand held out to her, then looked into Rolf's kind blue eyes and slowly extended her hand. His enveloped it gently as he led her to the door. "I'll be back," he said with a wink at Letty. "Don't let Jack eat everything."

As the door closed behind them, Jack noted that all three women were staring at it, Letty and Kristine from the middle of the parlor and Charity, turned in her corner of the divan, her mouth slightly open as though in surprise.

The women turned to each other in concert. "Do you think?" Letty asked Charity.

Charity smiled slowly. "It certainly seemed to be."

"What?" Jack asked.

"I would say so, ya," Kristine added, large, capable hands folded over her apron. "Ya."

"What?" Jack asked again.

"Rolf and Ming," Letty replied, moving to put a diagnostic hand to Charity's forehead.

"What about them?"

"Romance," Letty replied with a gently impatient glance at him. "Are you blind? Are you all right, Charity? Do you feel up to dinner or would you like Jack to help you to bed?"

Charity looked into Jack's eyes and saw precisely the suggestive gleam she'd expected to see.

"I'm famished," she said, swinging her legs over the side of the divan. Jack stood to help her up. "And after all we've been through to find the cursed gravy boat, I'd like to see it in use."

Kristine shrieked. "The gravy!" She headed at a lumbering run for the kitchen. Letty followed, assuring her that no one would perish if the gravy was inedible.

"We'll put cream in the gravy boat," she said, following the maid into the kitchen. "And pour it over our berries."

Jack laughed softly, keeping an arm around Charity as she walked to the table. "Good old Letty," he said. "Another crisis turned to creative purpose." He pulled a chair out and saw her seated. "There. Opposite me. Now I can gaze into your eyes all evening."

"You'll miss the food that way," she cautioned wryly.

"Your beauty," he said with a theatrical hand to his heart, "will give me sustenance."

She made a scornful sound. "On my beauty, a man could starve to death. Will you please be seated? Your hovering is exhausting me."

Jack walked around the table to stand behind his chair and look into her eyes. "Charity," he said gravely. "You're very beautiful."

"Jack, *please...*"

He frowned across the table at her. "Do you mean that none of your three husbands has told you so? No wonder you abandoned them all. Well, it'll be different when we're married, I assure you. I'll tell you every morning and every night. I may even come home during the day to tell you."

Charity looked heavenward in supplication. "Saints, preserve me."

"Even after the children come," he went on, "I'll continue to—"

"What children?" Letty appeared from the kitchen in a white apron, a platter of roast and vegetables in her hands. Jack moved the flowers in the center of the table to make room.

"Our children," he replied. "Charity's and mine."

"Ah," she said, straightening. "I trust they aren't arriving until after the wedding."

"Of course."

"Good." She dusted off her hands and headed toward the kitchen. "I do like to maintain a respectable household."

As the door swung behind Letty, Charity said quietly but forcefully, "If you say one more word about marriage or children, I will put pink plaid pockets on your white jacket!"

"As you wish." He took his chair, and Charity breathed a sigh of relief. Kristine came in with plates and a basket of bread. "I thought we'd go to Gearhart," he said when the maid had gone again.

"Where?"

"Gearhart Park. It's down the coast a short distance."

"Why?"

He looked at her blandly. "Because God put it there."

She closed her eyes to summon patience. "Why," she asked, opening them again, "would we want to go to Gearhart Park?"

"For our honeymoon," he replied.

When her eyes ignited, he calmly stood to seat Letty, who had shed her apron. "That wasn't on your forbidden list," he said, a suspicious twitch at his bottom lip. "You said we couldn't discuss marriage and babies."

Charity turned to Letty as Jack pushed Letty's chair in. "Excuse me. I think I'll eat in my room. Your friend is driving me to drink."

"Here." Letty put the carafe of wine in front of her, daring her, and sent Jack a scolding glance. "I won't be left alone with him when he's in one of his moods." She handed Jack the carving knife. "Put that rapier wit to good use, Mr. McCarren. I'm afraid the roast may be a little tough. The butcher doesn't approve of me."

Charity slept very little that night, her mind thoroughly occupied with thoughts of Jack McCarren. He'd been relentless all evening. She didn't know what to do about him. He was making it difficult for her to keep her distance—and, worse than that, he was making it difficult for her to *want* to keep her distance.

But she had to.

She rolled over for the tenth time and punched her pillow. She couldn't slip off her past like an old coat. It clung to her, lived with her. But she was determined she was the only one who would ever be harmed by it. Even if it meant having to leave Letty's house.

Heavy-eyed and irritable, she dressed in a brown skirt and white blouse and presented herself for breakfast the next morning. But there was no one at the table to greet her.

"Ming, that is not so!" The sound of Letty's angry voice came from the kitchen.

Surprised to hear Letty shouting at one of her employees, particularly gentle Ming, Charity followed the sound to the small table in the kitchen where Ming sat in a chair and Kristine pressed a cloth to her face. Letty paced back and forth, lecturing and shaking her finger.

"What's happened?" Charity asked.

Kristine lowered the cloth and Charity gasped at the sight of a large, livid bruise that ran from Ming's eye to her jaw.

"She says she fell again when she got home," Letty said, her cheeks pink with temper. "But it was Ah Chun, I know it was."

Charity felt anger well up inside her. It was incomprehensible to her, and reprehensible, that anyone could strike a creature as sweet and eager to please as the little Chinese maid.

"I do not believe these conditions are allowed to exist," Charity fumed. "How can people be imported like goods?"

"There are laws against it now," Letty replied. The kettle whistled and she went to fill the teapot.

Charity followed her. "Then doesn't anyone check the ships that bring them?"

"If word gets to the ships that federal officers are waiting, sometimes they turn around." Letty shook her head gravely. "Sometimes, they simply throw their illegal cargo over the side. Mostly, though, I think someone looks the other way. But Ming's situation is different. She needed help and Ah Chun provided it."

Letty put the tea aside to steep and took down a cup and saucer from the cupboard.

"But certainly that doesn't entitle him to hurt her like that."

"Of course it doesn't. She'll be staying here from now on. I won't allow her to go back."

Letty put the tea things on a tray and carried it to Ming. Charity followed.

"It *was* that Chinese devil," Kristine said, her blue eyes sparking fury.

"He see my new dress," Ming said, large tears streaming down her face, her soft pink mouth quivering. "He think I get more money and not give him proper share."

That did it. The anger bubbling in Charity since she saw what had been done to Ming boiled over. Fury coupled with the knowledge that the pretty dress she'd made for Ming out of friendship and that Ming had loved so much had earned her abuse in an already intolerable situation sent Charity stalking to her room for her cape and hat and purse.

Perhaps she was unable to put her own past behind her, but she, at least, was hale and hearty and capable of coping. Ming was tiny and fragile, set adrift in a strange country by a man who'd used her, then was set upon by another man who took advantage of her situation. She may not be able to do much about her own situation, but she was going to do something about Ming's.

"What are you doing?" Letty asked, chasing after her.

Charity pinned on her hat with care, hoping the familiar little ritual would calm her nerves so that she could think clearly. And she mustn't alarm Letty.

"I'm going shopping," she replied calmly.

Letty studied Charity's reflection in the mirror in concern. "Chinatown is not a safe place—"

Charity turned away from the mirror and swung on her cape. "I don't recall mentioning Chinatown."

Letty stood before her, hands on her hips. "Charity Butler, there is something in your eyes I don't like."

"Nearsightedness." Charity snatched up her purse. "From all the hours I spend hand finishing in the dim light. I suppose I must look into glasses one day. Do you need anything from town?"

Letty followed Charity as she crossed to the door.

Charity paused to look into her friend's uncertain frown and said with a bright smile, "Good heavens, Letty. You mustn't be so concerned. I go shopping several times a week."

Letty looked into her eyes. "You swear to me you're truly going shopping?"

Charity raised a hand and vowed solemnly, "I swear."

Letty relaxed visibly and smiled. "Very well. I wouldn't mind a treat from the candy shop if you stop in to buy Jon a cinnamon stick."

Charity pretended dismay. "Candy? Honestly, Letty. We'll have to bring back the bustle simply to hide your indiscretions."

Letty swatted her arm. "Don't dawdle. It looks like rain."

Charity started at a quick pace down the hill, fueled by indignation over Ming's plight and only mildly dismayed at having lied to Letty.

She *was* going shopping—for tea and silk. It just happened that the best bargains on both were in Chinatown.

Charity felt as though she'd crossed the street into China, so exotic were the sights and smells as she proceeded down Bond Street. Men and women in the traditional pants and jackets bustled in and out of shops filled with unusual wares and beckoning smells. Beautiful gardens were interspersed with the shops and dwellings. The expressive, tonal language filled her ears as people hurried about their daily business.

She was two blocks inside Chinatown before the head of steam that had brought her that far dissipated sufficiently for her to realize she had no idea where to find Ah Chun.

She saw a young woman on a corner, her face thickly rouged and painted. She appeared to be wearing a light wrapper opened to expose bloomers and a chemise. For a moment, Charity couldn't believe her eyes. Then she realized the woman's occupation and decided she was probably just the one to give her directions.

Charity crossed the street and saw the young woman frown as she approached. "Good morning," Charity said sociably.

The young woman did not respond, but looked at her as though she'd grown a second head.

"I'm looking for Ah Chun," Charity said. "Can you tell me where to find him?"

The woman looked Charity up and down, her expression clearly telling Charity that she understood now why Charity was looking for him. It also told her what she thought of her prospects in the business. Then she pointed her chin in the direction of the block ahead.

"The tea shop," she said. "In the back."

Charity nodded briskly. "Thank you."

On the next block, she found a store window filled with barrels and baskets of tea. The sign in Chinese characters was incomprehensible to her, but the illustration of the steaming cup was easy to identify.

Tables and chairs filled the small shop, though they were unoccupied at the moment. And all around the room were bags of fragrant tea.

Charity squared her shoulders, cleared her throat and walked into the shop. She felt herself relax a little when she found that it looked so ordinary. It was neat and orderly and made her think Letty had exaggerated dramatically about the danger.

A small man in traditional garb with the black skullcap all the Chinese men wore, bowed to her from behind the counter.

"Help you, missy?"

She approached him courteously and with determination. "I wish to see Mr. Ah Chun, please."

The man stared at her for a moment, as though he couldn't imagine what she could want with his employer. Then a little flicker of understanding crossed his face and he looked her over again—this time with the same doubtful expression the young woman on the street had worn.

"He busy today," the man said.

"I'll only take a moment of his time," Charity insisted.

"He busy," he said again.

Charity didn't budge. "I wish to speak with him about Chan Ming," she said firmly, "and I won't leave until I've done so. Now, please, tell him he has a visitor."

The man stared at her another moment, his expression growing increasingly hostile. Then he headed for a beaded curtain at the back of the store, muttering to himself in Chinese as he went. Extravagant hand gestures accompanied the words.

He was back in a moment, holding the beaded curtain aside and gesturing her into the shadows beyond it. She went, giving him a satisfied look as she passed him.

"Thank you," she said.

He responded in Chinese, and she got the distinct impression he hadn't said, "You're welcome."

The beaded curtain closed behind her with a musical clicking, leaving her to face a deep blackness, relieved only by a dim red glow at the back of the room. She had to resist the urge to run out again. She had the feeling that she'd taken one step from light into darkness—darkness not simply resulting from a lack of light, but generated by evil. A little shudder ran up her spine.

Then she remembered Ming and the terrible bruise she'd sustained through no fault of her own. Charity took several steps toward the red glow.

"Ah Chun," she said, purposely making the name a statement and not a question. She knew she could not appear hesitant.

There was silence for a long moment. Then a silky, low voice from the direction of the glow replied, "Come."

"Go!" was the instruction Charity's mind gave her, but she straightened and walked purposefully toward the glow.

As she drew closer, she saw that the glow came from an ornate, red-shaded lamp. She stopped in wonder as she saw that the lamp sat on a small table beside what appeared to be a throne. She stepped closer, unable to believe her eyes.

She stared at a very large chair of glossy dark wood carved with frightening winged creatures. A fat red and gold brocade cushion caught her attention and made her long to touch it. She was sure it was from the loom of some brilliant craftsman in China. Fear shuddered inside her again as she wondered if Lucifer sat upon such a throne.

Then a man stepped out of the shadows. He was elegantly garbed in a red silk robe embroidered with a dragon. A small hat sat upon glossy black hair tied back in a braid.

He took the chair, much as though he was a king about to pass sentence on an errant subject, and looked her full in the face. The little shudder rattled all the way down her spine.

His features were sharp and handsome, and a long thin mustache dangled all the way to the front of his robe. His fingers were long and slender and his nails were talon-like as he held the carved arms of the chair. His eyes were dark and cold and saw inside her. He knew she was afraid.

But Charity had dealt with bullies most of her life. Gripping her bag with both hands to steady herself, she swallowed and said firmly, "Good day, Ah Chun. I am Charity Butler."

"Miss Butler." His Oriental tongue distorted her name just a little. "You have no man to speak for you?"

The question took her completely by surprise. "I do not need a man to speak for me," she replied.

"A man does not do business with women, but with another man."

"I am not here to do business." She shifted, trying to look taller, bigger. "I am here to terminate your contract with Chan Ming."

She saw every muscle in his body stiffen under the elegant silk. He narrowed his eyes at her. "You are new contractor?"

"No, I'm her friend. Ming works in the house where I live, and I saw what you did to her because you thought she hadn't paid you enough. I wish to inform you that she will live at the house where she is working, and that her contract fee is to be considered paid in full. If any further injury comes to her over this incident or if you harass her in any way, I will tell the newspaper and the sheriff of your extortionist practices."

Charity waited for the explosion. It didn't come. Ah Chun simply uncoiled, like a snake, and looked at her across the small space that separated them.

"It is unwise," he warned quietly, "to stamp on the foot of the tiger."

Charity lifted her chin. "The tiger is brave and noble. You, on the other hand, sell your countrymen and women for a profit, steal their money and then hurt them. You are not the tiger, Ah Chun. You are the droppings one finds on the bottom of the tiger's cage. Good day."

She walked briskly through the shadows, through the musical, tinkling curtain of beads, past the little man in the shop and out onto the street.

Once on the sunny sidewalk, she leaned against the shop window and gulped in air. She took a moment to quiet her heartbeat and calm her nerves then started at a quick pace for home. She wanted desperately to be there.

She was two blocks from the edge of Chinatown and congratulating herself on having survived that frightening meeting when something hard collided with her shoulder and pushed her around the corner and onto a side street.

She was propelled by the momentum of the three men suddenly encircling her and shoving her into a narrow alley between the back of a shop and the side of a house. She smelled garbage and sickly-sweet smoke from the back door of the shop. She confronted the three men she guessed were in Ah Chun's employ, giving them her fiercest look.

"Let me pass," she demanded, "or I will scream so loud I will be heard across the river in Washington!" It was an idle threat, she knew. There were children screaming at play just up the block. No one would pay attention to her shouts for help.

The men advanced on her, trying to back her farther into the alley, but she stood her ground. She reached into her hat for a pin and held the lethal-looking thing up so they could see it. They looked at each other, grinned and continued to advance on her.

Then one of the men snaked an arm out for her, and Charity poised her hat pin. But he was yanked backward before he could touch her.

She blinked in surprise. There were suddenly two broad backs between her and Ah Chun's men.

From between Jack's and Rolf's shoulders she saw two of her attackers still standing, contemplating the tall intruders. They seemed to decide against a confrontation. One of them helped the man on the ground get to his feet, and all three backed out of the alley, shouting something angry in Chinese.

"What did they say?" Rolf asked Jack.

Jack shrugged a shoulder. "I don't know. I imagine it would translate to, 'We'll kill you next time.'"

Both men turned to look at Charity. She put her hand over her heart and felt its thudding quiet. "Thank you," she said. "For a moment there, I thought I was going to be beaten."

"Don't grow complacent," Jack warned, his eyes dark with purpose. "That danger hasn't passed yet. Come on." He took her arm in a firm grip and led her out of the alley to the street where the box factory's delivery wagon waited. He lifted Charity into it without his customary gentleness, and placed her in the back. Rolf climbed up beside him in the front.

Charity understood the message. He was not pleased with her. She was traveling as freight.

"What in the hell did you think you were going to accomplish?" They stood in her bedroom in the small space between the tester bed and the wall. He had marched her past the three women in the house: Letty, who had folded her arms in silent admonishment; Kristine, who'd shaken her finger and scolded excitedly in Finnish, and Ming, who hadn't noticed her at all as Rolf went to her, face set, and put a gentle hand to her bruised face.

Charity tried to stand her ground as she'd done in Chinatown. But Jack gave her shoulder a shove, and she landed on the edge of the bed with a bounce.

"Have you any idea what could have happened to you if Rolf and I hadn't been delivering a late shipment and seen you marching down Bond Street?" Jack paced back and forth in front of the bed, hands in his pockets, jaw set. "You could be in the hold of a ship at this very moment on your way to some slaver's den."

Charity pulled the last pin out of her hat, stabbed it into the grosgrain ribbon and tossed the hat aside.

"He was robbing Ming, plain and simple, because she's small and helpless with no one to defend her. Then he hit her because she wore a dress I made for her and he thought she'd gotten a raise in wages and hadn't shared the money with him." She glowered at him. "Would you have stood by and done nothing?"

"No!" He glowered at her. "But no one bothered to tell me, did they? Some featherhead took it upon herself to handle the most ruthless and dangerous criminal on the northern Oregon coast!"

"I did not try to handle him," she denied. "I simply told him he should consider her debt paid in full. I don't understand why the sheriff can't do anything about him."

"It's usually thought best to let Bond Street take care of itself."

"A perfect arrangement for the likes of Ah Chun."

"We're not talking about him at the moment," Jack said darkly. "We're talking about you. That was a completely foolish and irresponsible thing to do." He leaned closer. "People who cross Ah Chun have been known to disappear. People who owe him money and don't pay are relieved of a digit or two, or other vital parts of their bodies. He sees women as a useful commodity, worth a king's ransom in the Orient or in Africa where rich men will pay a high price for ivory-skinned . . ."

"Stop!" She covered her ears, more than convinced of Ah Chun's wickedness.

"You are not to seek him out again," Jack went on more quiety. "Is that clear?"

She bristled, but formed a careful answer. "At the moment, I have no wish to seek him out again."

He sat on the edge of the bed beside her so that they were eye to eye. She knew instantly that she had put nothing past him.

"If you are overtaken by a wish to do so sometime in the future," he said, "you will not do it."

She'd never been one to defy for the sake of defiance, but she decided he was taking liberties he didn't have.

"Jack," she said patiently but sternly, "you've no right to pass judgment on my actions."

"But I do," he insisted, his tone as stern as hers. "As the man who cares for you, I have an obligation to protect you and the right to insist that you follow my instructions for your safety. Not," he said loudly to cover her sputtering protest, "because I'm in any way superior, but because I know Astoria, and you do not. And because I can deal with three of Ah Chun's men, and you cannot."

"We don't know that for certain," she said quietly, folding her arms. "You stepped in before I had the opportunity to try to defend myself."

"*I* know for certain that you could not have held them off with a hat pin."

She raised a haughty eyebrow. "Perhaps I have fighting skills of which you are unaware."

He studied her a moment, something altering subtly in his eyes that she didn't like.

"Very well." He stood and pulled her to her feet. He removed his jacket and tossed it onto the far corner of the bed. Then he pulled her around to the foot of the bed where there was more room to move and took several steps back from her. "Consider me one of Ah Chun's men. Show me this fighting prowess."

It had been an empty boast, but pride rose instantly in her. She glanced at him while she unbuttoned the sleeves of her blouse and rolled them up. "You are a foot taller than most Chinese men," she pointed out.

"But there were three of them." He stood, arms loosely on his hips, then reached one out to beckon her tauntingly. "Stop stalling, Miss Butler."

Arrogant, egotistical male, she thought, prepared to show him a thing or two. Fingers curled to scratch, she lunged at him.

She had no idea what happened, but in the space of an instant the room tilted and she found herself dangling in the crook of his arm, her arms and legs flailing futilely.

"Now, that's an interesting approach," he said, holding her suspended in the air. "It might have had some effect if you were buxom and could count on your weight to tire me. As you are, I could hold you immobile until breakfast."

He set her on her feet and stepped back again. "I trust you've another tactic?"

Without giving him or herself a moment to think, she kicked, aiming at his groin. He sidestepped her easily. Chagrined, she tried again, with the same result. She flung herself at him, certain it would be easier at close quarters.

She found herself dangling from his arm again.

"I know girls are taught by their mothers to aim for a man's masculinity." She could tell by his voice that he was biting back a laugh. "Boys, however, are taught by their fathers to protect it carefully. A kick to the groin is not as easy to accomplish as women are led to believe."

He put her down again and stepped back, resuming his waiting stance. "But I'm sure you've a brilliant maneuver at your fingertips. I'm waiting for it."

Charity decided she'd been mistaken in her approach. Letty's words from several days ago came back to her. "Men have the muscle to execute their wishes. So we have to be clever and resourceful."

Remembering that Jack always had a small but lethal knife at his belt that he used at the factory, she took several steps toward him, smiling.

His eyes watched her with interest, his hands still resting lightly on his hips.

"Has it occurred to you," she asked, dropping her voice an octave and reaching a small hand out to his shirt front, "that a bedroom is not a place for combat?"

She could feel the steady beat of his heart under her hand, but his eyes never left hers, and she saw suspicion form there.

She raised a hand to the nape of his neck and brought the other up to meet it behind his head. She tried not to be distracted by the warmth of his skin, by the thick, wiry hair under her fingertips, by the steel cording in the muscles of his neck.

She rose on tiptoe, her eyes concentrating on his lips. Still, she couldn't reach them. He had to lean down to accommodate her.

"I think you may be right about the passion between us, Jack," she whispered, her lips hovering a hairbreadth from his. "I'm beginning to believe that pretending it does not exist—" she lowered her lashes for effect, then raised them and looked boldly into his eyes "—is futile. Can you see that in my eyes?"

He looked deeply into her eyes and she knew she had him. "Yes," he said, his whisper thick and dark. He took her lips and she reached around his waist for his knife.

She was completely surprised when his hand slapped over hers on the ivory handle. She looked into his eyes and saw that she hadn't deceived him for a moment. Then she felt herself spin around and fly through the air.

She landed on the bed with an oof, and lay there a moment on her stomach trying to collect her wits. She shrieked in protest when a stinging slap landed on her bottom. The next thing she knew she was on her back, her hands pinned to the mattress over her head.

Jack knelt astride her, his wide shoulders blotting out everything else in the room. He seemed as quiet and calm as he'd been moments before, while her bosom heaved as she struggled.

"The lessons to be learned here, Charity," he said patiently, "are that, despite your claims, you could not fight off one man, much less three, that though you're a very intelligent woman, you do not know much about men, and, that though we're vulnerable to deep feelings and strong passions, we're also creatures of pride and purpose—and retribution."

She wriggled under his hold, not trusting his tone of voice or his choice of words. That single slap on her bottom still stung.

"Now, you can admit that I was right and you were wrong," he said, holding her still. "And you can promise me that you won't go to Chinatown again unescorted. Or I can turn you over and finish what I started."

She hated to contemplate what could have happened to her in Chinatown had he and Rolf not appeared. And she hadn't needed their little skirmish to prove it to her. But it rankled to have to admit it to him.

"Jack McCarren," she accused, still breathless, "you're a brute!"

He grinned impenitently. "Yes, I know."

"All right!" she conceded. "You were right and I was wrong. Now, will you please let me up?"

"You forgot the promise," he reminded.

She expelled an exasperated growl. "I promise I will not go to Chinatown unescorted. There! Does that satisfy you?"

"Not entirely."

Why was she not surprised? "If you think," she threatened, despite her ungainly position, "that you can spank me like some errant child..."

"No," he said with a slow smile. "Although I have a feeling that the time will come one day in this relationship. At the moment, I like this side of you better."

She frowned at him warily. "What do you mean?"

"You taunted me with a kiss, then tried to stab me in the back," he said.

She pursed her lips. "You exaggerate. I meant only to steal your knife."

"Figuratively speaking, the result was the same. Now, I want the kiss."

She raised an eyebrow. "After I've been so reprehensible?" she asked with affected wonder. "How could you possibly?"

"I'm not sure," he admitted. "Except that every little part of you—even the parts that annoy me—have somehow become critical to my day-to-day existence. Now, will you kiss me, or must we discuss it until sundown?"

Physically, she'd been powerless against him. Some perverse little demon inside her required that she prove to him she could overpower him with emotion.

"Must I do it with my hands held over my head?" she asked softly.

Jack freed her wrists and slipped down next to her on his side, his upper body propped on his forearm. She turned toward him and contemplated his wicked smile.

She would show him, she thought. A little corner of her mind tried to remind her that she'd intended to *show* him she could have dealt with Ah Chun's men. She had even less skill romantically than she had physically, but it occurred to her that her lack of experience never seemed to affect her kisses with Jack. They acquired a life of their own and a perfection that astounded her.

And if she was ever to be allowed off this accursed bed . . .

She combed her fingertips into the thick black hair above his ear and put her lips to his.

Accustomed to his immediate reaction whenever their lips met, she was momentarily confused by his passive participation. Then she understood. *She* was to kiss *him*.

It wasn't difficult for her to recall just what it was about his touch that always called forth her response. It was his control of the situation—the knowledge that he knew what he was about—coupled with his artful hands and their delicious tenderness.

She drew herself even closer to him, stroking her hands along his shoulders and into his hair as he'd always done with her. She felt him lay his arm over her side to allow her to be closer.

She moved her mouth in little caresses along his lips, nudging, nibbling, trying to ignite the flame she was sure was inside him. Then she dipped the tip of her tongue between his lips and probed timidly. The stirring of his tongue against hers, the small, almost involuntary stroke of his hand against her back spurred her to shed her shyness.

She inched a little higher against him so that she could wrap both arms around his neck and give the kiss every last bit of energy she possessed.

Her tongue delved boldly into his mouth, her hands wound into his hair and held him while she gave the kiss everything she had. Sensing that he fought active participation with great difficulty, she pushed him onto his back, holding him there with her upper body, her mouth and her ardor.

His control was lost as he wrapped her tightly against him, bending one knee up and fitting her securely along the length of him.

There was heat in every little part of him in contact with her, despite the rigid armor of her corset. His body knew what secrets were hidden there even if they could not make contact. And that part of him he'd boasted of protecting just moments ago was now vulnerable and eager to perform.

He finally loosened his grip on her with a groan of pain and frustration. She tried not to let him see her smile.

She lifted her head and looked at him with apparent innocence.

He could see the smug satisfaction in her eyes. He couldn't fault her for it. She'd earned it well.

But he caught her wrist when she tried to roll off. As good a student as she was in some ways, she was very hardheaded in others.

"Tell me what you've learned," he ordered quietly.

She huffed impatiently. "You are a tyrant. I could not hold off a man by myself, I don't know everything about men, and using their vulnerabilities against them will earn me only their retribution."

"Very well." He sat up, still holding her against him so that she sat astride him precisely where he wanted her. He let himself enjoy the torment an extra moment.

"And what have you learned?" She wriggled slightly against him, and he wondered for an instant if the movement had been accidental or deliberate. Then he saw that falsely innocent expression in her wide eyes and he knew. But he felt it didn't diminish him to be honest with her.

"That in your own way," he said, "you've as much control over me as I have over you."

"Very well," she said, pushing against his shoulders to lever herself off the bed. "Then we're both wiser today."

"Charity." He rose and snatched his jacket off the edge of the bed. He held it over his shoulder by one finger. "There's a fund-raising dinner for me Saturday at the Occident Hotel. I'd like you to come with me."

She smoothed her skirt and tugged at the lacy bib of her shirtwaist. "I doubt it would help your campaign to continue to be seen with the hoyden who rents rooms in Letitia Donovan's house."

He grinned. "With my past, dangerous associations are part of my appeal. I'm sure you'll only contribute to my popularity."

"Jack," she asked seriously, the thought of making a public statement of their association raising a score of warning signals, "do you really think it's wise?"

He frowned at her. "I've explained that I'm not concerned what people will think. Why else would it be unwise?"

"Well," she said lamely, walking across the room to open the door for him. "You know."

"I don't." He reached past her to push the door gently closed. "Explain it to me."

She shifted her weight, folded and unfolded her arms. "Well, you've so much going on in your life right now. Guiding a successful business, running for office..." She smiled thinly. "Protecting Letty. It hardly seems the time to..."

He was watching her closely. "Yes?"

Pretending was useless. She leaned against the wall and stared at the carpet. "Time to fall in love."

He pinched her chin between his thumb and forefinger and lifted it. His eyes were warm and gentle and pleasantly surprised. "Is that what you feel, Charity? Love?"

In answer, she let herself melt against him, wrapping her arms around his waist and freely admitting without words that it was the only place she wanted to be.

He crushed her to him and kissed her with all the delight her admission brought him and all the easy affection he felt for her when they weren't vying for position in the relationship.

Then he simply held her and rested his cheek on her hair. "Well," he said, "you've also learned the lesson I'd despaired of ever teaching you. That you love me. It's been a fruitful morning, after all."

It wasn't until hours later, long after Jack had taken his leave and Charity had told and retold the story of her confrontation with Ah Chun and Jack and Rolf's rescue to Letty, Kristine and a disbelieving Ming, that she came to her rooms to work on Nell Johnson's dress.

She went from the workshop into her bedroom to retrieve the scissors she'd left there when she'd trimmed a thread off her hem and noticed the beautiful quilt that covered her bed in wrinkled disarray.

She put both hands to her face and turned away from the sight, only to catch her reflection in the mirror. She could hear her mother's voice.

"Charity Ross, what in the name of all that is holy have you done today?" She ticked off her sins as she used to do when Charity was a child. "You disregarded common sense, you went to the place of business of a dangerous criminal, you got yourself in an alley at the mercy of three thugs, you used your body to taunt a man, then you rolled around on your bed with him!"

Charity heard the long-suffering sigh that had marked the end of every one of her mother's litanies, followed by the inevitable question, "What's to become of you, Charity?"

Charity sank onto the edge of the bed, fell backward onto the evidence of her depravity and enjoyed the smell of Jack that lingered there. She put a hand over her eyes and groaned.

"I don't know, Mama," she said aloud. "I just don't know."

Chapter Eight

"Who are all these people?" Charity asked in amazement as she walked into the Occident Hotel on Jack's arm. Throngs of people crowded the lobby and flanked their short walk to the banquet room, calling greetings, shouts of encouragement and good cheer. "Are they all going to vote for you?"

He laughed softly as he waved and responded to the crowd. "I hope so. They've paid a fair amount to be here. Many of them are people I've come to know through business and through Connor. But most I've known all my life."

"But you led me to believe," she whispered, "that many people don't approve of you."

"Many people don't, but these people are my friends."

"Most of the town must be here."

He laughed again. "Not even half. My friends just make enough noise to make it appear so."

Jack was welcomed warmly, but Charity was treated to a subtle but noticeably remote courtesy, though the women to whom Jack introduced her studied her appearance with obvious interest and approval.

She wore an evening dress she'd fashioned for herself after a dress designed by Worth and shown at the Paris

Exposition Universelle. It was made of white accordion-pleated chiffon inset with strips of royal purple and a straight front of gold lace. Thin straps of the same lace held the low-cut gown in place, and several shallow tiers of the pleated chiffon ringed her upper arm above her long white gloves.

She'd dressed her hair in a bouffant upsweep and had starched a length of the lace to make a small coronet. Its effect was that of an expensive tiara.

Charity kept her head held high and her back ramrod straight as Jack led her to a room filled with tables covered with white linen and topped with garden bouquets. All heads turned as they entered, then the room was abuzz with gossip. If only she could relax in this foreign setting. She wanted nothing more than to run home to the comfort and security of her two rooms at Letty's. Her thoughts were interrupted by Dr. Parson, who greeted her warmly.

While Jack went in search of punch, the doctor introduced Charity to several younger couples standing with him.

"Friends of mine," he said with a wink. "We're in good company."

The women separated from the men immediately as one of the wives pulled Charity aside to exclaim over and inspect her dress.

"I fancy myself a seamstress," Anna Rickman said with a moue of self-deprecation, "but I'm limited to skirts and simple shirts. I don't think I could ever do all those insets, nor that perfect lace panel with the scalloped edges."

Unembarrassed, she leaned closer to lift the fabric of Charity's skirt and study the almost invisible stitches. "However did you do that?"

Relaxing, Charity explained that she had years of experience and that her new machine was capable of very straight and fine stitches.

"Do you give lessons?" Anna asked.

"Ah, no," Charity replied. That possibility had never occurred to her. "That is, I haven't yet."

"Would you consider it? Many of us know the basics, of course, but the fine tailoring is beyond us."

A young woman at Anna's side slapped her arm lightly with a gloved hand. "Anna!" she scolded. "Charity's in the business of tailoring. It isn't fair to ask her to show you what she knows. Then you wouldn't need her services."

Anna looked suddenly apologetic. "I hadn't thought of that."

Charity laughed and shook her head. "That's very considerate, but I don't feel that way at all. I usually reserve Fridays to catch up on odds and ends. If you'd like to come by, I'll be happy to let you try my machine and help in any way I can."

Anna looked delighted. "I'd pay you of course."

"No, that wouldn't be—"

"I insist. Otherwise I won't come. Oh, David would be so pleased if I learned to make my own gowns. We go out and entertain often, and he's always complaining that I've overspent my clothing allowance. The man is a darling, but a veritable—"

A sudden silence turned the women's heads in the direction of the men, who stood behind them in a half circle, apparently listening to their conversation.

Anna smiled at David's mockingly severe face and said sweetly, "I was explaining to Charity how brilliantly economical you are, darling."

"Were you?" he said wryly. Charity could see the indulgence under his pose of displeasure. "It sounded more as though you were criticizing my brilliant economy."

"Of course not," she said, turning to loop her arm in his. "I told her you were a darling."

David turned to his male companions with a wince, obviously considering the endearment a doubtful honor. Jack, Dr. Parson and the other young woman's husband made the most of it, hooting and patting his back.

Jack pulled Charity to him and they all chatted comfortably until it was time to be seated for dinner. The little group parted company with the promise that Anna would visit Charity the following Friday.

Dinner was succulent baked Columbia River salmon with parsley potatoes and asparagus. Eating it at the head table, however, made Charity uncomfortable—especially when she looked up to find people staring in their direction.

After dinner, Dr. Parson, the chairman of the committee to elect Jack mayor, gave a speech about the condition of life, business and society in Astoria.

"Even the governor," he said urgently, "has asked us to do something about the lawlessness of Swill Town. I think it's time we look the problem in the face and admit that despite all our efforts in the past years, nothing has changed because the administration of Astoria has remained the same.

"The incumbent mayor," the doctor went on, "has done nothing about the crimes that continue on the dock. One can only wonder why.

"This man," he said, resting a hand on Jack's shoulder, "is an honest alternative to the city government we've had so far. Listen to his ideas, and think about change."

Everyone applauded, a few of Jack's more raucous friends cheered. Jack stood, elegant in black-and-white evening dress, and told them with a quiet but riveting passion what he planned to do.

"The best thing we can do for Astoria," he said, "is make legitimate businesses so profitable that illegal ones will cease to exist. I want to add another dock so that we can increase the port's shipping schedule. I want to connect a main street from the center of the commercial district to Union Town." There was another long cheer. "And I'd like to find a way to bind us as a community. As it is, we exist as separate entities that function together only minimally—Upper Town, downtown, Union Town, and Chinatown. Imagine what we could accomplish if we worked together."

There was dead silence for a moment. Working together was an alien concept.

"Think about it," he encouraged. "With Chinese industry, Finnish determination, union solidarity and downtown financial backing there won't be anything we can't accomplish."

A smattering of applause grew to deafening proportions. Jack finally raised his arms for quiet.

"Let me give you details on how I see this coming about."

He spoke for half an hour and Charity stared, fascinated, almost spellbound. This was a side of Jack she hadn't seen before. She knew well the man who cared on an individual basis, the man who nurtured friendships, kept promises, cared for and protected the woman he loved.

But this glimpse of his social conscience was a touching revelation. Considering that all she'd known much of her life was the scorn heaped on the helpless people who shared the name of her father, a man who had *no* conscience, social or otherwise, the love she felt for Jack deepened and swelled. It no longer mattered that some people looked at her askance because she rented rooms from a notorious suffragist. All she was aware of was that a good man loved her. The place inside her that held pride and self-esteem had been vacant for a long, long time. She felt it fill suddenly, even overflow.

A bright light flashed, and a chemical smell filled her nostrils. A photographer at the foot of the podium smiled his apologies.

After Jack's speech, there were hundreds of hands to shake, questions to answer, agreements made to speak at men's groups and an invitation from Harriet and Henrietta Clune to speak to the Ladies for the Vote.

That one stopped Jack in his tracks. The crowd milling in the lobby of the hotel fell silent, awaiting his answer.

"We are another faction set apart from downtown," Harriet said bravely. "And we could make a valuable contribution toward bringing all of Astoria together."

"Of course," he said finally. "I'd be honored."

Anna and her friend and Dr. Parson applauded loudly. Others looked at each other, obviously unsure what to think.

Charity's mind was awhirl with the evening's impressions and with what she'd felt happen inside herself. As Jack handed her up into the hired open carriage, she felt herself lose all sense of security about who she was and just what she was about. She felt as though a large hand had taken her by the throat and shaken her.

Jack pulled the bright plaid blanket over her and tucked her tightly against him. Though it was early summer, the night was foggy and cool, moisture thick in the air.

"Drive slowly," Jack called to the driver. At Charity's look of surprise, he grinned and kissed her temple. "We have things to talk about, Miss Butler," he said.

"You're right," she agreed, leaning her head on his shoulder and inhaling a deep breath of the cool, wet air. "You were wonderful tonight, Jack," she said. "I feel almost guilty that I've enjoyed your friendship all these weeks and I've never really *known* you."

"Of course you have. Mercy!"

She straightened at his exclamation. "What?"

He tugged lightly at her little lace coronet. "Can this be removed? I've just kissed it and made a sieve of my lips."

She laughed and reached up to unpin it. She placed it atop her bag beside her on the seat.

"There." She nuzzled her nose in his neck and felt his lips on her forehead. "Now you'll never be able to eat soup again," she laughed softly.

"Or drink," he said, sounding stricken. "Horrors."

They laughed over the ridiculous exchange.

"Actually," Jack said, "tonight is not what I wanted to discuss with you."

She sighed against his throat, sublimely comfortable. "What did you want to discuss?"

"Our marriage."

She groaned. "Jack..."

He sat her up and frowned. He looked into her eyes. "Surely you can't be surprised that I want marriage. I'm certain you've heard of it. The union of a man and woman who..."

She turned away to sit stiffly beside him, staring straight ahead. "Jack, *we've* never talked about it."

He turned to look at her, his arm along the back of the seat. Her panicked mind noted the clop of the horses' hooves on the brick-lined street.

"We *have* talked about it," he said.

"Your imperious references to when we are married—" she spoke the last four words in an imitation of his deep voice "—do not count."

"Those references aside," he insisted, "we have discussed it."

"When?"

"The other morning in your bedroom when you showed me your poor excuse for self-defense." His voice had an edge of temper to it. "You told me you loved me."

"Yes." She glanced at him, her eyes softening with everything she felt for him. "I do."

Jack looked into her eyes and felt all the laws of reason totter dangerously. "Then what did you expect would happen next?" he asked, his patience strained.

She hid her nervous fingers under the blanket and pulled it up a little higher. The truth was she hadn't thought beyond loving him because the feeling was too new and the possibilities too unsettling.

She answered quietly. "I expected nothing."

"Wedding plans never entered your mind?" he asked, half teasing, half annoyed. "A beautiful confection of a wedding dress never formed in your creative eye?"

It hadn't. She knew it was impossible. "No."

"Then what," he demanded, his voice rising, "did you envision happening between us? Are we simply to go on as friends who just happen to be in love, going to the opera, meeting for fittings in your shop or at Letty's dinner table and parting every night to go to our separate beds like two celibates who never want anything more?"

That ugly possibility was the very reason she'd given the future no consideration. Because that was all it could ever be. "Of course not!" she said, angry with him for giving it form.

"I see," he went on crisply. "Then you've become that much of a suffragist that we'll take up residence together without benefit of marriage?"

"Suffragists do not endorse free love!" she snapped at him.

"Do you?"

"No!"

"Then tell me what you see in our future! I can't seem to come up with the proper solution."

Charity put a hand over his mouth to stop his shouting and put her cheek against his as hot tears filled her eyes. "Please," she whispered. "I would love to be your wife, Jack, but..." *But I have a past that would embarrass you, possibly even ruin your career if anyone were to discover it. I came here to start over, to build a new life for myself, but now yours is even more important to me than my own, and I wouldn't jeopardize it for my own comfort.* She wanted desperately to say it, but the words wouldn't come.

She felt his anger ebb, and his hand on the back of the seat curled around her shoulders as the other covered her hand. He kissed its palm, then lowered it to his lap.

"But what?" he asked quietly.

She groped desperately for an answer he would believe. "I—I left debts behind in Kansas. My business is just beginning to... to pay its way..."

"Charity, I can easily settle your debts. And if you want to maintain your business, that will be fine. You can even maintain it at Letty's if that would make you happy.''

She pulled away to look into his eyes, but he kept an arm around her. "Jack, I would be very difficult to live with.''

"Yes," he said, his tone grave despite a smile. "I know that.''

"You're a man who likes to control things." Her quick glance upbraided him for it. "And you would want to control me.''

He shook his head wryly. "Considering how I've failed in that so far, your concern seems misplaced.''

"The point is, you would want to.''

"The point is, I would have to," he corrected mildly. "As your husband, that would be my duty. But I would exchange the word control for... monitor.''

"It's much the same." Her soft brown eyes widened with emphasis. "I left home to be rid of all that.''

"No one is ever rid of all that." The night breeze blew a tendril of her hair across her face, and he reached up gently to brush it behind her ear. "We're all responsible to someone—all of our lives.''

"Really." Her expression dared him to prove it. "And to whom are you responsible?''

"My employees," he said without having to consider. "My customers, Connor, Letty, you...''

"Me?''

"Of course." He seemed surprised she should question him. "Because I love you, I'm responsible for being certain that you know it, for taking care with the love you give me in return..." He added with an amiable but level gaze, "And I'm responsible for keeping you safe." As she opened her mouth to protest, he put his hand gently but firmly over it. "I know. Among suffragists that is not a popular notion. But protecting his woman has been an instinct in man since Adam, and whether or not women get the vote, that will never change.''

"Then,'' she said practically, "there is no way we could make a life together with such an elemental difference between us.''

He smiled. "Charity, the elemental difference between man and woman is what life is all about.''

The driver pulled the horses to a stop in front of Letty's, then glanced over his shoulder at Jack with what Charity considered male commiseration. "Shall I drive on, sir, until you win your argument?''

Jack laughed. "No, it's late. And this argument could go on for days.'' He leapt out of the carriage, then reached up to swing Charity down. Then he paid the driver, took Charity's arm and led her slowly up the walk to her private entrance.

"If you would remember *before* you act that I love you and care for you and would no doubt waste away without you, then I will promise to give you as much freedom as you want,'' he said.

Charity couldn't help but smile at him, wondering if he realized that all he'd done was put control in very charming terms. Marriage to Jack would be bliss, despite his tendency to issue orders—she knew that. For all his autocratic behavior, he cared for her and in all honesty wanted only what was best for her.

She wished with a desperation that hurt that she was any other woman who could utter a resounding yes to his proposal without fear of one day destroying his future.

Jack saw the longing in her eyes, and the grim determination that closed over it. God, but she was a stubborn woman.

"I know promising to give me freedom is a great concession on your part, Jack," she said, standing on tiptoe to kiss him quickly on the lips. "Might I have a little time to consider?"

He frowned at her, wishing he could see what was going on in her head. "You may have as long as it takes you to reach a positive answer."

"Good night, Jack."

"Good night, Charity."

Charity bolted her door, turned down her lamp and lay in the middle of her bed in the darkness. She was arriving at a dangerous crossroad, she realized with a stab of genuine fear.

She smiled thinly at the thought of Jack's determination to protect her. He, like most men, thought of danger in physical terms. He had no idea that the greatest threat to her safety at the moment was emotional.

She had to tell him about her father before this relationship grew any more serious—and if she did, she would surely lose him. He'd already struggled up from scandal once to carve his place in Astoria society and to become a candidate for mayor. An alliance with her would destroy everything he'd achieved. That is if anyone was to learn that her name was really Charity Ross and not Charity Butler.

She turned onto her stomach, petticoats rustling, as she closed her eyes to escape thoughts of her last few years in Kansas.

Humiliated and destroyed, her mother had refused to leave the house after her husband had died. Charity, ever hopeful, had been sure that Calvin Ross's death would mean a new life for them.

She'd secured employment in a department store, refusing to feel embarrassed by the knowledge that the store was owned by the minister's zealous son and that he'd taken her on as a sort of rehabilitative project.

She'd been given every dirty and unpleasant job as a way to "redeem" herself and repent her criminal parentage.

Determinedly cheerful at sixteen, she had done everything asked of her and done it well. After all—her father was dead. She and her mother were finally out from under the specter of his reputation.

But she'd been too young to know that prejudice never died with whatever aroused it, and that it could reach beyond the grave.

She was still considered unsuitable company for other young women her age, and though her good looks drew suitors, they were soon discouraged by their parents or they learned very quickly that, despite her circumstances, she was not an easy tumble.

Heat flushed her cheeks as she remembered a particularly humiliating circumstance in which she had struggled against her employer's attentions.

"Mr. Hauser!" she'd shouted, pushing him away with one hand and holding the torn sides of her white lace waist with the other hand. "You're a minister's son! You preach in his church!"

"My wife's been visiting in Boston for six weeks," he explained calmly, trying to reach past her arm. "I shouldn't have to do without, and I shouldn't have to pay for it."

She'd backed away, groping for a weapon. "But it's wrong!"

He had laughed. "It's only wrong with good girls, not with bad girls."

Her hand had connected with a hoe leaning against the wall, and she'd swung it in front of her, holding him off with the sharp-edged tool.

"I am *not* bad!" She'd screamed at him, and in the sound she'd heard the anguish of her entire life.

He'd looked at her as though she was a fool.

"Charity, your father was hanged. His blood runs in your veins. Of course you're bad."

She'd struck him with the flat side of the hoe; she'd lost her job, and any innocent notion she still retained that her father's death had somehow freed her of the pall of his reputation and his deeds.

Charity cried quietly into the mattress, letting all her fragile dreams of life at Jack's side slip away. The people of Astoria might have forgiven him for being the son of a prostitute, but they wouldn't forgive him for marrying the daughter of a murderer.

Jack would not approve of this, Charity was sure. Marching with the Ladies for the Vote would be considered an abuse of freedom.

Letty and her ladies hadn't asked for her participation, but the Clune sisters, Ingrid Rasmussen and Agnes Butterfield had looked so forlorn as they'd gathered on Letty's porch to set out that she'd picked up a sign and taken the place of an absent member at the end of the line. These wonderful women had become her friends during the past month, and she felt an unreasoning desire to join ranks with them.

Even as she did it, Charity knew she was just trying to distract herself from thoughts of Jack and his marriage proposal. She wanted to prove that she could face life alone.

And, she thought, angling her chin, few women were better qualified to fight for equality than Charity Ross, who'd struggled her entire life against the inferior position in which her father's reputation had placed her.

Harriet reached to pull Charity in front of her. "For your first time," she said with a grin, "you shouldn't be in the back. The last lady often has objects thrown at her posterior."

They were in the middle of a rousing chorus of "The Battle Hymn of the Republic" when they rounded the corner onto Commercial Street. There, a crowd had collected to watch them pass.

"Stare straight ahead," Harriet told her from behind. "And remember that their insults are born of ignorance and fear. It will feel very personal, but it isn't truly meant that way."

Charity absorbed the advice and squared her shoulders, convinced it wouldn't be that difficult. A moment later, she was proven wrong.

Shouts of "Who's home with the children, hussies?" and "Votes for women means social disaster!" when Charity knew every one of the women marching to be sensible and responsible made it difficult not to react with an abusive shout of her own.

The crowd was composed of a cross-section of Astoria: the well-dressed as well as the dockworkers, men and women who called them hoydens and home wreckers. One man aimed a particularly crass remark at Letty.

Charity, sign raised like a weapon, took several steps in that man's direction.

"Back in line, Charity!" Harriet snapped quietly. "If we break formation, we lose our unity."

They had just about cleared the crowd when a missile thrown from behind a group of men made a clean arc to the back of Letty's head. She fell to the ground. Everyone gasped, including the gapers on the sidewalk.

The ladies gathered around her. Charity, trying to fan her with a handkerchief, was pushed aside by Dr. Parson, who knelt in the street and propped her against his chest. Her eyes fluttered open as he took her pulse.

"What happened?" Letty asked in a thin voice.

"Some fool hit you with a bottle," the doctor said, holding up the evidence with his free hand. "How do you feel?"

"I'm fine," she said. She got immediately to her feet, and the doctor had no choice but to follow. The ladies rose with her, still forming a protective circle around her.

"Letty, you should go home," Charity said, thinking she looked pale and slightly disoriented. "I'm sure Dr. Parson would take you."

"I'm not going home," she said, brushing dust off her white blouse. "I'm going to the temperance hall as we planned."

"Doctor?" Charity turned to him worriedly.

"You'll go nowhere," he said, taking Letty's face in his hands, "until I say you can. Now, be still and let me look at you."

He looked into her eyes, gently turned her neck from side to side, then reached fingers into her hair where the bottle had struck.

Letty winced.

"Going to have a mighty goose egg there in a few minutes. Can you see clearly?"

"Yes."

"Truth?"

"Truth."

"Good. I don't see any damage, but you could have a concussion. I think you should go home, Letitia."

Letty smiled at him and took the sign she'd dropped from Harriet. "I'm grateful for your help, doctor, and I appreciate your concern, but I'm going to Freedom Hall. We're having a rally today, and I hope the room is filled with women waiting to hear what we have to say."

The doctor glanced doubtfully at Charity.

"No one except Jack McCarren could make her go home," Charity confided quietly. "And he would probably have to carry her."

The doctor gave a long-suffering sigh, adjusted his hat, then took the sign from Letty. She squared her shoulders, about to do battle with him.

But he grinned and hooked his arm in hers. "Then it's fortunate I happened by. I suppose the best thing I can do is offer escort. Coming, ladies?"

Agnes Butterfield stared at him a moment in rapt adoration, then fell into line behind them.

As murmurs of disapproval and disbelief rose from those on the sidewalk, the ladies and gentleman closed ranks and continued the march.

Chapter Nine

Letty looked at her notes, blinked, then held them a few inches away. A hush had fallen over the meager handful of ladies waiting in the hall. Letty turned away from the podium to beckon Henrietta.

"I seem to be seeing two of everything," she said, trying to pass the notes to Henrietta. "You'll have to read the speech."

Henrietta looked horrified and pushed the notes back. "I'm afraid I'm not a very inspirational speaker, Letty. Maybe Harriet could."

Harriet shook her head adamantly. "Henrietta is far and away the better speaker."

"No, you are, Harry," Henrietta denied. "Your delivery of *The Song of Hiawatha* always brings tears to everyone's eyes at family reunions. You must give the speech."

"No," Harriet said simply.

The audience began to stir.

"Ladies," Letty pleaded. "Please. We've come all this way. Someone must give the speech."

If only so that they could finally go home again and put this difficult afternoon behind them, Charity took the speech from Letty and stepped to the podium. Silence fell again.

Charity began. The speech was familiar to her because she'd been Letty's audience as she planned and wrote it.

She read the words clearly and emphatically as she remembered Letty speaking them. The words promised hope for a better world if women were allowed a say in how it was governed. Letty envisioned new horizons for women when women were given a voice. She encouraged participation in the struggle to bring it all about. Attending the Ladies for the Vote convention when the northwest directors of the movement, Judith Vineyard and Coleen Hensley, came to town would make a significant impact.

The work would require their time, she said, their dedication and their courage, but it could mean a new world for their daughters, a better world for everyone.

Then Charity told them what had happened to Letty on the march to Freedom Hall.

"Please help us," Charity said, inflamed anew by the sight of Letty massaging her temples, "so that all people everywhere may express their opinions without fear of being attacked as Letty has been."

There was enthusiastic applause when she was finished, and all the ladies present signed Letty's enrollment roster for the convention.

Letty hugged her fiercely. "You did wonderfully," she praised, holding Charity at arm's length. "One would have difficulty believing you weren't completely dedicated to women's suffrage."

Charity no longer knew to what or whom she was dedicated. She loved Jack, she loved Letty, she loved all the Ladies for the Vote, and she'd truly felt the words of

Letty's speech move her as she'd read them. But, she reminded herself yet again, she'd come here for solitude and anonymity, not to take up an unpopular cause.

It became obvious that she'd acquired neither solitude nor anonymity when she was featured in the *Astorian Daily Budget* the following morning. Jack arrived, paper in hand, and entered Letty's house without knocking. Charity met him in the middle of the living room.

"Is she all right?" he asked in concern. "I just heard what happened from Emmett Parson. Why didn't someone come for me?"

"Because she wouldn't let us," Charity said quietly. "We're letting her sleep in this morning. She seems fine now, but she was seeing double at the temperance hall. She seemed fine by the time we returned home. Would you like some breakfast?"

"Thank you, no. I understand you marched with the ladies," he said.

"I did."

He studied her, his expression neither condoning nor condemning. Charity was momentarily confused.

"What?" she teased. "No limitations placed on my freedom?"

He grinned. "Presuming that if you *could* vote, you would vote for me, limiting your freedom would be self-defeating. It's a beautiful morning. Can we talk in the garden?"

"Of course. I see you've brought our paper in with you. Will you bring it along? My first advertisement should be in today." Charity led the way to the beautiful green lawn behind the house and the iron bench under a hawthorn tree, now in full bloom with starry pink flowers.

"So, you've become a soldier for the cause?" he asked when they were settled side by side on the bench. He put his arm around her, dispensing with the small space she'd tried to keep between them.

She'd reached her decision as she'd tried to keep a pale Letty in bed when she'd been determined to work on her speech for the convention.

It was bravado, Charity knew. There was hurt in Letty's eyes that someone had tried to harm her, and she fought it by assigning herself a task. Charity thought her very brave.

"Yes," she said thoughtfully. "Not out of heroism for freedom for womankind, but because I saw firsthand that we live in a society filled with supposedly civilized men and women who don't want to be bothered by hearing anyone's opinion but their own. Worse than that, they are willing to be violent to keep others silent."

"Yes," he said. "Civilization is just a word. The next time you ladies march, I'm going to see that you have an escort."

She looked up at him with a frown. "No."

"Charity..." He stiffened with impatience.

"Jack," she said reasonably, turning and leaning urgently toward him, "women are trying to prove themselves capable of making knowledgeable, intelligent decisions. If it looks as though we've gone crying to our men because someone in a crowd did a cowardly thing, we'll appear cowardly, too."

He tried to remain calm, but he felt temper stirring. "Charity," he said calmly, "I am not going to let you and Letty sacrifice yourselves on the altar of the movement."

"A bump on the head is hardly a sacrifice."

"This time it was *only* a bottle, the last time *only* a punch in the face," he said. "But the mood is irrational. As logical as it seems to you, the notion of a woman being able to do as she wishes without the support and protection of a man shakes the whole fabric of some people's existence. They think that common sense, the law and even the Bible dictate otherwise. They consider suffragists almost an evil threat to the American way of life."

"That's foolish!"

"The fact remains."

"What would be of more use to us than an escort," she said cautiously, her eyes on her lap, "would be men willing to march with us as Dr. Parson did yesterday. They'd provide not only protection, but they would lend us credibility." She looked into his face. He was already shaking his head. "Men like yourself and Rolf."

"No," he said quietly, firmly.

She wanted to shake him. "Why not?"

"Because, although I believe in a woman's right to vote, I can't honestly endorse all your other demands. I'm not sure it *is* sane for a woman to run freely in a world that can be dark and dangerous. I think a woman drinking and smoking and joining with men in commerce is a danger to them and to herself. I grant you your right to believe as you wish. You must give me the same right."

"Jack McCarren," she said forcefully, "I am every bit as intelligent and competent as you are."

He nodded agreement. "But you're smaller, softer, more trusting, less experienced ..." He grinned. "And you couldn't fight your way out of a paper wrapper."

She acknowledged his gibe with an elbow to his ribs. "I shouldn't have to fight. Business should be conducted with words, not fists."

"That would be ideal. But you must deal with the world the way it is. And to do that, you must be equipped. Women are not."

She stood impatiently. "Words have been known to overpower brawn."

"When?" he challenged, grabbing her wrist and pulling her gently but firmly down. "Where?"

She groped for an example to which he could relate. "Napoleon returning from Elba. He met Marshall Ney's army dispatched by the king to capture him and appealed to their loyalty. They joined his army and marched with *him*."

Jack felt himself losing the argument, and tried not to let her see it in his eyes. Not because he feared being bested by her—God knew she was a worthy opponent—but because winning might spur her to more dangerous endeavors.

"He was backed by an army of his own when they met," he said.

"But he was outnumbered."

"He had a reputation for toughness. His presence overpowered their willingness to fight."

"Exactly," she said smugly. "His presence, not his sword."

"Charity," he said patiently, "presence implies power. His power stopped them, not his peaceful nature. If you've studied Napoleon, you know this to be true." Then he frowned. "How does a seamstress know so much about Napoleon, anyway?"

"By reading," she said, exasperated. "Fabrics and skirts do not define me, Jack McCarren. After school, I continued to educate myself."

He smiled at her tirade. "Charity, it was simply a question."

"Very well, have it your way," she said. "But don't you dare send us an escort unless they're willing to join ranks with us. May I have the newspaper, please?"

Jack picked it up from the bench beside him and handed it over. "I take it the discussion is over because you're losing?" he teased.

"No," she said absently as she opened it. "Because you're being bullheaded and— Oh, my God!"

Jack leaned sideways to look at the front page. The About the City section, usually relegated to two columns, took up the entire top of the page. There was an illustration of a head table, a man standing, obviously giving a speech, and a woman garishly attired and seated beside him, chin on her hand, gazing adoringly at him. The headline read, "Jack McCarren 'marches' with suffragists."

Charity's and Jack's dark heads bumped as they read the long article. It told of Jack's relationship with Charity Butler, a newcomer to Astoria who had set up her seamstress business in the home of the notorious Letitia Donovan. It cited Jack's rescue of Charity from the bear, said they'd been seen together often around town and at social events and that she'd accompanied him to his fundraising dinner.

Included in the article was a quote from Jack's opponent, the incumbent, Walter Johnson: "It would behoove the voters to consider the integrity of a man who keeps company with a liberal hoyden."

"Oh, Jack," Charity whispered, stricken. She looked at him, dark eyes distressed. "I'm sorry. I told you this would happen."

"Don't be foolish." He folded the paper and put it aside. "Any publicity is valuable to a politician."

"Not derogatory publicity."

"It isn't derogatory," he said, pulling her closer. "It's beneficial. I told you that part of my charm is my scandalous past."

"But a scandalous present—"

"Will only make me more interesting." He pulled her closer, the newspaper article and their previous argument forgotten as his entire concentration focused on her mouth. "Will you be quiet and kiss me?"

Her eyes brightened. "I've a suggestion for your campaign, then."

He knew he'd regret asking. "What?"

"If scandal is good for your campaign, then marching with us carrying a sign that says Make Women Equal Citizens would gain you even more—"

He pulled her to him and silenced her with a kiss.

Charity lay in a delicious place somewhere between sleep and wakefulness, her dreams filled with Jack. She could feel his mouth against hers, and she imagined he was there beside her. She had only to stretch out her hand to touch his sinewy upper arm, to catch his hand and bring it to her breast...

At first she thought the scream was her mother's, from beyond the grave, because she had entertained such scandalous thoughts. Then she realized that it came from the other end of the house.

It came again, high and shrill and terrified. Ming!

Charity jumped out of bed and ran barefoot across the cold tiles of the moonlit conservatory and up the shadowy stairs as the screams continued. She collided with Letty, who was knotting the belt of a wrapper as she rushed out of her bedroom.

They raced together to the end of the corridor and arrived in Ming's room to hear the sounds of a struggle in the darkness.

Charity followed the sounds as Letty fumbled with the lamp. What sounded like Chinese epithets bounced around the darkness, some in Ming's shrill scream, others in two different and very angry male voices.

An arm struck at Charity and she grabbed it blindly in the darkness. As light finally bloomed from the lamp across the room, Charity realized she gripped the arm of one of the men who'd trapped her in the alley. His other arm held Ming's legs.

Ming's arms were stretched wide, her hands firmly grasping the window frame, thwarting the efforts of the second man whose muscular forearms were around her waist, attempting to pull her through the window.

Charity immediately clawed at the arms that pulled Ming as Letty snatched a blanket from the bed and dropped it over the head of the man holding Ming's legs. He dropped her legs, giving Ming the ability to prop her feet against the wall and pull harder against the man holding her.

There was a scream as the ladder apparently supporting him clattered to the ground. Charity pulled Ming inside as Letty, arms and legs around the intruder enshrouded under the quilt, beat on the man's head with her fist.

Their captive flailed his arms and legs and shouted angry words in high, hysterical Chinese.

Charity and Ming helped Letty push him onto the bed. As Ming and Charity held him down with their bodies, Letty gathered opposite corners of the bed sheet and tried to create a primitive straitjacket.

Then Jack burst into the room, barefoot and barechested, dressed only in denim pants, a gun in his hand. He took one look at the struggling bundle under the two women and, finding kicking feet on one end of it, brought the butt of his gun down on the other end. The struggle stopped. Charity and Letty sank against opposite edges of the bed, breathless with nerves and relief.

Jack leaned over the bed and yanked the coverlet down to reveal Ah Chun's henchman.

He looked from one woman to the other, his expression clearly indicating that he was not pleased at being dragged out of bed in the middle of the night. "What happened?" he demanded.

Letty frowned at him as she got to her feet. "What are you doing here?"

"Jon came for me," he said. "I made him wait downstairs. What happened?" he repeated.

"All Ming's fault," Ming said, coming out of the shadows. She was disheveled, her healing bruise livid against her pallor. "Ming is going home."

"No, you are not," Letty said firmly, catching her wrist as she tried to go past her to the door. Ming dissolved into tears against her.

Charity then recounted everything from the moment she'd heard Ming scream.

Jack nodded grimly, his glance going to the inert figure on the bed, then to Charity. "I presume since I found the two of you atop him, pummeling him," he said significantly, "peaceful reasoning had no effect."

Charity lifted her chin, unaware that in her flowing but thin cambric gown, the action was sensual.

"This is no time to be smug, Jack. Another man fell out the window."

Jack carried the lamp to the window and looked down. The ladder lay on the grass, but there was no sign of a man.

"The rhododendron must have broken his fall. He seems to have gotten away." Jack handed the lamp to Charity, then the gun. He hefted the still unconscious man from the bed onto his shoulder. "I'm taking him to the sheriff. I want all of you to stay inside until I come back. No wandering outside to look for the other man. Is that clear?"

They nodded in unison.

He looked at Charity. "Do you know how to use that?"

She shrugged. "Point it and shoot?"

"Basically," he said with a grim smile. He shifted the burden on his shoulder and reached a hand out to indicate the hammer. "Pull that back to fire."

"I understand."

"Don't pull it until you're ready to fire."

"Of course."

Jack thanked the impulse to take one of the factory's delivery wagons home that night. He dropped his burden into it, then drove down to the sheriff's office.

As he rode up the hill, he wondered if there'd ever been two women more prone to disaster than the two for whom he was directly responsible. He doubted it. History would have recorded it.

He might have kept one of them safe. But with two of them, their propensity for danger increased astronomically. They were becoming more than he could handle while maintaining a business and a campaign. He needed help.

He stopped at home, gathered a few things, then returned to Letty's.

The three women and Jonathan were drinking hot chocolate when he arrived. Letty handed him a cup she'd kept warm for him on the stove. She looked in alarm at his valise.

"What are you doing?"

He put the bag on the floor and took a place at the table. Jonathan, eyes still wide from the night's excitement, came to sit on his knee. "I'm staying until things quiet down."

"You can sleep in my room!" Jonathan shook with excitement.

"Your constituents won't like this, Jack," Letty warned.

Jack inclined his head as though that was a possibility. "Losing an election is preferable to having Connor kill me if I let anything happen to you."

Letty rolled her eyes. "I doubt he'd even be concerned."

Jack shook his head. "You're not very bright sometimes, Letitia."

Jon leaned sleepily against Jack. "This is going to be fun," he said, his voice as heavy as his eyes.

"I'm certain it will be an experience," Jack said, putting the boy on his feet. "And you'd better rest up for it."

Jon grasped the hands that tried to push him toward the stairs. "I don't want to go to bed," he complained, exhaustion warring with excitement. "You're going to talk about those men who tried to kidnap Ming, aren't you? I'm not too young to listen. I helped, remember! I went to get you."

Jack nodded. "You were very smart. But you're going to have to help Rolf guard the ladies when I go to work tomorrow. You'll need your rest."

Jon's eyes widened. "Will I have a gun?"

"No."

"You gave Charity your gun, and she's just a girl." There was scornful emphasis for her gender.

Jack looked at Letty, grinning. "A viper in the bosom of the suffragist camp."

She rested tired gray eyes on her son in resignation. "Heredity is difficult to overcome. Ming, will you put him to bed, please? If you are forced to defend us, Jon, you can use Papa's baseball bat."

Ming stood and took his hand. "Come. Ming will help you."

Jon confided in her as she led him away, "They just want us to leave so they can talk about things they don't want us to hear."

Ming ruffled his hair. "Yes," she said.

The moment they were out of earshot, Letty pushed her cup aside and leaned toward Jack in concern.

"Do you think Ah Chun will try again?"

"Yes," Jack replied. "That's why Rolf will be here when I am not. And I insist that none of you goes anywhere without one of us along."

"Jack, I will have several hundred women converging on Astoria in less than a month for the convention. I have an address to give at the Fourth of July picnic. I have another rally to prepare before the convention, meetings to—"

"That's all very well," he said amenably, then cast a challenging glance at Charity. For a moment, Charity didn't understand why. Then he went on. "Do what you must do, just see that you give me sufficient warning so that I can assure that you're escorted."

Letty stiffened in her chair. "Jack, I will not have my footsteps dogged by—"

"Then you will remain at home," he said quietly, implacably. "The choice is yours. I might remind you that you have a child and the rest of your household to consider. Anything that endangers you at this point endangers them."

Charity cast him a dry glance as she reached out to pat Letty's hand. "Much as I hate to admit it, he's right, Letty. It's only common sense."

Letty scowled.

"The sheriff promised to investigate," Jack said.

"We know how far that promise will go," Letty said skeptically.

Jack looked hopeful. "I'm a candidate who's gaining more popularity every day. I believe he'll make an effort, on the chance I am elected. He won't want to work with a mayor who has a grudge against him."

Letty sighed and got to her feet. "Well, we'll see, won't we?"

As Jack stood, she reached up to loop her arms around his neck and kiss his cheek. "I know you have our best interests at heart. It just seems that I fight my way out of one tangle only to get into another." Then she smiled and hugged him. "Thank you for moving in. Those men did frighten us, and I'll feel much better knowing you're here. Good night, Jack."

"Sleep well, Letty."

Jack grinned at Charity, who was placing cups in the sink. "I know how you feel about escorts," he said, amusement in his voice, "but I thought I might walk you to your rooms."

"So that you can scold me for something, no doubt," she said, grinning as she turned down the lamp then preceded him out of the room.

"No," he said, catching up with her and putting an arm around her shoulders as he led her through the darkened house to the conservatory, "for the pleasure of your company."

"Well, what a surprise," she teased. "I was certain you would somehow hold me responsible for that altercation with Ah Chun's men."

He stopped her in the middle of the moonlit conservatory, laughing softly. "I do. You're the one who ruffled Ah Chun's feathers, remember? I saw no point in bringing it up again."

She made a face at him. "Generous of you."

"Have you given thought to our marriage?" he asked. The moonlight glossed her loose dark hair and made gossamer of her practical gown. He felt desperate to make love to her, whether they were married or not.

"I thought I made it plain the last time we spoke," she said, trying to imbue her voice with conviction. "Marriage between us would be disaster."

She stood quietly under his hands, trying hard not to look at him. One side of his face was burnished by moonlight, its strong planes and angles captivating in the quiet of the night. The other side was in shadow until he smiled, and his bright white teeth reminded her that his strong nature was tempered by warmth and humor.

Jack McCarren was perfect. He consumed her thoughts every waking moment now. All her practical arguments for why they shouldn't—couldn't—marry were beginning to disintegrate, and she had to fight to hold them together.

"That's what you said," he agreed softly. "But your eyes, your touch, your heartbeat tell me a different story."

In the wedge of moonlight, he leaned forward to touch his lips to first one eyelid, then the other. Then he kissed the tip of her nose, her cheek, her jaw, her mouth.

She lost coherent thought as he kissed her lips with tantalizing slowness, dipping deeply with his tongue, then withdrawing to nibble at her mouth until she reached a hand behind his head and pulled him down to her. He'd taught her a considerable skill, and she used it mercilessly.

He withdrew slightly, his mouth just hovering over hers, and placed his hand beneath one of her breasts so that he could cup it while still touching her rib cage.

"Your heart pounds for me, Charity," he said, his warm breath fanning her face. "Why are you determined to keep us apart when your body wants me."

"Because..." She couldn't remember.

His thumb stroked across her breast, and the reason she'd almost grasped fled again. She gasped as sensation raced through her, causing little shudders that seemed to go everywhere.

"If you'd given me an answer in the beginning," he whispered, lifting her against him so that her hip rested on the arm with which he supported her, his other hand exploring her hip, "we'd be married now. I wouldn't have to escort you to your bed and leave you there."

He walked slowly to her rooms as he spoke, pausing to plant a kiss on the cambric-covered breast within easy reach of his lips.

"We do so well together," he prodded quietly. He continued his artful ministrations until Charity found herself wondering if all the moral strictures with which she'd been raised were nonsense. What could possibly be wrong with feeling this way?

She was vaguely aware that they had passed through her sewing room and that Jack was standing at the foot of her bed. The room was dark and cool, and the warmth and strength of the arms around her made her feel as though nothing would be worth letting him go.

He put a knee on her bed, slid a hand up to support her shoulders, splayed the other across her buttocks and set her on the soft quilt.

"If we were married," he said, hovering over her, taking a piece of her gown between his thumb and forefinger and giving it a disparaging shake, "I would take this off you and show you the mysteries of love and life. I would show you that all your fears are unfounded."

He tugged the hem of her gown against her left thigh and stroked his warm palm on her cool, silky flesh.

"Instead, I have to leave you. And because I have to suffer that way..." He slipped his other hand under her back and pulled her against him as he knelt in the middle of her bed. "Because it's all your fault..." He gave her a kiss that left her gasping. "I want you to lie awake and wonder what it would have been like had I the right to rip this gown off you."

Firmly, deliberately, the hand that had lifted her gown slipped under it, and he ran his hand up the back of her thigh, over her soft, round bottom, then down again, never touching that part of her Charity was disconcerted to find ticking like a clock. His fingers molded the back of her thigh and slid slowly to her knee.

He was satisfied that she was a quivering, gasping little mass when he laid her down again. He leaned to kiss her quickly, then pushed himself off the bed.

"Sleep well, my love," he said. "We'll discuss it again tomorrow."

Chapter Ten

For the next several days, Letty's household was never without either Jack or Rolf in attendance, and often both men stayed for dinner and spent the evening.

Because of their presence, the house on the hill took on a convivial atmosphere. Breakfast was served in the conservatory, and lunch on the back lawn was followed by croquet or badminton, or simply lazy conversation on blankets spread in the sun.

They made a fuss of dinner and gathered around the grand piano that Letty played with more enthusiasm than skill. They sang and laughed and forgot that their enforced incarceration was supposed to be unpleasant.

Charity noticed that Rolf's eyes followed Ming possessively and that if she turned and caught his gaze, she returned all the longing she saw there. Then a frown would inevitably mar her doll-like face and she would turn away and find something to do in another part of the house.

On those occasions Rolf would observe her retreating figure, then return to the task at hand.

Charity confided her concerns about the couple to Jack one afternoon as they tied the badminton net in the backyard.

"Would she be an outcast if she married a man who wasn't Chinese?" she asked as Jack, dressed in white shirt and suspenders and brown pants, forced one of the poles that supported the net tightly into the ground.

The pole secured, she threaded the strings on the edge of the net into the holes in the pole.

"I think so," he said, holding up the weight of the net to make her task easier. "And many of our people would be as reluctant to accept her as the Chinese would be to accept Rolf. But I think she has other reasons."

Charity glanced away from the knot she was making to demand, "What other reasons? Rolf is wonderful."

He met her gaze steadily, blandly. "Who knows? Neither of *us* would be ostracized if we were to marry, and I'm also wonderful, yet still you resist me."

She swatted his shoulder and started across the yard with the second pole. He followed, stretching out the net as a measure. She stopped when it was held taut, and Jack drove the pole into the lawn.

She toyed with the strings on the edge of the net. "I've said nothing of resisting today, have I?" she asked casually.

The truth was, she could resist no longer. After he'd put her to bed two nights before she'd been plagued constantly with thoughts of what might have happened had he stayed. Though she worked at her sewing machine, or helped in the kitchen, or played with Jon, she never forgot the tremors he'd created inside her, which never quite went away. The situation was worsened by the fact that they'd never had the discussion he'd promised the following day. In fact, he'd been circumspect and polite and behaved almost as though he'd forgotten the entire incident.

Every time she looked at him now, she felt a warm languor in her lower body that made the casual smiles she gave him a travesty. She was a quivering mass of unfulfilled desire, and today, Sunday, with Jack in attendance all day, she was about to expire with frustration.

Jack glanced at her, his expression deceptively casual as he wiggled the pole to test its solidity. It didn't move. "Haven't you? It's become so much a part of my daily life, I suppose I hear your protests whether or not they're spoken."

As he took the strings from her to thread them through the holes, he saw her little pout of annoyance and firmly suppressed the triumph. It was working. Leaving her alone after that little lesson that had almost debilitated him for life, in mind as well as body, had been a sound decision, however difficult to execute. He couldn't help teasing her. "Perhaps Rolf and Ming would be happier single." He said it casually as his big hands struggled to thread the string through the holes in the pole.

Charity stood on tiptoe to lightly swat his hands away and do it herself.

"That's nonsense," she said firmly, pausing long enough to thread the pole with unerring precision. She pulled the string through and tied the knot. "They're in love. I can see it in their faces. How can you imagine they'd be happier apart?"

Jack wrapped one hand around the pole and threaded the fingers of the other into the net on the other side of her. The knot tied, she turned to find herself effectively trapped, her dark eyes wide, her cheeks pink with her emotional defense of her friends. Or was it something else?

Jack didn't understand her completely. He was becoming convinced she was hiding something from him.

As long as it wasn't a husband, he didn't care what it was. Had she run away from a cruel, wastrel father? There seemed to be more to it, though. He didn't know what it was, and as long as it didn't keep her from him, it didn't matter. He'd had the feeling all morning that she was about to capitulate.

He looked at her now, pressed as far away from him as she could get into the net—all eyes and quivering lips.

"Then you believe lovers should be together," he challenged softly.

Around them bees buzzed, Letty's roses spilled wonderful perfume, and laughter came from the house.

He saw her eyes register the fact that he'd caught her. She glanced at him, exasperated, then accepting. She fidgeted in the little prison he'd made for her. "Of course," she said softly.

"Only other people?" he asked. "Or us, as well?"

Charity looked into his eyes with longing. Did she dare marry him and hope that her father's identity was never discovered to destroy Jack's career and their life together?

The thing to do, she knew, would be to tell him that she was Charity Ross, daughter of the notorious Calvin Ross of Dawson, Kansas, and let him decide.

But she knew the words simply wouldn't come—partly because it was a little late now for guilty admissions. They loved each other. How could she explain that she'd been too cowardly to tell him the truth?

And partly because there was always the chance that the life he'd planned and worked for would be more important to him than she was. He loved her. She was absolutely certain of that. But he'd dragged himself up from the docks against impossible odds to be where he was today. He'd endured gossip and scorn and made friends anyway. Whether or not he was elected mayor, he was a success. She wasn't sure how he'd react to the fact that public knowledge of her background would put him right back where he'd started.

Jack, seeing the turmoil in her eyes, tasted panic. Was she going to change her mind again? He forgot the tender diplomacy he'd been determined to employ on her today and leaned over her intimidatingly.

"I will get down on my knee," he said, pinching her chin between his thumb and forefinger, "and ask you to marry me one more time. But if your answer is no, I will turn you over that same knee."

She stared at him for one interminable moment, then she threw her arms around his neck and held on, giggling. "A proposal of marriage," she said, "accompanied by a threat. You are quite an individual, Jack."

He pulled her away from him and set her on her feet, holding her arms firmly as he looked into her eyes. "What is your answer?"

The doubts he'd seen there seconds ago were gone and love brimmed in them. "Yes," she said.

With a shout of laughter he crushed her against him, unable to believe he'd finally won.

"Say it again," he ordered.

"Yes," she repeated.

"Thank God!" They laughed together as he swung her around in the middle of the sunny, perfumed backyard. "Right away," he said. "Next weekend."

"But I'll have to make a dress and see that—"

"Jack McCarren!" Letty exclaimed as she came into the yard with a tray bearing glasses. Rolf followed her with a pitcher of lemonade. "Put her down. She isn't goods to be toted around and stuffed into one of your boxes."

Swinging Charity into his arms, Jack strolled to where Letty and Rolf sat at the table under the hawthorn tree. "She's just agreed to be my wife!"

The tray clattered to the table as Letty looked at them openmouthed. Her eyes registered first surprise, then delight, then a vague sadness that was quickly squelched.

"Well, put her down so I can offer my congratulations," she demanded, her eyes filling.

Jack obliged, and as Letty and Charity hugged and laughed and wept, Rolf shook Jack's hand.

"Good for you," he said. "Now, I suppose, you'll be obliged to march in suffragist parades."

Jack lowered his voice. "Remind me talk to you about that."

Rolf raised an eyebrow. "You mean you do intend—"

Jack shook his head. "I swear, Kauppi, there are times you don't have the brains God gave a salmon. No, I will not be marching in suffragist parades, but we have to get an escort together for the next time *they* do."

Rolf frowned. "But I thought the women said they didn't want—"

"An escort," Jack added, "that will remain close but out of sight. Charity and Letty don't even have to know."

"Ah." Rolf nodded and grinned. "Has it occurred to you that our lives are beginning to resemble a novel? Intrigue, danger, romance..."

"Romance?" Jack asked.

Rolf shrugged, looking away toward the trees up the hill. "Well, for you, at least."

"Ming is being difficult?" Jack ventured.

Rolf looked surprised. "How did you know?"

Jack laughed. "A good guess. Is she afraid Chinatown will not approve of you? I can understand her concern."

"No, she's afraid Ah Chun will kill me, and she will not listen to reason. The fact that I'm twice his size, that I have friends on the docks who could be more deadly than his henchmen doesn't influence her. She says he has power that reaches beyond size and number."

Jack put a consoling arm around his shoulders. "When we finally succeed in putting Ah Chun in jail where he belongs, she'll come around."

Rolf groaned. "All I have to do is be patient."

Jack grinned. "Can you manage?"

Before Rolf could reply, Letty launched herself into Jack's arms. Rolf turned to give Charity a hug.

"You'd better be good to her, Jack," Letty warned, "or my ladies and I will make you rue the day you met me."

He gave her a hearty hug. "I do that regularly already, Letitia."

She slapped his arm and turned to Charity with a dramatic frown. "You're sure you want to tie yourself to this man? That gentlemanly polish is simply a veneer. At heart he's a brigand, just like Connor."

"I remember one balmy night," a deep, masculine voice said, "when you told me women found brigands more exciting than gentlemen."

Everyone turned to the sound of the voice. Charity saw a tall, big man in white trousers and a blue jacket. His face was rugged and square, his eyes a startling dark blue. Thick dark hair caught red highlights from the sun, and he had an elegant mustache, more red than brown. Over his shoulder was a stout duffel. He dropped it at his feet.

Letty gasped. She took several steps toward the man, stopping well away from him.

"Connor," she said, her usually strong voice high and unsteady. "What brings you here? Have you wrecked your ship and washed up on shore?"

That had not been the welcome Connor Donovan had expected. His eyes flashed and snapped, and his square jaw set. But before he could reply, the back door opened and Jonathan and Ming emerged with a plates of sandwiches and cupcakes. When Jon spotted his father, the cupcakes fell to the grass as he shouted with heart-wrenching delight, "Papa!" and ran into his arms.

Connor's expression softened as he reached down to lift the boy high against his chest.

"Mama!" Jon called to his mother, reaching an arm out for her to join them. "Papa's home!"

Charity struggled to resist an urge to push Letty in Connor's direction. Jack, as though reading her mind, slipped an arm around her waist and held her at his side. He, she noticed, did not seem at all surprised by his friend's sudden arrival.

"What is it you want?" Letty asked, taking several steps closer in response to Jonathan's continued beckoning. Still, a distance remained between her and her husband.

"I heard you'd been hurt on a march," he said. "And that someone broke into the house."

Letty glowered at Jack, then turned to her husband. "By your confidant, I suppose."

Connor sent a look across the yard at Jack, a fractional smile on his lips. It vanished when he looked at Letty. "Yes. He was only doing what I asked."

She folded her arms. "Yes," she said coolly. "That is what you like, isn't it? Someone who does what you ask."

He drew a deep breath. "Titia, I didn't come here to argue."

"Well, that's unfortunate, because if you remain that's precisely what will happen."

Connor studied her without speaking for a moment, and Charity felt Jack shift his weight, as though he knew something was about to happen.

Connor put Jonathan on his feet and pushed him gently toward the door. "Go inside, son," he said.

"But, Papa..." The boy resisted.

"Go on. Mama and I will be right in."

Jonathan went, dragging his feet, looking over his shoulder.

Connor fixed his bright blue eyes on Letty, who remained straight as a fireplace poker several yards from him.

"I'd just come off the Los Angeles to Portland run," he said, his voice quiet but curiously menacing, "when I received Jack's letter. I took the ship that afternoon, and had to bring her in myself because the captain was ill."

"I'm sorry, that we've caused you any inconvenience, but you will remember that Jack sent for you, not I," Letty said stiffly.

His dark blue eyes grew darker. "I'm not in the best of tempers. I'm tired and hungry and completely out of patience. You would be wise to come inside with me and tell me what has happened. Otherwise—" he smiled dangerously in the direction of their unwilling audience "—we will be the entertainment for our friends at this lovely lawn party." His eyes went to Letty, their expression significant. "Do you really want that, Titia?"

Letty resisted a full ten seconds, then marched in the direction of the back door. Connor watched her go, expelled a sigh, then waved in Jack's direction. "Hello,

Jack," he said, his voice tinged with grim humor. "I won't forget that you're responsible for this."

Jack smiled back. "What are friends for?"

"Indeed. Please excuse us." He started for the door.

Jonathan, who'd been sent outside by his parents, joined the others. They ate sandwiches and played badminton while a battle raged within the house.

The shouting went on for some time. The argument seemed to have moved upstairs, for the sounds of something delicate breaking came from Letty's open bedroom window. There was an oath, a scream, then silence.

"Jack?" Charity said worriedly, twirling her racket as their opponents chased the birdie into the azalea bushes. Jonathan lay asleep under the hawthorn tree. "What do you suppose has happened? It's awfully quiet."

He did not seem concerned. "He's either taken her to bed or strangled her."

"Jack!" She swatted the top of his head with the netting of her racket.

He pulled her to him, laughing, and kissed her. "Connor would never hurt Letty, but she's a woman who needs a man who is as firm and as stubborn as she is. They'll be fine once they start talking."

"Letty did not look receptive to peaceful conversation." She sighed, still watching the house in concern. "You're certain sending for Connor was a good idea?"

Jack followed her gaze. "I didn't precisely send for him. I simply wrote a letter telling him of the various scrapes Letty had been in, that Ah Chun's men had tried to take Ming, and I knew he'd be here on the next ship."

"I don't know..." Charity said doubtfully.

He pointed across the net with his racket. Rolf and Ming seemed to have forgotten the game. The search for the birdie had somehow become a kiss under a shady flowered bush.

Charity smiled. Maybe all the romantic problems in Letty's household would solve themselves. She looked into Jack's eyes as he leaned to kiss her again. It occurred to her that she was being naive and overly optimistic. But she was in love. It all seemed so right.

When Letty and Connor finally came downstairs for dinner that first evening they insisted that Jack and Rolf stay for the meal. Letty, her cheeks hectic with color, reacted by chattering gaily and endorsing Jack's wish for an immediate weekend wedding. She promised Charity that she would take care of all the details.

Connor watched his wife with a moody but starkly possessive look in his eye. He talked with Jack and Rolf, joked with his son, made polite conversation with Charity, but his eyes always strayed to Letty, who hadn't looked in his direction once since the meal began.

With Connor in residence once again, Jack moved home. The lively atmosphere of the last few days was replaced by a curious kind of quiet.

Ming and Kristine went about their duties with their usual efficiency, and Charity spent much of her time in her rooms, preparing for the wedding.

Determined to give Letty and Connor their privacy, Charity slaved to repair the white dress to wear for the ceremony and to create a bathing costume to wear to Gearhart just down the coast, where Jack wanted to spend their week-long honeymoon.

When she'd finished those tasks, she packed the few possessions she would move to Jack's house. Then she spent the remaining time fighting off second thoughts.

She shouldn't be doing this—at least not without telling Jack the truth. But she feared the truth would change everything. This was what she wanted. Jack loved her. If it all blew up in their faces one day, he would understand. She hoped.

Letty ran into her shop from the conservatory, still dressed from a trip to town. Her cheeks were pink, her eyes bright under a turquoise and black Gainsborough hat. She held out a package wrapped in paper.

"Look what I found for you at the Bee Hive." Letty met her in the middle of the room. "I know you were planning to make your own, but time is growing short and this was so beautiful, I couldn't resist it. What do you think? Do you love it?"

"Oh, Letty!" Charity unwrapped a nightgown of white Victoria lawn. It was trimmed with eyelet lace and white silk ribbon.

Charity looked into her friend's face, thinking how blessed she'd been to have found Jack and Letty. She'd experienced more happiness and laughter in the six weeks she'd been in Astoria than she'd known in the whole of her life.

But she could see that Letty, despite the gaiety and chatter, did not feel as blessed at the moment as Charity did.

Charity wrapped her arms around Letty and held her, wishing she could somehow mend the breach between her and Connor. They loved each other; it would have been obvious to a blind man. But the wounds their year apart had created would need time to heal.

Charity's empathy reduced Letty to noisy, gulping sobs. Charity sat her down on the edge of the bed and poured her a cup of the tea that Kristine had brought earlier.

"Stop that," Charity ordered gently as Letty dabbed her eyes with a lace-edged hanky. "I don't want my matron of honor having red cheeks like the men who spend all their time at the Sunset Saloon."

"Oh, Charity," Letty said, covering her mouth with the hanky as fresh sobs shook her. Charity sat beside her and put an arm around her. Letty sniffed and lowered the hanky and heaved a deep sigh. "When he appeared that day...I thought he was back because...because he truly loved me and missed me...and..." She shook her head and her face contorted. "But he came because Jack sent for him."

"Jack didn't send for him," Charity clarified. "He merely wrote him a letter and explained what had been happening at home. Connor's decision to come back was his own."

"Because he didn't want me embarrassing him further."

"Did he say that?"

"No." Letty stood, twisting the hanky around her index finger and pacing the width of the bed in the small space between it and the wall. "He doesn't talk to me unless we're at meals. He sleeps in the library."

Charity didn't know what to say, so she remained silent.

Still pacing, Letty wrapped the hanky around the index finger of the other hand. "The afternoon he came home, he ordered me into the house... Well, you saw that!" She turned to Charity for concurrence. Charity nodded dutifully, though she thought the word "ordered" was a bit strong. "He spoke to Jon a few minutes, told him how much he loved him and missed him and that from now on they were going to do so many things together. Then he asked Jon to go outside so he could talk to me. But he didn't want to talk, he wanted to accuse me of outrageous behavior, of flying in the face of danger, living like a bachelor woman..."

Charity bit back a smile.

"I dragged his bag upstairs to get it out of the middle of the room and to get away from him, but he followed. I had to put the bag in my closet since I'd rented you the storage rooms, and he came with me into the bedroom, still railing."

She stretched the hanky and tried to tie it in a knot. "I'd finally had enough and I threw my glove box at him. He pushed me onto the bed, intent, I was sure, to do me an injury, only..." She gulped a sob and the hanky tore apart in her hands.

Charity stood and went to her. "He made love to you instead."

Letty fell into her arms. "I thought it had solved everything. But afterward we were both awkward and... and now he makes his bed in the library!"

Charity sat her down and forced the teacup into her hands, waiting until she'd disposed of half the liquid before suggesting carefully, "Perhaps you should try to talk to him. Tell him honestly how you feel, tell him how much you love him, how lonely you've been without him and how much you hate this distance between you."

Letty looked horrifed. "Charity! That would be admitting... defeat."

Charity coaxed her to drink the rest of the tea. "Maybe it would just be admitting how much you need him and that if you could do it over again, you'd have found a way to be a hostess to his friends while still attending your meeting that day."

Letty's brow pleated tightly between her delicate eyebrows. "It was the principle of the thing."

"The principle of the thing," Charity said, taking the empty cup from her and putting it aside, "is that you love one another. He came back because he thought you were in danger. You can bend a little."

Letty pulled the pins out of her hat, upturned it, dropped the pins inside the crown and tossed it toward the pillows. Then she fell against the mattress with a sigh.

"I was always the one to bend," she said petulantly. "He always got things his way. I'm fighting for women's rights. I can't back down from him now."

Charity sat beside her and leaned down to rest her weight on an elbow. Sun streamed in through the lace curtains and made strange patterns on the bed.

"Living here," she began, "has taught me so much. I've learned a lot about women's rights and responsibilities. But it seems to me that we aren't fighting for our rights because we're superior, but because we want to be able to do things we're smart enough and strong enough to do without being ridiculed. We don't want to be free of good men who try to protect us because they love us, do we? Only of cruel, tyrannical, ignorant men who would hold us back because they think we aren't good for anything but bed service."

Letty was silent for a long moment, then she propped herself on an elbow and frowned at Charity. "Did Jack tell you to say that?"

Charity laughed lightly. "No, but I do believe he taught me that."

Letty pushed herself to a sitting position and sighed. "All right, Charity, I'm going to follow your advice. But if it fails me," she said, turning a look of mock ferocity on her friend, "I'm going to come looking for you."

Charity laughed again, sitting up. "I won't be far away."

Letty suddenly became grave. "I'm going to miss you being in these rooms. It has been wonderful having you here."

"I've loved being here." Charity patted her hand. "You'll have to come to my house every other day for tea, and on alternate days I'll come to yours."

"It won't be the same."

"No, it won't. When I first came here, we were both at a loss. Now you and Connor are going to start over," she predicted firmly. "And Jack and I are on our way to the governor's mansion."

"Hmm." Letty looked severe. "Salem is a long way for me to have to go for tea."

Chapter Eleven

She was married. Charity absorbed the wonder of her hours-old status as Jack wrestled their bags from the train. In a kind of trance, she took her small portmanteau from him and followed him to a waiting wagon. The driver stowed their bags, then helped them onto the old but comfortable leather seat.

The afternoon sun was hot, but the coastal breeze stirred around them as the wagon left the depot and headed down a planked road lined by tall cedars and firs. The breeze sighed in the treetops, and sunlight dappled the road.

Jack let out a contented sigh as Charity settled against him. The day had gone precisely as he planned. Charity belonged to him. He'd been certain something would happen at the last moment, feared she would change her mind.

Nonetheless he'd waited near the altar at Grace Episcopal Church, Connor stalwart and smiling beside him, Rolf escorting guests to their seats, and there were no surprises. Though they'd had a brief week to prepare, word had spread among his friends, and they'd all appeared for the ceremony.

The music had begun and Letty had appeared in the doorway in a yellow gown, looking uncharacteristically shy and reserved. Then Charity had walked in on Dr. Parson's arm and Jack's world seemed to stop, to freeze. For an instant nothing moved and he was able to look his fill.

She wore the dress she'd torn the night she and Ming had fallen in the kitchen. She'd made a little beaded jacket to go over it, and tufts of veiling bloomed out of a coronet of beads in her hair. The netting obscured her features until she reached the first pew and Dr. Parson sent her the rest of the way on her own.

He stepped forward to meet her and finally saw her dark eyes peering at him, her sweet, loving smile that was just for him, and at that moment Jack McCarren, bachelor, disappeared. Jack McCarren, husband, was born. He felt the change like a physical thing. And despite all the bawdy jokes and dire warnings offered by his friends the night before in the back room of the St. Charles club for gentlemen, he did not feel confined or in any way diminished. He felt as though the whole world had opened at his feet.

"I just thought," Charity said, bringing him back to the present, "that it looks like the cover of a novel I read on the train coming to Oregon."

"One of those syrupy love stories?"

She slapped his chest halfheartedly. "Don't be scornful. I feel syrupy about you, and you don't seem to mind."

"As long as you don't get syrupy about a character in a book."

"How could I?" she asked with all apparent sincerity, "when I have the genuine gentleman?"

He rewarded her with a kiss, then as they settled back to enjoy the ride to the Gearhart House Hotel, he prayed he would be able to remain the gentleman. Since their honeymoon began, he'd been consumed with lust, and impatient to finally, after many frustrating weeks, take her to bed.

But she would be nervous and he would have to be considerate and patient. He loved her so much that he was determined to control his passion, to make it wonderful for her. He just prayed his body would cooperate.

There were people everywhere in the two-story white frame structure. Guests sat on the porches that wrapped around on both levels, and children played in the sand near the road that ran down to the beach.

The elegant lobby was handsomely furnished in oak. Groups of people were seated around tables quietly talking, and guests came and went up the stairs.

Charity stood beside Jack while he registered, and caught the grinning glance he sent her when he wrote "Mr. and Mrs. Jack McCarren."

They followed a bellboy to their room at the far end of a wide, breezy corridor on the second floor.

Long lace curtains fluttered from the windows as they walked into the room. A brass double bed covered with a colorful quilt dominated the room. Charity's eyes went to it with a paradoxical combination of excitement and trepidation.

She swung her apprehensions away as she pretended to inspect the rest of the room while Jack tipped the bellboy. Vaguely, she noted a plain but serviceable dresser with a mirror, a washstand and a chair next to a window that opened onto the porch.

She opened it and looked out. The ocean lay like a silver blanket that stretched to the horizon, embroidered with sunlight, tipped with the lacy rill of waves. Bathers in bright bathing suits and caps walked along the road that led to it, towels over their shoulders, food hampers carried between them. It was the most delightful sight she'd ever seen.

She felt Jack come up behind her and wrap his arms around her. He planted a kiss on her temple and squeezed gently. "Are you thinking about a swim?" he asked. That was the last thing he wanted to do at the moment, but he was ready if that was what she wanted.

She leaned against him with that little sigh of contentment that made him feel invicible—and desperate to make love to her.

"No," she said lazily. "I was just thinking how beautiful it is. When I was a young girl, I was so sure I'd never see the ocean. I expected to live my whole life in Kansas."

"You were obviously unaware at the time, that you had a wild, adventurous streak that would put you on a train headed west—and right into the path of a hungry bear," he teased.

She laughed as she thought back on that day. She turned her head to kiss his chin. "And an even more dangerous wolf," she said.

He growled and nipped her earlobe.

Charity turned in his arms, her heart swelling, overflowing. Her mind filled with cherished impressions of their quarrels—the playful and the real—their conversations on subjects men often considered women too silly to discuss. Her body was suddenly filled with a curious, liquid warmth.

She looked into his dark, devilish eyes and knew that she hadn't left home when she'd left Kansas, she'd come home.

"I feel so fortunate to have found you, Jack," she said, her voice heavy with sincerity. "Not just because you've saved me from a bear, and Ah Chun's men, and the loneliness I'd expected to face when I came here. But because you've saved me from . . . myself."

He could feel her heart fluttering against his ribs. He tried not to be distracted by it because, though he didn't understand it, he felt sure she was revealing something important.

He raised an eyebrow. "Yourself? Had you such dangerous plans for your future?"

No. Not dangerous. But she'd been so sure there'd be nothing for her but work and anonymity and a solitude she'd thought she wanted. Then he'd leapt into her life, and she hadn't had a moment's peace since. And she no longer wanted one.

She couldn't explain, because that morning when they'd exchanged their vows, she'd put Kansas and her father behind her forever. Jack was her life now. She wouldn't think of the past again.

She smiled, feeling a delicious new ease fill her being.

"Well, I was twenty-five, after all. I was sure all I would find in Astoria was self-employment and spinsterhood."

"Twenty-five?" he asked, pretending to be shocked. "Such an advanced age. I hope your faculties will continue to serve you until our honeymoon is over. I believe the management can provide a chair with wheels—"

"You will be the one in the chair," she threatened, giving him a push.

"I? You were the one who—"

She pushed him again. "Yes, I was the one who raised the subject, but must you always take wicked advantage of everything I say? Well, now that I am your wife..."

She pushed him once more and he let himself fall with martyred abandon atop the sweet-smelling quilt on the bed. She knelt beside him, leaning over him, her beautiful face formed into a threatening grimace. "You will learn that you've married a termagant who said yes only to repay you for all the times you've tormented me."

Jack caught her wrists and pulled her across him then down on the other side of him. He held her there while she squealed and giggled, then he rose over her thinking her plan was working. He felt fairly tormented at the moment. If they didn't get out of this room, he might forget that she hadn't eaten since before the ceremony.

"And you might discover," he said, feigning ferocity as she had done, "that you haven't married a gentleman at all." He laughed wickedly.

She looked at him a long moment, the sparkle of humor in her eyes turning to the glimmer of something else entirely. She gave him a smile that turned his heart over. "I don't believe that for a moment."

He thought there was a message in her eyes for him, but he dismissed the idea, certain it was simply the product of his impatience to make her finally, irrevocably, his.

He sighed with theatrical disappointment. "Well, it was worth a try. I suppose now I'll be like Horace Frampton."

She blinked, still trapped under him. "Who is Horace Frampton?"

"One of my customers," he replied. "He's a haberdasher. A brilliant man with sound business sense, but his life is completely managed by Cornelia."

"His wife?"

"Yes. He was playing poker with Rolf, Connor and me one evening, and Cornelia came for him and dragged him home by his ear."

"You're joking."

"I'm quite serious. We haven't heard from him since. I believe we've been deemed bad company."

"Hmm." She pretended to consider. "Perhaps I should call on Cornelia for a few lessons."

"If a woman ever did that to me," he interrupted, "she would find herself on the next ship to Anchorage—without a return ticket."

Charity's eyes widened innocently. "Perhaps Cornelia had plans for him that evening that he enjoyed far more than playing poker with three itinerant bon vivants."

The suggestion was there in her eyes again. He felt fairly certain he wasn't imagining it this time.

He rolled onto his back, pulling her over him. "Are you telling me, that you're entertaining such plans for me?" he asked softly.

She dropped her eyes, a subtle blush rising from the lacy neck of her blouse. Then she looked at him and conceded with a little grin that was decidedly mischievous, "I have been since that afternoon in my bedroom when you taught me the fine points of self-defense."

He smiled, brushing away a silky tendril of her hair, delighted with her. "I thought you might want dinner first."

She crossed her forearms on his chest and admitted candidly, "I had thought to tell you I was famished because I was... I am... nervous."

He ran a thumb gently over her cheekbone. "I would never hurt you, Charity."

She leaned into his touch. "I know. I'm not frightened, I'm simply nervous. And not because of you, but because I . . . well, my performance may not be . . ."

He turned her again, cradling her in the crook of his arm. Looking into the concern in her dark eyes he felt weak with tenderness and desire. Balancing the two, he thought wryly, was going to prove a challenge.

"There is no performance required of you, Charity," he said gravely. "We will simply show each other how we feel. There are no standards to meet or rules to follow. I'll love you, and you'll love me." He smiled slowly. "We will be brilliant."

She looped her arms around his neck and pulled his head down. "Then I think dinner can wait," she said.

She met his mouth eagerly, artfully. Knowing that he now belonged to her and she to him, she let her hands explore as she'd never done before. Her hands combed into his hair, felt its wiry strength curl around her fingers. She swept downward to the steely column of his neck, the warm, oaklike solidity of his shoulders under the linen shirt, the long length of his muscled back to his narrow waist. She encountered the waistband of his pants at the same moment that he took the tail of the bow that tied the neck of her blouse and pulled.

She lost all ability to move. He was going to undress her and make love to her. Everything inside her began to tremble, and though she was innocent, she knew it wasn't from fear. It was excitement, anticipation . . . desire.

One by one, he unfastened the small buttons that closed the front of her blouse. His large fingers operated with surprising dexterity. He pulled the blouse out of her skirt and opened it.

Charity felt a breeze from the overhead fan on her shoulders and the tops of her breasts not quite covered by her lace-trimmed chemise. But Jack's gaze warmed her immediately.

He leaned down to plant a kiss at a madly beating pulse at her throat. Then he traced her collarbone with kisses and followed the lacy edge of her chemise over the gentle rise of her bosom. She made a little sound of pleasure that brought his mouth to her lips.

Slipping an arm under her blouse to hold her even closer, he leaned up abruptly, frowning.

"What?" she asked in concern.

He frowned at her waist. "This," he said in obvious displeasure, his big hand placed across the tight pink brocade.

"It's my corset," she said, smiling teasingly at him. "You're not going to try to convince me that you've never seen one before."

He lowered his hand to gently swat her hip. "It's tight enough to render you unconscious," he said, unceremoniously rolling her over and quickly, deftly unlacing it. He unfastened her skirt and turning her over again tugged it from her and tossed the corset aside.

"You will not wear that while we're at the beach," he said, rubbing her waist through the delicate chemise.

"Fashion demands it, Jack," she argued reasonably. "And since fashion is my business, I cannot appear inappropriately dressed."

"If you insist," he said agreeably, undoing the buttons at the cuffs of her blouse. He slipped a hand under her to hold her up to him as he pulled the blouse off. "I'll simply keep you in bed the entire week so that you have no occasion to dress and present your plump little body to the public."

"Plump!" she protested indignantly, then lost the will to scold him when he lay her down and slipped his fingers under the waist of her chemise to pull it up.

"A joke, my love," he said, leaning over her to plant a kiss in the slender concavity between her ribs.

He pushed the thin fabric higher and Charity raised her arms to allow him to remove it.

It was ironic, he thought, that she'd been concerned about performance when just the sight of her was pushing him to the edge of insanity.

Two beautiful little globes, flushed pink like her cheeks and tipped with darker pink like the center of a flower, lured his mouth to her once again. He kissed her breasts gently, reverently, and felt the little buds tighten into beads.

Charity felt a flush sweep over her from head to toe. She ran her hands up his arms, needing to feel his steadiness as the world seemed to tilt a little sideways. Sensation raced from the tips of her breasts to her arms and legs, making them feel weighted and languid.

Jack straightened and reached to pull off her slippers and toss them toward the growing pile at the side of the bed. Then he stood and, leaning over her, untied the drawstring of her bloomers, slipped his fingers into the waistband and pulled them down her hips, over her stockings and off. The cotton hose were dispensed with in an instant.

Entranced, Jack placed one knee between hers and a hand on each of her thighs. His fingers swept up her silken skin, up the length of her leg, over the swell of her hip to the indentation of her waist. He leaned over her and said in fascination, "You are a masterpiece, Charity McCarren. More beautiful than in my dreams."

"Oh, Jack." She sighed in acceptance of the compliment, knowing it was far from the truth but convinced by his sincerity that he believed it to be so.

"And what about *my* masterpiece?" she whispered, tugging at the tie still at his throat. "You are still fully clothed."

He dropped onto the mattress beside her and turned onto his back, both hands raised in helpless acceptance.

"I am yours to unveil," he said with a smile.

Charity struggled against an instinctive shyness as she got to her knees beside him, sat on her heels and considered where to start.

Jack put a gentle hand to her face. "I am yours, remember," he coaxed.

That was true, she thought. And though the unknown was daunting, she knew she would want to do this with him often and for hours; she applied herself to the task with honest enthusiasm.

Deftly, she removed his tie and linen collar, then unfastened the buttons of his shirt.

He arched a brow at her efficiency. "You do this," he said, "as though you have experience."

"Oh, I do," she replied with an air of innocence, though she knew he was teasing her.

"What?" he demanded quietly.

She would have continued the charade, but her lips quirked traitorously. "To make extra money I dressed windows at a department store in Dawson. I often put them on a form in the window."

He grasped her shoulders and pulled her to him. "I can see," he said sternly, "that you're going to require a firm hand, probably applied somewhere discreet, to make you behave."

She giggled and used his shoulders to lever herself back to her knees. "I'm all atremble," she said, reaching for the buckle of his belt. She untied it, then, faced with the buttoned fly on his pants, looked at him uncertainly.

"Yes," he said. He was capable only of a word of one syllable. As her fingers worked the buttons, her small knuckles moving over that part of him already swollen for her, he had to concentrate to continue to breathe.

Then she had the pants unfastened and tugged them down his legs. Braced on his elbows, he lifted his hips to help her.

Her cheeks were bright pink, her hands unsteady as she carefully folded the pants and laid them over the back of the chair. Then she came back to him, one knee on the bed beside him, the other foot braced on the floor. Then he saw her eyes widen as her hands touched the fabric of his short-legged union suit.

"Silk?" she asked in what seemed to be appreciative amazement.

He smiled wryly at himself. For a moment he'd thought her wide eyes were appreciating his magnificence. Under the fragile fabric it was difficult to hide.

It occurred to him that that was why he loved her. She was so guileless and so dear.

"Yes," he replied. "I have them made at Wah Sing's at home."

"What a wonderful fabric," she said, her fingertips running up his thigh. They stopped abruptly when she reached the juncture of his leg and torso and noticed his obvious excitement.

She looked into his eyes, her blush deepening but her interest apparent. He couldn't stand another moment.

He unbuttoned the garment and pushed his way out of it. He tossed it away, then lay on his side and pulled her down to face him.

He brushed back the hair now coming loose from her pins and noted that though his hands were steady, a curious trembling was taking place inside him. Probably, he guessed, because though making love wasn't new to him, feeling love was. And receiving it.

She reached with tender fingers to stroke his cheek, then run her thumb lightly along his bottom lip.

"I love you so much," she said, her voice a whisper in the lengthening shadows of the golden afternoon invading their room. "Now...I don't think I could bear my life without you in it."

"You will never know that possibility," he said, pulling pins out of her hair and tossing them. "I will not let you more than two feet away from me the whole of our lives."

She smiled, her eyes heavy-lidded as he combed his fingers through the mass of rich, dark curls he'd loosened. Her hair smelled of roses.

"Then which of us is changing professions? Am I going into the box business, or are you going to become a seamstress?"

He was kissing her throat. "Perhaps we will combine resources and sew boxes together. What do you think?"

She didn't answer. She couldn't. While one of Jack's hands cradled her against him, the other had wandered over her breasts and now seemed to be making its slow way downward.

She was already a mass of emotion so intense and so new that she felt like someone else—not Charity Ross at all, or even Charity Butler. Then it occurred to her. She was Charity McCarren now.

She leaned trustingly into him as his warm hand slipped between her thighs to cover the mound of her femininity. Every nerve ending seemed to jump at the intimate touch.

Then she remembered what he had said. "I will love you, and you will love me."

She put a tentative hand to the mat of hair on his chest. She heard the smallest sound deep in his throat and felt a muscle leap under her hand. Inspired, she stroked circles over his chest as he had done to her.

Jack couldn't believe what the stroke of that little hand did to his body. When he'd been a child, his body had withstood the elements and the occasional kick of a shopkeeper unhappy to find him asleep in his doorway.

As an adult, it had worked slavishly, hard physical work that strained his muscles and formed them into iron ropes.

But under her fingers, his entire being turned to jelly—except that part of him that wanted her touch so desperately. Fire traveled under her hand, and he felt it roaring in his ears, burning in the pit of his stomach.

In her attempt to follow his lead, she began to explore downward. He closed his eyes and let himself consider the prospect for a moment with shuddering anticipation, then he reached down when she got to his belly and caught her hand. He placed it against his chest.

Her eyes widened in confused surprise. "No?"

"No." He laughed lightly in self-deprecation. "Or I won't have time to prepare you."

She had a vague idea what that meant. She'd overheard conversations in the fitting rooms when she'd done alterations for the department store. Attitudes had varied. It was wonderful, or it was frightening.

Because she couldn't imagine Jack ever being frightening, and wonderful would probably be too much to expect for someone who'd not done this before, she prepared for it to be something from which to learn.

And learn she did. When his finger slipped inside her, she learned that no words could ever have prepared her for what it felt like to have Jack's touch within her.

"It's all right," he reassured her gently, kissing her cheek, her ear, her temple.

"I know," she said against his throat. "It's just that it's...that I..."

The finger inside her began to move and she lost every thought in her head. Her entire body tensed and seemed to focus on that small, mysterious space.

The notion that she no longer knew herself swelled and for just an instant startled her. Who was this woman, taut as a bowstring, feeling a curious pleasure and an odd discomfort and unaccountably waiting, yearning for...what?

Jack felt the tension in her, heard the little gasp of surprise and mild alarm.

"Easy," he whispered, holding her to him when she tried to draw back.

"Jack, what is..."

If he answered her, she didn't know it. She lost all sense of who she was or wasn't. All she knew was what she felt, and she felt curiously, unaccountably greedy.

She wanted whatever it was that little movement of Jack's hand was promising. Her body, of its own accord, began to turn on that movement like a little mill, trying to make something.

As the movement quickened so did everything inside her, and all focus narrowed on Jack's hand.

Then it burst over her, stroke after stroke of delicious pleasure she'd had no idea existed. It claimed her again and again, seeming to open and close her like kiss after kiss. She felt her body convulsing and heard her little drawn-out groan of pleasure as not an inch of her seemed to be free of the delicious, tremulous well-being.

Then, slowly it began to ebb. And she became aware of Jack smiling at her with a look of pleased possession.

She said his name, but could say no more. Instead, she tightened her arms around him and breathed again, "Oh, Jack." She drew a deep breath, then added ingenuously, "I believe I'm prepared."

He laughed softly. "Now you may touch me."

It almost amazed her that her hands could move, that her fingers worked, that her body could simply return to normal after such an experience. But it did, so she did as he asked.

Jack had thought he'd braced himself for her touch. In truth, he realized, as her slender fingers explored him with tender interest, rubbed and stroked, then closed over him, there was no way he could have known that he would feel this way—hotter, harder, more desperately eager than he ever remembered being.

He turned her onto her back and rose over her, poised before her, exercising every last vestige of his control. More than anything, he didn't want to hurt her.

Then he saw her smile at him and felt her hands run gently up his thighs. He knew she was reading his mind. "It's all right," she whispered. "Come to me, Jack."

Then he couldn't have stopped if he'd wanted to. He entered her with a swift thrust and scooped her against him as her sharp little cry bit into his shoulder.

She breathed hard against him as her body adjusted to his.

"One moment," he said, "and it'll be better. I promise."

He lay her against the mattress and tipped her hips up as he began to move inside her. She smiled at him with that trace of humor that surprised and pleased him.

"I'm not certain I could bear feeling better than I felt a few moments ago," she said, instinct already taking over and making her move with him.

"Wait," he prophesied.

He saw the return of pleasure stiffen her body, glaze her eyes, still her movements. Then he lost all awareness himself as her body tightened around him, and his own pleasure exploded inside her, shaking him like a force of nature, taking everything he thought he'd known about himself and erasing it. He felt as though he was being drawn through a velvet tunnel, and when the shudders abated and he came out the other side, he was no longer the same. Some vital change had taken place inside him he couldn't quite identify or understand. Except to know that he felt new.

He reached to the head of the bed to yank the quilt down and lifted Charity so that she rested on the pillows, then he lay down beside her. He pulled the quilt over them and tucked her into his shoulder.

She lay heavily against him, obviously spent. He kissed her forehead and stroked her hair. "Sleep for a while," he said. "We'll have a late dinner."

Charity snuggled against him, feeling, she imagined, like every woman felt when she finally understood the mystery other women whispered about in front of their unmarried sisters.

So that was what love was all about.

"No wonder lovers leap off cliffs together," she said lazily, hooking an arm over Jack's waist as she found just the right spot in the hollow of his shoulder. "Or kill those who would keep them apart, or pine for each other for a lifetime when they are separated."

He smiled at her thoughts. "Love is a formidable power."

"It makes you feel," she said, "as though you've been slain and reborn without all the darkness that once plagued you."

"Darkness?" he asked, turning her chin up so that he could look into her eyes.

"Dramatically overstated," she said quickly, lowering her lashes then smiling at him. "As though your problems died with your old self, and the new one has a long sunny path ahead." She kissed his chest and rested her head again.

He stroked the silk of her hair as the approach of evening darkened the room. The heaviness of her thoughts sometimes surprised him. Though she'd quickly made a jest of it, she'd been serious about the darkness of her old life.

He'd once thought whatever it was she kept secret about her past would never matter to him. But now he'd made love to her. They were two separate beings, but one life spirit. He would feel more comfortable when she trusted him sufficiently to tell him. Not because he doubted her, but because he wanted to know that she didn't doubt him.

"I hope," she said with a little sigh that soothed his concerns and made him smile, "that when we awaken, the sunny path leads us to dinner."

Chapter Twelve

They swam, flew kites and picnicked on the beach with other guests of the hotel. One day they took a carriage to Seaside and rode the carousel, ate pastries from the bakery and played a kind of piano machine that banged out a tinny tune for a penny.

As the tune ground to a halt, Charity shook her head at the contraption in amazement. "Isn't it something that a machine can make music without anyone to play it?"

He tucked her hand around his arm and drew her up the planked sidewalk. "It's a new century," he said. "I imagine it'll be filled with all kinds of things that are now beyond anything our minds can conceive."

Charity stopped walking and closed her eyes, raising one gloved hand dangling a beaded pouch and placing her index finger to her temple.

"My mind is conceiving...wait, wait," she said dramatically. "It's coming in clearer. There it is!"

Jack shrugged a shoulder at a stodgy-looking man and woman who frowned at Charity's antics as they were forced to walk around her, barely dodging her elbow.

"Yes?" Jack encouraged. "Some new disaster? Some wild notion that will bring me running halfway across town when you attempt it and it fails?"

She opened one scolding eye, then closed it again. "I see . . ." She winced as she pretended to concentrate. "A bed," she finally finished quietly.

Instantly, Jack felt the stirring in his groin. She had an uncanny ability to do that to him with a glance, a word, an artlessly graceful movement of her body that related in no way to lovemaking, but which brought it to his mind with a sharpness that almost caused him pain. When she did or said anything overtly suggestive, he was lost.

She was proving an eager and talented partner in bed as well as out, and he was enjoying every second of their time together; it was beyond anything he'd imagined.

"And who is in this bed?" he asked softly.

Two children came out of a candy store, and he took hold of Charity's elbow to steady her as they raced by on either side of her.

Her brow furrowed and her mouth pursed. "My goodness. It appears to be me."

"Truly? And is there a gentleman with you?"

She frowned as though thinking. "No," she finally replied, "but you're there."

"You'll pay for that," he threatened as he took her elbow and bustled her across the street toward a waiting carriage.

She giggled, as eager as he was for the confrontation.

"Must we go home?" Charity whispered. It was the middle of a rare sweltering night, and though all the other guests of the hotel had managed to fall asleep, judging by the silence, Jack and Charity sat together in a chair on the porch beyond their window, wide-awake.

Charity sat between Jack's knees, her bare feet under her nightgown stretched to rest atop the railing of the porch. Jack, one foot braced beside hers, had both arms wrapped around her.

"I'm afraid so," he said very quietly, sounding as reluctant as she. "We both have businesses to run."

"Can we come back?"

"For certain."

"Even if you're mayor?"

"Particularly if I'm mayor. I'm sure there'll be occasions when Astoria and I will need a respite from each other."

Charity reached back to stroke his face. "I'm not sure I will like you working all the time. I've grown used to being with you every moment. Perhaps you could give up the box factory, and I could support us with my dressmaking."

He laughed softly and squeezed her. "If I was home with you every moment, my love, you would have no time for dressmaking."

She sighed, but he could hear her smile. "We do do that often, don't we?"

"Not as often as I'd like."

She slid her head sideways along his chest to look into his eyes, her own wide in the moonlight. "Jack, you can't be serious. Several times a day isn't enough?"

He kissed her forehead. "I doubt I will ever get enough of you."

"It's been a lovely honeymoon," she said dreamily, turning to wrap her arms around his neck. He lifted her to settle her comfortably. "Thank you."

"Please," he said. "If anyone deserves thanks, it's you. I've never felt the way I feel at this moment. Full of life and love and hope. You're a magician, woman, and not simply with a needle."

She kissed him long and lingeringly, thinking that she could never seem to fill herself with him, either. When she wasn't in his arms, she longed to be. When they walked side by side, or the Promenade in Seaside, she felt as though she owned the world and everything in it. Her marriage to Jack was like a deed to a new life. They were so right together, she thought, that after a mere week as his wife, she felt more settled and secure than she'd felt in all the twenty-five years that had gone before.

"Well," she said lazily. She drew her lips away but tilted her forehead against his. She felt his hand slip under her nightgown and wander up her thigh. "I've a particularly delicious spell to make you sleep."

His hand slipped over her hip to the inside of her thigh. Her pulse was already thrumming, her body leaning into him to allow him access.

"To help me sleep," he asked, his breath a little short, "or to bring me wide-awake?"

She leaned sideways, dipping her tongue into his ear. "First one," she said, "then the other."

"In proper order, I trust."

"Of course. Let's go inside."

"No." He took advantage of her stretch to dip his fingertips inside her. "We'll stay here."

"Jack!" she whispered, trying to sit up. "We can't stay out . . ." But his touch was already paralyzing her.

"Shh!" he cautioned in a grinning whisper. "We can if we don't wake anyone. Now, hush. And pay attention."

With a little moan of pleasure she fell back against his arm and did just that.

Jack's home was less elegant than Letty's, but large and roomy and filled with big furniture, comfortable chairs and every modern convenience. It was all scrupulously cared for by a plump older woman named Lily who'd worked for him for some time.

Charity discovered Jack had a telephone that he used primarily for contact with the factory.

For one instant, its presence on the parlor wall alarmed Charity. The notion that people long distances apart could communicate without having to send a telegram, which was by necessity brief and free of detail, or post a letter that could require days or even weeks to reach its destination, was sobering. It occurred to her that the new century was making it more and more difficult for anyone to hide.

Then she dismissed the thought and went back to the task of getting used to her new residence. She'd resolved when she married Jack that nothing would ever draw her thoughts to the past again, and she did her best to hold to that resolve.

Temporarily, at least, it was decided to leave her shop at Letty's. "But, Jack," Charity had protested, "they're trying to restore their relationship. I'll be in the way. I know you're concerned about my safety, but I'll be—"

Jack had cut her off, "Con and I have talked it over. He's planned to spend the next few months at home, and he'll be there to keep an eye on you and Letty. While I'm at the factory, I'd prefer you were at Letty's."

She'd almost forgotten, during her idyllic honeymoon, that the threat of Ah Chun still existed.

She'd opened her mouth to offer further protest, but he'd shaken his head.

"That's final," he said with the quiet authority of a man who did, indeed, consider his word to be law.

She had dropped the argument, knowing the effort would be futile. The right time to challenge his attitude would come, she knew.

"I have to make a delivery this afternoon," she said one morning as Jack walked her to Letty's on his way to the factory. "It's an easy walk, just a few blocks away. Near the courthouse."

He frowned as they turned up the walk. "I thought your customers usually came to pick up their purchases."

She nodded, avoiding his eyes. "This one hasn't responded to my messages, and the gown is paid for. I'd like to see that she has it."

He raised an eyebrow. "Someone who resents your suffragist involvement?" he asked. "Certainly she knew that when she hired you to make the gown."

She sighed and glanced at him wryly. "I believe she resents my involvement with the man who is running against her husband for mayor—and gaining much attention and support."

"Ah. Nell Johnson." He stopped her at the door to her shop and took her face in his hands, his eyes dark and troubled. "I wonder sometimes if I did you a disservice by bringing you here to Letty. The quiet life you envisioned as a successful seamstress has been thwarted at every turn, first by Letty and then by me."

She punched a gloved fist into his shoulder and frowned at him severely. "Jack McCarren, if those words come out of your mouth one more time I won't be responsible for my actions. Letty's friendship has blessed my life, and your love has...has..." Her eyes filled with the intensity of the emotion for which she had no words. When she couldn't speak, she punched him again.

Laughing, he wrapped her in his arms. "All right! I retract the statement. You didn't tell me, my love, that you've trained as a pugilist since our discussion about your self-defense skills."

She kissed him soundly in forgiveness. "I have qualities you've yet to discover," she said, "unless you insist on talking such foolishness. In which case I'll be forced to remove myself from hearing distance."

His grip on her tightened, and his eyes darkened. "You will not even say such a thing in jest. I would track you down and make you sorry you'd conceived such an idea, believe me."

"Honestly, man, have you no finesse?" Connor and Jonathan appeared from around the back of the house, croquet mallets in hand. Connor frowned at Jack with feigned disapproval. "Letty would not like to hear of you threatening Charity with bodily harm. It's against the new rules of society, you know. No matter how deserving the woman." Connor gave Charity a quick hug. "Good morning, Charity. Have no fear, I'll protect you from this bully."

"Ha!" Letty's head and shoulders appeared from the lace curtains at the open window of Charity's shop. "You've enough bullying tactics yourself to make that notion ridiculous." Letty smiled excitedly at Charity. "Hurry inside. Your watered silk arrived from Paris on this morning's steamer. I was just putting it away for you."

With a gasp of delight, Charity gave Jack a quick kiss then ran up the porch steps and into the house.

Nell Johnson greeted Charity with a surprised stammer. Charity stood alone, the paper-wrapped package in her arms, as Jack waited at the picket fence that surrounded the deep lawn.

"I...I didn't expect you to... I mean, you needn't have..."

Charity handed her the package with a smile. "You've paid for it, Mrs. Johnson. I wanted you to have it."

Nell Johnson's formidably handsome face softened and flushed. "Yes, well, I haven't been able to get to you, you see...I..."

Her husband had forbidden her to pick up the dress. Charity nodded. "I understand." And she did. She'd lived on the outside all her life, and so had Jack. But if they made careful choices now, and behaved with dignity and nobility, they would have a chance at belonging—whether or not Jack won the election.

One had to stand up for one's beliefs, she'd decided, but there were areas where it was possible to make concessions. "I hope you enjoy the dress."

"Charity!" Nell called to her as she started down the porch steps. She turned halfway with a look of inquiry.

Nell looked a little sheepish as she clutched the package to her. "It will feel good to replace my bland old taffeta dress I wore all last year." She smiled hesitantly and came to the edge of the porch. "Thank you, Charity. It was thoughtful of you to deliver it."

"I value your business, Mrs. Johnson," Charity replied. "Good afternoon."

"I've never seen the dragon look so warm and approachable," Jack said as Charity tucked her hand in his arm for the walk home. "More of your magic?"

Charity dismissed the praise. "Of course not. Women are all the same. A new dress makes us all more amenable."

"Well, that's a clever ploy. You mean if a man wants his wife on her best behavior, he has to buy her a new frock?"

She laughed, pleased with her success with Nell Johnson, ecstatic with her life in general. "Or lunch at the Parker House."

He turned in that direction. "Does this allow me," he asked, lowering his voice as a gentleman passed them, tipping his hat at Charity, "to take you home and be on my own bad behavior for an hour or so?"

"It not only allows it—" she grinned at him "—it anticipates it."

"Well, then. I may adjust to this husband business after all."

Charity had just returned to her shop when Letty came in with a tea tray and closed the door behind her.

Charity put a hand to her stomach, already full with wonderful Columbia River salmon. "Letty, I can't eat another bite," she said plaintively, "Jack and I just had lunch."

"That's all right," Letty said quietly, placing the tray on the table then coming with a chair to sit beside Charity at the sewing machine. As usual, she was forced to displace yards of fabric—this time a snowy-white handkerchief linen. "This was just an excuse to talk to you about the Founder's Day dinner."

Charity pinched a seam together and ran a quick, flawlessly straight line of tiny stitches. She lifted the feeder foot, pulled the fabric out and cut the thread.

"What about it?" For days she'd been listening to the speech Jack had been invited to present that night. Walter Johnson had also been invited to speak.

Jack had told her that Connor would be receiving an award in honor of his family, who'd established regular shipping routes between Portland, Seattle and Astoria. And she was working on new dresses for herself and Letty to wear to the affair.

"Did you hear they've changed the date?" Letty asked, her eyes dismayed.

"To what?" Charity felt a grim suspicion forming.

"To the same weekend as our convention. The night Judith Vineyard and Coleen Hensley inspire our ladies to work to the bone for woman's suffrage, your husband will be giving the most important speech of his campaign, and mine will be accepting a tribute to his family and explaining his plans to improve freight service even further."

Charity closed her eyes. "No."

"Yes."

Charity opened them again and drew a breath. "The men of this town have done this on purpose to diminish attendance at our convention."

"Of course. But, frankly..." Letty stood moodily and went to the window. Desultorily, she poured a cup of tea, then walked toward Charity, sipping it. "Connor and I have worked so hard to reestablish peace that I'm not going to fuss about it. The problem is, how are we to be in both places? Connor's trying very hard, but he wouldn't understand if I didn't attend with him Saturday night."

Charity also stood to pace. "Well... if the two ladies will be speaking that night, they won't need us. We'll just make sure that they have everything they need ahead of time. You can give your speech that morning, and I'll see that they get to the train the next day."

Letty put her cup primly in its saucer and smiled a little stiffly at Charity. "I wanted to talk to you about that."

Charity didn't like her expression.

"Connor's uncles will be arriving that morning from Portland to attend the dinner. They worked with his father to found Donovan Shipping. I promised him we would entertain them in grand style when I thought the dinner would be the week *following* our convention." Letty shook her head, obviously miserable. "Charity, if I tell him I have to be at the convention that morning, it will be last year all over again. I know it's selfish of me to ask, but please, will you give the speech for me?"

"Oh, Letty, I do that so poorly..."

"Poorly?" Letty repeated, setting her cup on a shelf that held lace and other trims. "Everyone thinks of you as my second in command. You're the one who saved the rally that afternoon, you're the one who makes everyone look wonderful whenever we appear in public, you're the one who fought for Ming and made what we preach a reality."

Charity sank into her chair. "Letty, please. Bring the curtain down. Such drama. All right, I'll do it."

"Oh, thank you!" Letty crushed her with a hug. "I'll do anything you ask in payment. I'll sew on buttons for you, I'll make hems, I'll—"

"You will keep your destructive fingers off my gowns, thank you very much. The last time you sewed buttons on for me, you attached them through the back of the dress."

Letty pretended hurt feelings as she went to pick up the tray. "Very well, Princess Charity. Just because Nell Johnson, the doyenne of Astoria society, will be wearing one of your creations to the dinner, there's no need to snipe at those of us of lesser consequence."

Charity frowned at her. "How did you know that? I delivered the dress only hours ago."

"Word just came to me from Agnes Butterfield, who happened to be at Nell's when you left the dress. They're cousins, you know, so though Nell doesn't approve of Aggie's politics, loyalty requires that she receive her. Anyway, it seems Nell was quite overcome by your consideration in dropping it off. Apparently Walter had forbidden her to pick it up. If Aggie is true to form, everyone will know by morning."

Charity shook her head as Letty left the room. How did these things happen to her?

As the weekend of Letty's convention approached, Charity sewed from morning until night. Jack called the Portland office of Sears Roebuck to purchase a second sewing machine for Charity to use at home, and Connor arranged to have it rushed downriver on the *River Rose*.

They had quickly made a work area out of a morning room, and Charity split her projects between those she worked on at Letty's and those she worked on at home in the evenings.

She left the simpler projects for home because there she was endlessly distracted by her large, handsome husband, who was usually lounging in a chair across the room, sipping brandy and working on his speech while she sewed.

"At last!" he said with emotion one evening. He met Charity's eyes across the small room. "Have you the patience to listen to it all, one final time?"

She did, of course. The sound of his voice was now more dear to her than the air she breathed, and she thought his ideas brilliant and forward-thinking. But there was such fun in teasing him. It usually ended with her being caught in a deliciously punitive hug, or wrestling on the carpeting with him as he tried to show her the error of her ways. It was usually a prelude to wrestling upstairs.

She glanced up with a straight face as she backstitched a hem. "Do you advocate women's suffrage in your speech?"

She knew he didn't. He'd been reading her portions of it all week. Then he saw the glimmer of humor behind the steady expression.

"No, I don't," he said, putting the sheaf of papers aside and getting to his feet. "Actually, in elegant and exciting prose, I advocate the imprisonment of women who believe such nonsense."

"Oh, dear," she said mildly, snipping a thread. "I suppose this calls for a march on the Founder's Day dinner. I'll tell Letty to gather the ladies..."

Jack leaned over her to remove the fabric from her hands and pull her to him. "This is an important evening for me," he said. "You're the only suffragist I want beside me."

She reached in to the hair at the back of his head to tug him to her. "I promised I'd be there even though your cronies changed the date to conflict with our rally."

Jack shook his head, unconsciously rubbing her back. "It had nothing to do with your rally. It was something about two events scheduled for the same evening in the hotel, so our dinner was moved forward a week."

She looked skeptical. "So they say." Then she went on to relate her conversation with Letty. "I promised Letty I would give her speech Saturday morning." She winced at the thought. "I hate the very idea, but she and Connor have a fragile peace, and I wouldn't want to be responsible for shattering it."

Jack nodded. "As long as you're with me Saturday night."

"I will be. I promise. Our two visitors are speaking Saturday night, so Letty and I will be free to join you and Connor."

"Excellent." He swept her up in his arms and started for the door. She had little doubt what his intentions were.

"Jack, I have another hour's work on that dress," she said halfheartedly, pointing toward the sewing machine as he carried her out of the room and toward the stairs.

"I'll wake you an hour early in the morning."

"That's kind of you," she said dryly. "What about your speech?"

"I'll wake you two hours early."

Chapter Thirteen

"There they are!" Letty, her arm hooked in Charity's as they stood on the depot's platform with a full contingent of the Ladies for the Vote grouped behind them waving welcoming signs, pointed to the front of the train where two women, one dressed in pink, the other in yellow, made their way down the steps.

Charity gaped. She wasn't sure what she'd expected of Mrs. Vineyard and Mrs. Hensley, but the cheerfully smiling women who started toward them in response to Letty's wave did not fit her mental image.

Judith was tall and slender with straight dark hair covered by an outrageous straw hat decorated with birds and flowers the same color as her yellow dress.

Coleen was shorter by a head, and wore a pink traveling costume topped by a straw hat that must have come from the same milliner as Judith's. A family of pink birds lived around it, one small one on the brim still in its nest. Over her arm was a straw lunch hamper.

Once Charity was over the initial shock of seeing the two suffragists dressed like dance-hall girls, she was captured by the cheer they exuded.

There was laughter as the women, who'd obviously met Letty's ladies previously, exchanged greetings.

Then Letty introduced Charity. "She moved here from Kansas almost three months ago, and though she knew our organization existed, she'd never been involved before. Then she rented a room from me to open a seamstress shop, and was coerced to join us in a march one afternoon when our numbers were thin." Letty squeezed Charity's shoulders. "I was injured that afternoon when a bottle was thrown at us..." Judith and Coleen shook their heads and looked at one another in dismay. "But," Letty went on in heroic tones, "when I couldn't deliver my speech at Freedom Hall, Charity did it for me, and she was *brilliant*." Letty's ladies confirmed that with quick applause.

"In any case. We've found her to be a woman to count on, and we know you will, too."

Charity held her sign out of the way as Judith hugged her, then passed her to Coleen. "Welcome to the cause," Judith said, looking very pleased. "You're the type of woman who can do us the most good." She pinched her cheek. "You're young and pretty. You look like everyone's daughter or sister. Because we're older..." She eyed her friend and they exchanged a wry look. Charity imagined they'd been through a lot together. "The press and the public tends to think of us as a group of disgruntled old ladies who could never snare a man or suckle a baby, and they think our fight therefore must simply be inspired by discontent because we never quite made the grade as women."

Coleen smiled at Charity. "Are you married?"

"Yes."

"Wonderful. Your face will tell the newspaper people and those who like to poke fun at us quite another story." Coleen patted her shoulder. "Wonderful."

The ladies walked en masse to the Parker House where Letty had registered their two guests.

"I know you'll want to rest," she said as they left Judith and Coleen with a bellboy. "My husband will come for you this evening to bring you home for dinner. If you need anything, Charity has a telephone. " The women appeared impressed. "Her husband owns the box factory on the wharf. Will you be all right?"

Judith nodded and said with disarming innocence, "Perfect. Tell your husband he'll find us in your famous Swill Town, looking for men."

Coleen elbowed her viciously. "Judith, really!"

Judith laughed and hugged her friend. "Honestly, Coleen. Those hours on the train have ruined your sense of humor."

Charity was dazed as the group disassembled. Signs tucked under their arms, she and Letty started in the direction of the Palace Restaurant.

"Aren't they wonderful?" Letty said excitedly.

"I couldn't believe it!" Charity laughed. "I expected them to look like the temperance ladies or photographs I've seen of Susan B. Anthony."

"They believe that the quest for justice and equality calls for 'soldiers dressed like a garden' because the reality of woman's suffrage is growing steadily despite weeds and bad weather."

Charity shook her head in wonder. It would be almost difficult to take them seriously if she hadn't looked into their eyes and seen that light of determination and conviction.

Letty pulled Charity to a stop with a startled gasp.

"What?" Charity demanded, following Letty's gaze. Angling toward them down the street were two large men dressed like dockworkers. The smell of alcohol preceded them by half a block.

"They're the McGee brothers," Letty said, backing away and pulling Charity with her. "They do dirty deeds for whoever will pay them. Ah Chun, this time, I'll wager."

Charity felt an almost undeniable urge to go forward instead of backward, to confront them with her fingernails and the solid heels of her shoes. To swing her purse at them and tell them to tell Ah Chun to get out of her life once and for all. But she remembered her self-defense efforts with Jack that afternoon in her bedroom. She had been less than impressive. And in the mid-afternoon quiet, there was no one about to lend a hand. As satisfying as a confrontation might be, she wasn't prepared to spend the convention weekend in the hold of a ship headed for a sultan's harem.

She backed away with Letty. A warehouse door squeaked open behind them, and Charity saw a thin, bony hand reach out to cover Letty's mouth. As she cried out and moved to stop it, a hand covered her own mouth, muffling the sound, and yanked her backward into the gloom of a large, windowless room.

She drove her elbow into a rib cage and heard a satisfying grunt of pain. She wriggled away from her captor, only to come up short against a shadowy figure that was rocklike though not much taller than she was. She caught the fragrance of sandalwood.

Letty was shoved toward her and they clung together as a lantern light bloomed out of the darkness to reveal the shallow planes of Ah Chun's face.

Charity swallowed a gasp of alarm. Letty covered her mouth with her gloved fingertips.

"What do you want?" Charity demanded, deliberately raising her voice in an attempt to cover its tremor.

"Only what is mine," Ah Chun replied in a smooth, quiet voice. His manner reminded Charity of the slickness of oil, or the slime that clung to the wharf pilings when the tide went out. She experienced the same shudder of revulsion she'd felt in the back room of his shop.

"Ming is *not* yours," she said.

"You do not understand," he corrected amiably, "how things are." He touched a long, pointed fingernail to the chest of his silky robe. "What I wish to be mine is mine." He paused. The dank air pulsed. "And what I wish to disappear..." The finger at his chest he now flicked away from him in a gesture of removal. "Is gone."

Despite her fear, Charity felt rage. She could not believe rules protected a culture that prevented the law from destroying this man.

"Ming is our friend," Letty said, clinging tightly to Charity. "We will not let you harm her."

He smiled. Charity felt cold to the core of her being.

"I do not speak of Ming," he said.

In a swift movement that made both women scream, he produced a knife with a long, thin blade and a vicious point that caught the lantern light.

He made a graceful circle in the air with it, then brought it down to rest its point on Charity's chin.

"This is a cannery knife," he said quietly, running it lightly down her throat to the ruffled lace collar of her waist. "It is used to filet the fish. It works well with those who trouble me also—like the man who accepted my money for his passage here, accepted the work I found for him, then tried to take one of my women with him when he ran away."

Charity's heart pounded in her throat, her blood ringing in her ears. She was vaguely aware of Letty telling him that Jack McCarren would kill him if he hurt his wife.

One of Ah Chun's men came to him at a run, speaking swiftly and anxiously in Chinese as he pointed toward the door.

Ah Chun replied quickly, darting a glance in that direction.

The man spoke again, pointing toward the door.

There were loud shouts in the street.

Ah Chun turned his attention to Charity. She swallowed against the point of the knife.

"You will remember not to interfere with me again." He turned to Letty. "And you. Or you will both be found in a net with the salmon."

Then they were plunged in darkness, and he and his companions were gone. Seconds later, the door burst open to admit Rolf and several men Charity recognized from the box factory.

Rolf pulled Charity and Letty outside as the men pursued Ah Chun to a trapdoor that opened onto the river.

"What happened?" he demanded. "We lost you when the cable car passed. One moment you were there and the next you weren't."

Letty explained. Charity fought an overwhelming need to be ill.

"How did you know..." Letty began. Then her eyes narrowed. "Have our husbands put you up to following us?"

"They have," Rolf replied without apology. "It was Jack's idea when you were hit by that bottle. When you began having trouble with Ah Chun, he and Connor armed us. We've been right behind you since you left the house this morning."

Charity drew a deep breath, felt her stomach settle down again and exchanged a smile with Letty. "I believe we won't complain about their hovering this time."

Jack held Charity in his lap in the big chair by the fireplace and brooded in front of the empty grate.

Charity was relaxed in his arms, no longer the taut, wide-eyed bundle of nerves Rolf had brought to his office. He was grateful for that.

This was it. He was going to settle this score with Ah Chun, and quickly. He soothed Charity as she shifted sleepily in his arms. And if it couldn't be done legally, he'd find another way. He and Connor and Rolf would be making plans in the morning.

Friday, Charity ran in Letty's wake from sunup to sundown. Women arrived at Carnahan's Hall all day long. There was a gratifying number of local women, and several hundred women from other parts of the state. There were accommodation misunderstandings to be untangled, missing name tags to be found, box lunches to be served and hundreds of questions to be answered. Charity found it indescribably exciting and utterly exhausting.

Ah Chun crossed her mind only once. She had dismissed the thought quickly, sure Jack and Connor had hired the men wandering the four sides of the hall.

Jack stopped for Charity in the carriage that evening. "Would you prefer to have dinner at the hotel?" he asked as she slumped against him on the seat, the ribbon on her hat tickling his nose.

"Oh, Jack, I'm too tired to eat," she groaned. "Would you mind if we just went home? There must be something in the icebox we can shape into a supper for you."

"I wouldn't mind at all. But you must eat something if you're to give a brilliant speech in the morning."

She groaned as the horses clopped up the hill. "I wish I was on a boat to Alaska instead. There are so many more women than I expected."

He grinned at the road. "I'm sure it's your magnetic qualities as an orator that are attracting followers to you like bees to a flower."

She yawned. "I think many of them are just curious about what the movement is up to."

"You'll win them over," he said. "Just as you've won me."

"I have?" she asked softly in surprise.

He hunched a shoulder with vague uncertainty. "In part, at least."

"Jack," she said, sitting a little closer. "That's wonderful. Will you come in the morning? It's Letty's speech, but I've added a few embellishments. It would mean a lot to me, and it would do so much for the cause if the most popular mayoral candidate came to hear what we have to say. The ladies love you, you know, since you came to speak to us."

Politically, he knew it could very well be suicide. Although the density and enthusiasm of his growing support was beginning to surprise even him.

Personally, he couldn't refuse her. In spite of her tendency to trouble and a propensity to speak her mind that many other men would have found dismaying, she was as perfect a wife as any man could hope for. She was loving and warm and as interested in everything that filled his dreams as she was in what occupied her own.

She was good-natured unless crossed—or followed—and loved him with an intensity that enclosed him in its comfort and still left him feeling curiously free. Love, he thought, as he lifted her sleepy form from the carriage and carried her into the house, was a complex and curious thing.

"I'll escort you to Carnahan's Hall in the morning," he said, putting her on the divan. "And I'll stay to hear you speak. Lie still and I'll talk to Lily about supper."

Charity could not imagine life being more perfect than it was at that moment. She was loved by a very special man, she had a little army of friends she felt so fortunate to know, her shop was successful, considering the circumstances, and she'd adopted a cause that made her feel as though she belonged to the world instead of simply occupying space in it.

For the first time in her life, she felt as though her past no longer existed. Almost as though it had never been at all.

Jack returned a few moments later to carry her upstairs.

"Lily will be bringing up a tray with roast beef sandwiches and wine."

Charity sank into the middle of the plump bed, a hand flung out on each pillow as Jack unbuttoned her shoes. "That sounds heavenly," she said, then uttered a little "Oh!" of pleasure as Jack rubbed the throbbing sole of the foot he'd just freed. "If only we lived on a tropical isle where I could run around barefoot all day."

He lifted her other foot, removed the shoe and did the same. "That sounds appealing, but at this moment you'd be lying on the floor of a lean-to and looking forward to a supper of sliced coconut."

She frowned as she considered that. "Must you be such a realist? I imagined that I had this wonderful bed in our lean-to." She closed her eyes. "With proper encouragement, I could probably conjure the image of you in it beside me."

A rap on the bedroom door prevented him from following her suggestion.

"Come in," he called.

Lily bustled in with a tray heaped with food, a bottle of wine, glasses, napkins and a small plate of cookies.

"Here we are!" she sang cheerfully as she placed the tray on the bedside table. She noticed him rubbing Charity's foot and asked solicitously, "Would you like a footbath, Mrs. McCarren?"

Charity smiled, waving away the suggestion. "Thank you, Lily, but I'm enjoying this more."

Lily smiled like a woman who understood completely. "Well. If you need anything, ring."

"Thank you, Lily."

The fragrance of the succulent beef on freshly baked bread stirred Charity's appetite. She made a weary sound of approval. "Perhaps I could force down half a sandwich."

Jack propped her pillows and pulled her up against them. He handed her the sandwich plate, then uncorked the wine and poured.

Charity tugged a piece of beef from between the slices of bread and put it into her mouth. She chewed, frowning at her sandwich.

Jack handed her a glass of wine. "Where were we?"

"We were contemplating life on a tropical island, but I'm afraid the food has brought me back to reality. And I've been meaning to talk to you about Rolf. How is his relationship with Ming faring?"

Jack, glass and sandwich in hand, walked around the bed to the other side and sat, leaning back against the headboard. "I know what I've already told you. That she won't even consider it. She thinks she would be a danger to him. She already feels very guilty that she's a danger to you."

"*She* isn't the danger to me," Charity said. "Ah Chun's greed and vindictiveness are the danger." She took a bite of sandwich, chewed, swallowed, then took a sip of wine. "What about Connor? Has he said anything to you about how things are progressing with Letty?"

Jack gave her a mildly impatient look over the rim of his glass. "Charity, men don't spend a lot of time discussing their women. All I know is what you've told me from your conversations with Letty."

Charity put the rest of her sandwich and half-empty glass aside and leaned into the pillows. Weariness was overtaking her, and she rolled toward Jack. "I'm falling asleep," she said, nuzzling into his side. "Will you nap with me?"

His sandwich finished, Jack put his glass aside, tugged the spread and blanket out from under her, then removed his shoes and climbed in beside her. He pulled her pillows into place, then drew her into his arms. His hand encountered the steel-like rigidity of her corseted waist.

"You can't sleep in this," he said, tossing the blankets back again and turning her gently onto her stomach.

"I can," she said sleepily into the pillow. "You don't have to..."

But he was already unfastening the row of buttons down her back. She vaguely she felt his fingers unlace her corset and the delicious relief as the constricting garment finally lay open. Then she slipped away into a dream of palm trees, exotic flowers and coconuts on a mat woven of grass and palm fronds.

Jack frowned at the silky, ivory skin of her back and waist roughly embossed with the pattern of her corset and its laces. He rubbed gently to soothe the angry red marks, and she made a low sound of contentment.

Placing a hand under her ribs, he pulled her gently up while pulling down on the dress and tossing it aside. She made a small sound of protest, then settled into the pillows in her bloomers and chemise.

He stripped down to his union suit, then pulled the blankets over them and settled her in his arms. Her breasts softened against the side of his rib cage and he wondered idly if there was a more satisfying feeling in the whole world. Then he closed his eyes as she unconsiously burrowed even closer to him. He fell asleep, feeling very much as though he had everything the world had to offer.

He was awakened by a kiss. It touched his eyelids and ran over the bridge of his nose, nudging him relentlessly from the comfortable velvet of sleep. He brushed at it, turned his head away from it. Then it began an insidious invasion of his ear. It nibbled at his lobe and up along the outer rim, then the tip of a tongue traced inside, sending a shudder all along his spine.

"Jack?" Charity's voice whispered. "Jack, are you asleep?"

"Yes," he said, anxious to see what other ploys she might use to claim his attention.

In a moment she had undone the bottom two buttons of his union suit and slipped her hand inside. He came to swift and definite awareness.

"Are you still asleep?" she asked. He could hear the smile in her voice and the little edge of wickedness he was pleased to know he'd put there.

She knew the answer to that. She felt him rise and swell in her hands.

Before she quite knew what had happened, she'd been divested of her bloomers and he of his suit.

"I hope you're awake, young lady," he said, pulling her onto him. "You're about to find out what happens when you wake a man out of a deep dream about long-haired maidens and tropical islands."

His hands swept possessively from the backs of her knees up over the trim mound of her buttocks to her slender back, crushing her to him.

"Clever me," she whispered when he gave her the chance.

His warm hands, fingers spread wide, swept up and down her, again and again, and it was only moments before the yearning, which dried her mouth and quickened her heartbeat, began.

He hitched her knee up, then swept a hand down her inner thigh. He repeated the action only once before she strained against him in anticipation.

He dipped his fingers inside her, and that was enough. She tightened her arms around his neck and moaned his name. He rolled them over and entered her just in time for the world to explode around both of them. It convulsed for long moments as they clung together, not separate in their pleasure this time but together in hot, rolling release.

It was a long time before they were willing to move apart.

"I wonder what time it is?" Charity asked finally, her head on his chest, her hair across his face. He couldn't remember ever feeling quite this perfect.

He gently moved her hair aside to reply. "Still early evening," he said. "I can hear Lily working in the kitchen."

"I should look over Letty's speech again," she said, but made no effort to move.

"Mmm. I brought home paperwork." He ran a caressing hand over her bottom as he spoke.

"We could bring our work to bed," she said, kissing his collarbone. "And finish our sandwiches."

"Excellent idea."

"But I'm not ready yet."

"No."

It was half an hour later when Jack finally pulled his pants on and slipped into his shirt. For a moment Charity lay propped on an elbow, taking pleasure in watching him walk back and forth from his desk to the bed. His shirt was hanging open, exposing his strong, hair-covered chest, and she wished she had nothing to do tomorrow but remain in bed with him and explore the delicious new heights of sexual endeavor they'd reached that evening.

He finally stopped in the middle of the room to warn her with a grin, "One more glance from your languid eyes and I will be back in bed with you. Then you will have to create your speech as you go tomorrow, and I'll have to deal with unbilled customers."

She sat up and reached to the foot of the bed for her dressing gown. "Humiliation and poverty," she sighed. "Strong motivators."

A frantic rap on the door interrupted them.

"Yes?" Jack asked.

Lily's voice was high with concern. "There's someone on the telephone contraption for Mrs. McCarren."

Charity stood, frowning, trying to finish buttoning her gown. "Who would call me on the telephone?"

Frightening possibilities sprang to her mind as she hurried downstairs. All the fears she'd determined never to consider again sprang to mind. She'd been found out. Someone knew who she was and was calling to blackmail her. Jack's sturdy footsteps right behind her provided little support. She'd lied to him. He would hate her.

"Hello?" she said into the receiver, her voice a little shaky.

"Charity?" A cheerful feminine voice asked.

"Yes?"

"It's Judith."

When she didn't respond for a moment, confused, the laughing voice added, "Judith Vineyard! At the Parker House Hotel."

Relief swept the length of Charity's body. Then concern reappeared. "What's wrong? Are you and Coleen all right?"

"Actually, we're wonderful! We've just gotten word that the governor, with whom we've been trying to gain an appointment for *months,* wishes to see us tomorrow!"

"Tomorrow?" Charity felt all the careful and tedious planning for the weekend fall apart. "But your address to the Ladies for the Vote. They'll be—"

"We were hoping," Judith went on, "that you would be agreeable to changing the schedule. If Coleen and I could speak in the morning, then we could be on the eleven o'clock train."

For a moment, Charity could find no difficulty with the plan. Then Judith added innocently, "And you would simply give your speech in the evening. These ladies have come from far and wide to be here. We wouldn't dream of disappointing them."

Give her speech in the evening. The evening of the Founder's Day dinner. She put a hand to her forehead, at a complete loss for words.

"Charity?" Judith called. "Will that be all right? I know it's an inconvenience at the last moment, but we feel it would be important for us to have time with the governor. Can you accommodate us?"

Charity couldn't see how she could refuse. Judith and Coleen had important work to do; they had a chance to convince the top political figure in the state that the women of Oregon deserved the right to vote.

And the women who'd traveled to Astoria from all over the state would be expecting to hear at dinner how the battle for the vote was faring in Oregon. They deserved details and praise and encouragement—and Letty's speech was filled with all three.

She glanced at Jack, wondering if he would understand that she had to break her promise. It was impossible to tell. Frowning at her from the middle of the room, he simply looked concerned because he knew she was, though he didn't know why. Certainly her generous husband would understand her dilemma?

"Yes, of course, Judith," she said finally. "You and Coleen make your plans, and I'll see that there is a carriage to take you to the depot immediately after your speech."

"Thank you, Charity."

"Good night, Judith."

"What is it?" Jack came to turn her toward him the moment she replaced the receiver.

She smiled at him hesitantly. "Judith and Coleen have received word from the governor."

"Ah." He smiled. "He's having them shot?"

When she didn't respond to his joke and remained concerned, he found himself stiffening with worry. "You mean they can't stay to give their address?"

"They want to give it in the morning instead of the evening," she said. She looked at him expectantly, as though that news should trigger some reaction in him.

"Is that a problem?" he asked.

She sighed. "I believe that depends on you."

Now he was confused. He dropped his hands from her arms. "How is that?"

She swallowed and drew a breath. "Because now I will have to give my speech in the evening."

It finally fell into place. "Instead of coming to the dinner with me," he said.

"Yes."

Charity had little difficulty reading his eyes, though he didn't move a muscle otherwise. He simply looked at her, anger and disappointment darkening and hardening his gaze.

Reasonably, she repeated to him all the arguments she'd just gone over with herself. When he said nothing, she asked quietly, imploringly, "Do you understand?"

His answer was swift and concise. "No," he said. "I don't."

Chapter Fourteen

"What you're saying—" Jack paced away from her to the divan, stopping there to turn and pin her with his eyes "—is that in order of importance in your life I'm number three? Or is it four? The dressmaking business also has had more of your time lately than I have."

He hadn't raised his voice, but his anger was apparent. Charity felt both pain and the beginnings of her own anger.

"That isn't fair," she said, stalking across to him.

He watched her come toward him, his eyes calm. "But it's accurate."

"Stop behaving as though I did this deliberately!"

He walked away from her. "The situation isn't a deliberate act on your part," he said, stopping at the table that held a bottle of brandy and a tray of glasses. He glanced at her, his eyes condemning as he yanked the stopper out of the decanter. "But the decision to not accompany me is."

"Jack!" She followed him to the table, grabbing his arm and yanking him around before he could pick up the decanter. "It was not a choice to make you go to the dinner alone, it was a choice to carry through with what would best serve the hundred women who altered the schedules of *their* lives to come here!''

He yanked out of her grasp and poured the brandy. ''Precisely. You chose their convenience over mine.''

''Jack,'' she said reasonably, ''there are over a hundred of them. Many of them had to save all year just to come here!''

''I'm your husband.''

''No, you're not!'' she shouted in his ear as he bent to replace the stopper. ''The man I married would never behave this way!''

He put the half-filled glass down with a bang that spilled brandy all over the table's beautiful veneer and brought Lily running from the kitchen.

''You question *my* behavior?'' he roared.

Lily ran back into the kitchen.

''I have turned my life and my business upside down for months to see that you and Letty were safe, and all I've asked in return is that you be at my side at the dinner. You decide instead to regale your ladies with your successes, which have been due in large part to my cooperation, and you question my behavior?''

Guilt rose in Charity and tried to supercede her anger.

''Jack,'' she said, making an effort to lower her voice and establish calm, ''when the convention is over I will be available to go everywhere with you.''

''Tomorrow night's speech is important,'' he said implacably.

''So is the convention.''

He confronted her, arms folded. ''You mean to tell me,'' he asked quietly, ''that in that sturdy little line of ladies that marches with you everywhere, there is not one who could give the speech in your place?''

She replied as quietly, "This requires someone in authority, and Letty is unable to do it."

He looked at her a long moment, then lowered his arms. "Ah," he said, his tone and his manner causing her to take a step backward. "So, it's a matter of authority. Then, if you're going to wield yours, I must be called upon to wield mine as your husband."

She swallowed and took another step back. "A marriage is not about authority," she said.

He followed. "Every organization, no matter how small, is about authority."

Charity found herself backed up against the newel post.

Jack towered over her, his eyes filled with a dangerous light. "A ship needs a captain, a work crew requires a foreman, every household needs someone at the head."

He bent to put his shoulder to her waist and lifted her off the floor. She flopped over him with a little squeal of surprise and trepidation.

"Jack!" She kicked and wriggled as he ascended the stairs. "What do you think you're doing?! Put me down this instant or I will never attend anything with you again, I swear it!"

He proceeded down the hallway and turned into their room. It was in semidarkness now, lit only by the weak fire in the fireplace. It was cool and filled with shadows.

He dropped her into the middle of the tangled covers.

She braced herself on her hands and bristled at him. "And if you think for one moment that I will allow you to exert your authority by making love to me, you are very much mistaken!"

He put a knee on the bed and pushed her onto her back, imprisoning her with a hand on either side of her. Her small breasts heaved under the silky gown, and he could hear the alarm in every breath she drew. For a moment he took satisfaction in it.

"If that was what I wanted," he said, taking the hem of her gown and yanking it up in his fist, "I could make you want it, too. But my point," he said softly, "is that authority abused is an ugly thing. Wisely used authority is always careful not to hurt." Then he pushed himself up and stomped out of the room.

Charity wept for hours. She lay alone in the middle of the bed that only an hour before had been a warm and magical place. Now it felt cold and hard and empty.

The blankets were pulled up to her chin and her eyes burned from staring into the darkness. She railed against Jack's hardheaded, hard-hearted attitude one moment, then wondered if he could possibly be right the next. Was she behaving as though she was more interested in her place among the Ladies for the Vote than as Jack's wife? In the long hours until dawn, she changed her mind about the issue a dozen times.

Stretched out on the divan in the library that was an uncomfortable eight or ten inches too short for his frame, Jack glowered at the ceiling.

He was furious with Charity but disgusted with himself. After a lifetime of being called names and having to suffer the disdain of those who considered him unworthy of their company, he'd thought nothing more could injure his pride. It was demoralizing to find that his wife had done it so easily.

Was he being selfish? He didn't think so. He'd been more than tolerant of her outspokenness and radical behavior. No one could accuse Nell Johnson of being a weak-spirited woman, he reasoned, yet one would never find her carrying a sign in a march across town or in the back room of a dark and smoky shop in Chinatown, telling a red-gowned thug he was tiger droppings. His wife had no sense.

With a small groan, he dropped an arm over his eyes and closed them against the images that had plagued him since the quarrel.

What Charity did have was beauty and charm and, when she wasn't defying him, a sweetness that made him feel for the first time in his life as though the world was a truly welcoming place.

The image of her soft eyes filled with tears and her bottom lip trembling just before he'd left her in the middle of the bed lived behind his eyes like a photograph.

The longer he looked at it, the more selfish and guilty he felt. And the more determined he became that it would be a cold day in Hades before he went to her.

As Charity bathed and dressed for the day, she heard Rolf arrive and Jack leave for the factory. She stopped in the act of settling her slips at her waist and put both hands to her face; the need to sob until the burning lump in her throat disappeared almost overpowered her. Her head ached abominably, and her eyes burned from lack of sleep.

But she had a hundred details to see to today. She hoped wryly that Letty was enjoying Connor's relatives.

Rolf was attentive but quiet as he drove her to Carnahan's Hall. She doubted that Jack had told him what had happened between them, but she was certain all he would have had to do was look at either one of them to know that bliss no longer reigned in the McCarren household.

"I'll be back for you at four o'clock," he said, lifting her from the carriage. "Wait for me inside. I'll find you." He tucked her arm in his and walked her into the building. Then he stopped and smiled at her, sympathy apparent in his blue eyes.

"Everything will be all right," he said gently. "Sometimes his temper gets the best of him."

She thought he was being optimistic, but she nodded. "That's also true of me."

"You know, he's been trying to help me build a case against Ah Chun so that I can get him out from between Ming and me." He twirled his hat in his hands, obviously uncomfortable in attempting to explain her husband to her.

Charity's eyes widened in surprise. "He hasn't mentioned it to me."

Rolf shrugged. "It hasn't exactly been safe or easy work. But we've found out Ah Chun has an Astoria official helping him smuggle some of his countrymen in illegally. If we can find out who it is, we can call in the federal officers." He shifted his weight and leveled an imploring look on her. "He's been working very hard and he's had a lot on his mind. He didn't have to do this for me, but he told me he was so happy with you, he wanted me to know what it was like to be with the woman I love."

Charity felt the tightening knot in her stomach stretch even tighter.

"I know he loves me," she said, her voice quiet and strained. "But I thought he understood me, too."

Rolf nodded, then added mildly, "And I guess he thought you'd understand that he's finally getting what he's fought for for so long. Not the winning. That's not the important thing. But reaching the point where he's finally appreciated and accepted for his intelligence and his progressive ideas. That's what he's proud of. And he's proud of you. He wanted you with him."

Rolf drew a deep sigh and grinned sheepishly at her. "If you tell him I told you all this, I'll deny it. Four o'clock. Be sure to wait inside."

The morning was interminable. Judith and Coleen were brilliant. They told the gathering they were responsible for the endurance of the movement despite the odds against it.

"The state needs women," Judith said, "because we care about social interests and moral development."

"Only a mother who exercises her own rights as a citizen," Coleen added, "can truly teach citizenship to her children. Get involved! Get us the vote!"

Charity wanted nothing more than to run to the factory, throw her arms around Jack and tell him she'd find a way to be there that night.

But the day's activities went on until the middle of the afternoon, and she was responsible for coordinating the workshops and the panels. She hadn't a moment to herself. If she wasn't called upon to find another table, add more chairs or locate another pot of coffee, someone had a question and someone else felt faint.

By the time Rolf picked her up at four, she was mentally and physically exhausted.

"Has Jack gone home?" she asked Rolf.

He shook his head as he guided the team up the hill. "He has a meeting with a customer this afternoon, so he'll be bathing and changing clothes at the hotel."

Charity made an instant decision.

"Turn there!" she said urgently, pointing to the block two streets before theirs.

Rolf sawed on the reins to comply.

"I'd like to pay a call on a friend," Charity said, sitting on the edge of her seat as the idea began to crystallize in her mind.

Rolf glanced at her suspiciously. "What kind of a friend, Charity? Is Jack going to kill me for taking you there?"

She slanted him a dry smile. "At the moment, I don't think he'd mind if I got myself into a scrape."

"You're wrong," Rolf said. "Believe me."

Charity smiled at the concern in his face. "Relax, Rolf," she said. "This is the home of a very delightful little sixty-year-old suffragist. There!" She pointed to a modest white cottage under a tall cedar tree. Colorful flowers surrounded the porch and lined the stairs in clay pots. "Wait right here, please."

"Charity..." Rolf tried to tell her to give him a moment to help her down, but she'd already sprung lightly to the ground, skirts and all, and was hurrying up the walk.

Charity knocked on the front door with its leaded glass window. She peered into the clear heart of the fleur-de-lis, its etched glass petals preventing snooping.

She saw the tidy interior of a living room, but there was no sign of Agnes Butterfield.

"Oh, please!" she muttered under her breath, knocking again. She thought the rap held a note of the desperation she felt. Closing one eye, she pressed the other to the clear little circle of glass once again.

After a long moment, she caught sight of Agnes, a wrapper clutched around her, coming laboriously down the stairs. She peered through the clear piece of glass from the other side until she and Charity were eye to eye.

Charity heard her little expression of pleased surprise, then Agnes opened the door.

"Charity, now nice! Do come in." Agnes had an aureole of curls that were probably gray but had been somehow colored a very unlikely shade of crimson. Letty guessed that it was done with henna, but even knowing how it was created didn't prevent her from staring for a moment whenever she encountered her. It sat atop a plump but pretty face on a rotund little body that covered the sweetest soul ever created.

Just inside the door, Charity put her hands on Agnes's shoulders. "Aggie, I need you," Charity said without preamble.

Agnes was terrified of her own shadow, but generous to a fault and highly susceptible to flattery. And Charity had seen her eye wander to Dr. Parson on more than one occasion.

Agnes looked at Charity, belting her wrapper. "What is it? You look upset. But it's been such a wonderful convention so far. Why, Judith and Coleen were absolutely inspiring this morning, and I learned so much at the—"

Charity cut her off. "I desperately need someone to take charge at the banquet tonight until I can get there. I must attend the Founder's Day dinner with my husband, but I'll leave right after his speech."

Agnes didn't seem to see the problem. "Well, surely Letitia will . . ."

Charity shook her head. "She'll be at the Founder's Day dinner with Connor. I was hoping you could take charge, Aggie."

Agnes took a step backward. "Oh, Charity, I couldn't possibly. I've no public speaking abilities whatsoever. Why, the very notion absolutely terrifies me!"

"You could lead them in singing. Just until I can arrive. It won't be more than an hour or so."

"An hour! But I've a voice like the horn on the *River Rose!*"

Charity felt hope begin to diminish. She used her most powerful weapon. "Dr. Parson will be there, you know."

Agnes blinked, her expression softening. "He will?"

"Yes. I'm certain if I asked him to help you keep everyone entertained, he would do it." She added casually, "He's told me on more than one occasion how much he admires our group."

Agnes stood a little straighter and squared her shoulders. "Yes. And he did march with us that day to the temperance hall."

"He's single, you know."

"Yes," Agnes replied, her eyes losing their focus.

"He would probably appreciate the company of a competent, intelligent woman," Charity went on. "I've heard him express an interest in water birds. I'll bet he'd love to hear about all your bird-watching expeditions."

Agnes's eyes focused on Charity with sudden determination. "I'll do it." Then she added, "But do try to hurry."

Charity hugged her, thinking maybe this evening—and her life—was going to work out after all. "Thank you, Aggie. You're a darling. I'll see you as soon as I can. Oh! And I'll get word to Dr. Parson to call for you to take you to the hall."

Agnes closed her door, a beatific smile on her face.

"Thank you, Rolf. No, don't get down. You're certain it's not a problem for you to come back for me in an hour?"

Rolf shook his head, looking confused. She knew he had no idea what to make of her plea that he stop by Dr.

Parson's and ask him to pick up Agnes in his carriage on his way to Carnahan's Hall.

"Charity," he said with a shake of his head, "when you're involved, I have difficulty recognizing problems. The most innocent things seem to turn into them. But I'll be here."

She blew him a kiss, then ran up her steps.

Jack would have preferred to be anywhere else. As he made his way in white tie and tails down the stairs of the Occident Hotel to the ballroom, he could hear the low murmur of early arrivals gathered in the lobby. The last thing he wanted to do tonight was smile and glad-hand and pretend to be in charge of his destiny—and theirs. The quarrel with Charity, the long, cold night that had followed and the interminable day without contact with her had left him feeling adrift and alone.

He imagined her dressing for her convention banquet and the speech she would give. His mind's eye conjured a picture of her delectable curves in her lace-trimmed bloomers and the thin little chemise he could lure off her while they were preparing for an evening out. She would scold and giggle and protest and finally succumb to him with that trusting inclination of her body that still reduced him to porridge.

He groaned as he reached the lobby, then ran a hand over his face to dismiss his thoughts. He owed the people who had gathered tonight his good humor and his optimism.

Connor and Letty met him at the foot of the stairs, making it easier for him to force a cheerful mood. Or so he thought. It was only a few moments later, while Connor was talking with a friend, that Letty pulled him aside and asked pointedly, "What's wrong? You look terrible. Where's Charity?"

Briefly, he told her about the telephone call last night and their resultant argument.

Letty gasped. "She should have told me! I could have done something to—"

"She knew you wanted that time with Connor and she didn't want to do anything to upset that." As he spoke the words, it occurred to him how much Charity must care for Letty to have done that. In that light, it seemed far less like abuse of authority and much more like assumption of responsibility. Guilt bit him hard.

Letty frowned at him. "So, instead, you let her cause a rift between the two of you? Well, I won't have it. I've got to do something." She started to turn away, but he caught her wrist, holding her in place.

"You will do nothing," he said under his breath. "You have to stay with Connor. What's done is done."

"Well, McCarren." Walter Johnson suddenly materialized out of the growing crowd, his wife beside him. "How are you this evening?"

Jack suspected what was coming. He felt Letty stiffen beside him, and out of the corner of his eye he saw Connor making his way to them.

"I'm well," he replied politely. He noticed the formidable Nell looking very elegant in the dress he'd helped Charity deliver. He dipped his head at her. "You look lovely tonight, Mrs. Johnson."

"And where is your wife?" Johnson asked more loudly than was necessary. Everyone around them turned to look. "Championing the cause of harlotry and free love at Carnahan's Hall, I imagine."

Jack balled his fists and wondered idly, as he felt his arm prepare to rear back in an instinctive move he couldn't control, if breaking Johnson's nose would end his political career or enhance it.

But before he could test the possibility, a slender arm slipped into his and hooked around it, aborting the action.

"Here I am," Charity said cheerfully, taking an instant to smile at Jack before turning her attention to Johnson. "I apologize for being late. Harlotry takes so much time and attention." She looked Nell over with sincere appreciation. "Mrs. Johnson, you're stunning." Then she looked at Jack and asked softly, "And how are you?"

She was wearing a silky lavender gown with wide, ruffly sleeves that dripped lace. There was lace at the low neckline, the barest swell of ivory flesh appearing as she took a deep breath. Her eyes were bright, her lips smiling for the crowd. For him they were dark with apology, warm with love and anxiously uncertain as she waited for his reaction.

Love swept over him, seeping inside him, building a little fire in the pit of his stomach that he was going to have difficulty banking for the evening.

Ignoring the societal convention that frowned on public displays of affection, he leaned down and kissed her with slow deliberation. He felt her relax against him and reach a gloved hand up to touch his cheek.

He raised his head, ignoring the grins of Connor, Letty and Rolf and Johnson's expression of disdain. Mrs. Johnson, he thought, looked envious. Everyone else laughed and applauded.

But he had eyes for no one at that moment but Charity.

"I'm fine," he said softly, "now that I can look at you." He glanced at their friends with a look of apology. "Excuse us a moment."

Taking Charity by the hand, he led her away from the growing crowd, pulling her with him into the shadows under the ornate staircase.

"Jack, I—" she began, but he interrupted her with another kiss, a modicum of privacy allowing him to give this one all the passion and emotion that had swelled in him when he had thought himself alone and looked down to find her standing beside him.

When he raised his head, she opened her mouth to speak again, but he covered it gently with his hand.

"I'm sorry," he said, almost surprised to hear the words come from his lips. "I was selfish and wrong. I knew how important the convention is to you. I think I just wanted to know I was more important."

"Oh, darling, you are," she said anxiously. "It's just that everything got so confused, and I—"

He covered her mouth again. "I know. It doesn't matter." His eyes grew dark and grave. "It's been a hellishly long and lonely day, Charity."

"For me, too."

He enfolded her in his arms and simply held her, marveling that all was well between them. Then he reminded himself that she shouldn't be the only one making concessions. He put her back a step and forced himself to do the noble thing.

"Now I want you to go to the convention, give them a rousing speech, and I'll pick you up when this is over." He grinned. "We'll continue this conversation at home."

She shook her head at him, tucking her hand in his arm. "Someone is covering for me until after your speech. Then I'll have to go and give *my* speech." She stood on tiptoe to kiss his jaw. "Then we'll go home and...speak to each other."

"You're certain?"

"Yes."

He leaned down to kiss her once more, wishing he could take her home rather than into the crowd. His eyes were dark with desire. "I'll have to reward you especially for this."

She smiled at him. "I was hoping so."

Jack's speech was enthusiastically received. He promised to work toward creating better working conditions in the canneries, enforcing safety regulations in the logging camps and improving Astoria's docks and commercial areas.

"We can make Astoria a model of beauty and industry in the twentieth century," he said, the crowd watching him with rapt attention. "We can make a place that will be safe for our children, that will hold our young people with its promise of work and a healthy future." He paused. The silence pulsed. He turned to Charity and gave her a look of such love that a blush started at the neckline of her dress and slowly rose to her hairline. Then he ran his gaze over his audience. "That will show our women we value their wit and intelligence and their concern for social and governmental issues by moving ahead of our lagging state government and endorsing women's suffrage."

There was a collective gasp then murmurings of disapproval that were countered by smatterings of applause.

"We can't move into the next century," he went on, "unless every American is equal under the law—and that includes our women. Join me," he said eagerly, "in taking Astoria into the future."

The applause began politely, uncertainly. Then, as he resumed his chair beside Charity, it rose to rattle the windows. Letty was standing, as were several dozen other women in the room.

Charity gave him a hug and a quick kiss as the applause continued.

"When you said you intended to reward me," she whispered, still stunned by his words, "I thought you meant to do it...at home."

He grinned, his eyes filled with promise. "I did. This is just common sense. Now, go. I'll see you later."

As Walter Johnson approached the podium, Charity slipped behind a trellis that had been raised behind the head table and hurried along it to the wall of the dining room. Then she ran lightly against the wall, smiling apologetically at the diners distracted by the rustle of her skirts.

"Charity Ross!" a voice shouted.

Charity stopped in her tracks, startled by the sound of Walter Johnson's voice calling her name. She turned to him in confusion. Only his look of smug satisfaction made her realize she'd responded to her real name. A cold chill of dread touched every vertebra on her spine.

Chapter Fifteen

A hushed silence filled the room. Charity knew what was about to happen in front of half the population of Astoria. Unable to defeat Jack fairly, and knowing the voters had accepted his past, Johnson had probably decided to check into Charity's background on the chance she had something to hide. She thought with a grim sense of fatalism how gleeful he must have been over what he'd discovered.

Now her worst fears were about to be realized. Not only would she be discredited and humiliated in front of all her friends and much of the town, but she was about to lose Jack, as well.

She turned to him, her eyes filled with misery and acceptance. The look of confusion on his face cut her like the stroke of a razor.

"Do you deny you are Charity Ross?" Johnson demanded in a loud voice, "and not Charity Butler?"

She swallowed and raised her chin to answer. But before she could form the words, Jack got to his feet and replied for her, sharply and clearly. "She is Charity *McCarren*, Mayor Johnson."

Johnson pointed a condemning finger in her direction. "She is Charity Ross, the daughter of Calvin Ross of Dawson, Kansas!"

Silence fell again for just an instant, then the rumbling sound of a meaty scandal began to build. There'd been a time when that name had spread like a curse throughout the country. Johnson stilled the murmurs as he continued.

"Ross, an unconscionable thief much of his life, was a plague on the railroad for years, perpetrating dozens of robberies in the Midwest. Ten years ago he was caught and convicted of stealing fifty thousand dollars from the Atcheson-Topeka Railroad. During that robbery, he killed two guards, one of whom had ten children. Ross was hanged in 1891." He leaned over the podium, fixing his audience with a watchful eye. "If you vote for Jack McCarren—" he again thrust his finger in Charity's direction "—that kin of a thief and a murderer will be your mayor's wife!"

Charity fought the desire to run. With every pair of eyes in the dining hall staring at her, she walked to the head table, not slipping behind the trellis this time but walking in plain sight of everyone as a sort of self-inflicted punishment.

Jack had control of his surprise now, and except for a slight loss of color in his face, Charity thought it would be impossible to tell from his expression that his wife had just been revealed to him as a fraud in front of several hundred people. Charity knew what he must be thinking about her, but she could read nothing in his stoic expression.

He asked her one quiet, simple question. "Is it true?"

A sob rose in her throat and closed off her air. "Yes," she whispered.

Anger and disappointment darkened his eyes. He pulled out the chair she had vacated. "Sit down," he ordered softly.

He seated her, then turned to the audience. "What Calvin Ross did," he said reasonably, "has nothing to do with her. She's offered all of you nothing but kindness since she's been here."

He pointed a finger at himself. "My mother was a prostitute, but you all know me as an honest man, and I appreciate the fact that you've let me prove that to you. I expect you to give my wife the same chance."

The room buzzed with conversation. Guests leaned out of their chairs and over tables to whisper to one other.

"What do you think is really behind McCarren's plans to improve the waterfront and downtown?" Johnson asked, stopping the buzzing. "Where will he get the money, and where will he and Charity Ross go with it if and when he gets it?"

Jack started for the podium, but Connor reached it first. One powerful blow from his big fist sent Johnson sprawling backward. Half the room rose to its feet. When Connor yanked Johnson to his feet by the lapels and drew his fist back to hit him again, several men came forward. Jack pulled Connor backward as Johnson shook off the other men and suggested that the audience take note of the ruffian style of his opponent and his opponent's friends.

The evening's chairman, a portly man seated near the middle of the table, banged his gavel for order. "Ladies and gentlemen, please!"

After a few moments, the sound quieted to a low roar. Then a gentleman in the middle of the room stood.

"I don't hold her father's guilt against her!" He shouted to be heard. "But we've had a past full of graft and self-serving politicians. We should have candidates who are above reproach—who have not even the hint of scandal attached to their names."

"Then you should know something about Mr. McCarren's opponent."

Everyone turned to Nell Johnson in surprise. The tall woman stood, glanced at her husband with a bland look, then turned to the audience.

She looked magnificent, Charity thought in her misery. She, Charity, had done an inspired job on the dress.

"I've heard whispering around town that my husband is in the pocket of Swill Town," Nell said. "I assure you that isn't true."

The crowd buzzed again. Johnson went to the podium, looking righteously pleased with himself and pleased with how the scene he'd carefully researched and staged was developing. He waited for the glowing endorsement he thought his wife would give.

"He's in the pocket of Ah Chun of Bond Street," Nell added, without even looking in his direction. His indignant yowl of *"Eleanor!"* filled the large room. "He is supplied with women and money if he allows certain establishments to function without police interference." She stopped for emphasis. "And if he sees that certain ships come into port without being searched by federal officers."

She turned to him then, her eyes filled with scorn. "If you're looking for a man who is above reproach, you'll have to look elsewhere."

Now the sound in the room was deafening. Nell Johnson started toward Charity, and Charity rose to meet her halfway.

Johnson, white-faced, caught his wife's arm and spun her around. "Eleanor! How could you?"

Nell slapped his hand away. "How could *you*, Walter? How could you destroy this young couple? Jack McCarren's only crime is that he's better and more honest than you. Charity's only crime is that she's the daughter of a man who probably wasn't very different from you. She went out of her way for me, Walter. That's something you've never done in all our married life. Goodbye."

"Now." Nell straightened the bodice of her dress and turned her imperious expression on Jack. "Mr. McCarren. While you and our illustrious citizens decide what to do about my husband and this most extraordinary dinner, I'll walk Charity to Carnahan's Hall. I understand she's to give a speech."

Charity looked at Jack, her eyes filled with misery. "I'm so sorry," she said. "It would have been better for you if I hadn't come after all."

Anger still stood stiffly in his eyes. He opened his mouth to speak to her, but the sheriff, the chairman of the election committee and the county clerk were all trying to claim his attention.

"We'll talk later," he said. "Go on."

Go on. She heard the words again in her mind. A temporary suggestion, she wondered, or a permanent directive?

The several hundred people attending the dinner were crowded around the head table. And every single one of them was staring at Charity.

Nell put an arm around her. "Come on, now," she whispered. "Chin up!"

Letty appeared to flank Charity's other side, and together with Nell led Charity through the crowd and into the balmy summer night.

"Well!" Nell said, as they bustled her across the street. "That was a do they'll be talking about for months."

"I'm sorry," Charity said breathlessly. "I know that must have been difficult for you."

Nell's voice was as brisk as her pace. "It was and it wasn't. I closed my eyes to what he'd been doing, in deference to my marriage vows. But I began to overhear things, so I spent an entire afternoon in his office at home checking the desk drawers that are always locked. It was very enlightening." She shook her head apologetically. "What he did to you tonight was unforgivable."

"But I *am* Calvin Ross's daughter."

Nell shrugged dismissingly. "I'm Byron Baldwin's daughter. He was no thief, but he was a pompous and bigoted bore. Almost more of a crime than stealing, if you ask me. Society has such curious standards."

"What if your husband goes to jail, Mrs. Johnson?" Letty asked.

"My dear, I'm counting on it. I'll visit the Continent, possibly go on safari. The possibilities are limitless."

Charity turned to Letty. "Letty, I'm so—" she began.

Letty doubled a small fist and shook it at her. "If that's an apology, I don't want to hear it. As if whose daughter you were would make a difference to a woman with my reputation. Incidentally..." She yanked them to a stop just outside the doors of Carnahan's Hall. "I wish I had known about the problem with Judith and Coleen this morning. I asked you to cover for me at one meeting, I didn't ask you to assume my responsibilities."

"I didn't want to upset—"

"My tenuous peace with Connor. I know. I should pound you with a croquet mallet."

Nell urged them up the steps. "Goodness. What a hideous image. Although that might be a good idea to use on Walter." Even from outside the building, the strains of a high-spirited song could be heard, sung at full voice by a large group of enthusiastic women.

"Listen to that!" Letty said, her eyes aglow with excitement.

Charity did. At any other time it would have pleased and thrilled her to know that the Astoria chapter of Ladies for the Vote had made a substantial contribution to the cause—that through their efforts, women across the state had had their fervor renewed and local women had been spurred to action. Judging by the strength of the sound, they were strongly allied in their quest for equality for women.

The final chorus was ringing to a close when Letty, Charity and Nell tiptoed into the hall.

At the podium, Dr. Parson lent his powerful baritone to Agnes's shaky but heartfelt soprano. Dinner had already been cleared away, Charity noted.

As the last note died, Agnes looked up and spotted her salvation. "There they are now!" she cried.

Letty waved from the side of the auditorium as she and Charity made their way up the aisle to join the group.

Charity took the notes she'd folded tightly in her evening bag and tried to hand them to Letty.

Letty pushed them back at her. "I'm not giving the address," she said, trying to shoo her toward the stage. "You are."

Charity pulled her behind the grand piano. The audience laughed, probably thinking that this was some small comedic performance for their benefit.

"Letty, it's your speech," Charity said with what firmness she could muster from the depths of her despair. "And I am in no mood to stand in front of an audience and sound heroic."

Letty raised an eyebrow. "Stop being theatrical. So you chose not to tell us about your father. Who do you imagine will care?"

Charity shook her head at Letty's attempt to minimize the crisis. "You, of all people, should know the answer to that, Letty. My father was a murderer! Everyone will judge, and everyone will care. I'm sure Jack cares. Not only have I lied to him and married him under false pretenses, but I've just ruined his campaign."

Letty rolled her eyes. "What rubbish! Do you truly have such little faith in your husband and your friends?"

"I know what life was like in Kansas when everyone knew who I was. That's why I came here. To start over."

"Well, this is Oregon, not Kansas. If you want to start over, then you must start with your attitude. Trust us to have the decency to love you for who you are and not care a damn about who your father was."

Weary of the argument, Charity slapped her notes on the piano. "This is your speech, Letty. You wrote it. I was to give it only because we expected you would still be at the dinner"

Letty nodded. "I haven't looked at that speech in days. In fact it went out of my mind the moment I turned the responsibility over to you. You've led these ladies through the weekend's activities. You have to give this speech, Charity." Letty picked up the notes, and placed them in Charity's hands. "Now, straighten up. You forced me to face myself and my relationship with Connor. Now you have to face yourself and your place in this town."

She swept a hand toward the stage. "The podium is yours." Then she went to join their friends seated in the front two rows.

Charity wanted more than anything to run home and hide under the bed. But several hundred women were waiting expectantly, and she wasn't certain she could still call Jack's house home in any case.

She headed for the podium. Enthusiastic applause began. She'd made many friends in the past two days, and they were generous with their affection.

She opened her notes and spread them on the polished oak stand as the applause died down. She looked out at the sea of faces and had difficulty seeing them. Her mind couldn't rid itself of the image of the crowd in the hotel dining room and Jack's look of disappointment and anger.

Charity drew a deep breath and told herself that this evening wasn't about her. It was about an injustice that had been allowed to continue too long. About a country filled with women who were powerless to effect a change, waiting for women like herself who had the means and the opportunity to make a difference.

She squared her shoulders and cleared her throat. She gave Letty's speech, filled with news of the movement. She spoke about the petitions distributed to lawmakers, the statewide enrollment that had reached five figures, and about men who'd come over to their side and were bravely lending their support.

Then, when she was supposed to thank the ladies for coming, remind them that there would be a prayer breakfast in the morning and a small brooch for everyone who'd attended, she began to think that she might find some redeeming value in what had happened to her tonight by sharing it with the women who had become her friends. For the first time she could remember, she was able to put her past to good use.

She told her audience what had just happened in the hotel ballroom across the way.

"Of course I was very embarrassed," she admitted, "because I wanted so much for Astoria to be a new start for me. I've spent so much of my life regretting my past, and I believe now that I came here trying to hide from it. But that made me realize that I can't, that it's as much a part of me as my strengths and my good qualities…" She smiled tentatively. "Few as those might be."

The audience seemed interested—confused, perhaps, but interested. She drew a breath and went on.

"What I want to impress on you tonight is that we presume so much about each other because we've heard the same untruths over and over. Many men believe we're inferior to them because their fathers have told them so. It's wrong of them to believe that, just as we are wrong to believe *all* men would hold us down. Many won't, if we make enough of an effort to show what we can do." She smiled in Dr. Parson's direction. "Like our noble baritone, Dr. Parson."

Cheers, applause and a few whistles rose from the assembly.

"The important thing to remember here is that we shouldn't seek the right to vote, the right to work and to be paid fairly for it, the right to a good education, simply so that we can wield power. We must want to use it as a platform for social reform and justice for every man and woman."

She paused as the back doors opened and a large group of people streamed in. She frowned, recognizing many of the couples who'd been in the hotel dining room. Among them were Rolf and Connor—and Jack. They took seats toward the back and she stiffly offered a welcoming smile.

Charity went to the middle of the stage and tried not to think about why Jack had come. Was he here so that she would be unable to escape him after her speech? So that he could confront her about her true identity and berate her for her lies? Because he intended to send her away?

She kept her eyes resolutely from him and tried to wrest from deep inside her what all the weeks with Letty's ladies had taught her.

"You men should know," she said, addressing the new arrivals, still keeping her eyes clear of Jack, "that you will not be completely free in this world until your women are free."

There was a roar of applause from the ladies. "That you will never legislate or administrate with true strength until you are strong enough to allow us to legislate and administrate beside you. You will never know a stronger partnership in your lives than you will if you take us into your confidence and give us your full trust and the freedom to be your equals in every way.

"My husband," she said, still carefully looking everywhere but at him, "told the guests at the Founder's Day dinner that if Astoria voted to support women's suffrage, it would show the state and the country that we are a forward-thinking society, a spearhead for the twentieth century.

"Go home," she said, "and make that a reality in your hometown. Find out what's happening and support whatever will benefit most and hurt least. Find a need and fill it. Learn where the problems are and expose them. Don't attack people, attack *problems*. And, most importantly, don't hide from anything. Good night."

They were on their feet for her, their applause deafening. She tried to take her place with her friends, but the applause continued and they pushed her back to the center of the floor. Uncertain of how to show her appreciation of their support, she bowed, feeling a little like an aged diva on the night of her swan song. Then she went to her seat.

Letty stood and raised her hands to quiet the crowd. "We'd like to hear testimonials from those of you who feel you've been enriched by this weekend."

A woman from the southern Oregon coast stood to say how much she'd enjoyed their hospitality, and that their strength and dedication had convinced her that the cause couldn't fail. It might take time to succeed, but it couldn't fail.

Several other women rose to admit that their faith in the ultimate success of the cause had wavered over the past few years, but that they felt their own dedication rekindled because of their weekend.

Dr. Parson spoke, too. He told the crowd that he thought women should go a step further and demand freedom from the corset. "You need to be free of them as well as all other means of oppression. Good health is dependent upon good breathing and good and happy living!"

Then Connor Donovan stood, and the entire hall fell silent. Everyone present knew about the situation that had separated Connor and Letty for the past year.

Color filled Letty's cheeks, but she tilted her chin and asked politely, "You would like to testify, Mr. Donovan?"

"I would," he said clearly, tall and handsome in his evening clothes. He glanced quickly around the room, seemingly at ease despite everyone's stare.

Charity forgot her own problems for a moment and prayed he wouldn't do anything to embarrass Letty.

"I'd like to go on record as supporting the Ladies for the Vote," he said. Mouths fell open. Letty looked very much as though she might faint when he locked his gaze with hers.

"Because of my association with a brave, intelligent, eminently capable woman, my manhood has been enriched, not diminished. I was forced to struggle against my own ignorance to understand that her assumption of power over her own life did not exclude my influence or my protection. Love gives us the right to affect each other's lives. But God gives her the right to live hers in her way."

Letty's teary-eyed gasp of "Connor!" was soundless as the crowed roared once again. Then chaos reigned for an hour before everyone began to leave.

Charity and Letty shook hands, accepted hugs and exchanged addresses. Then they looked at each other a little glassy-eyed when the last conventioneer walked out the door.

Letty wrapped Charity in a hug. "You did it," she praised gently.

"You made all the preparations and did most of the work."

"But you carried it off. You made peace of a situation that could have upset everything, and helped us land on our feet. I'm so proud of you. And I'm so proud that you're my friend."

Charity hugged Letty and thought wryly that she'd saved the situation but ruined her life. Ah, well. It had been pretty well doomed from the beginning anyway. As she'd told the ladies, it was impossible to hide from what was a part of you. She'd been foolish to try, and deserved whatever came now for having deceived everyone, particularly the man she had vowed to love and honor.

They pulled apart to find Connor and Jack standing in the doorway. Connor opened his arms and Letty ran into them. Jack, hands in his pockets, stared at Charity, that look of anger still in place.

"We'll wait for you two in the carriage, Jack," Connor said quietly. Letty looked at Jack doubtfully, then gave Charity an encouraging smile. Connor closed the doors, shutting Charity inside alone with Jack.

Charity made herself look at him, really look at him, because it might be the last time. She let her eyes wander over the perfect symmetry of his face—all sharp planes and hard angles in his anger—over his broad, square shoulders in the elegant evening clothes. She let herself absorb the strong and easy presence that so defined him, even in his fury.

Everything inside her trembled, as though it had knowledge that her entire life stood on the brink of a dangerous precipice. Emotion pulled at her throat and her eyes, but she held it back.

"I'm sorry." She'd wanted to say it strongly, firmly, but it came out as a whisper.

"As well you should be," he replied. His voice was as hard as the fingers that closed around her elbow and pulled her toward the last row of chairs. He pushed her into the second chair and took the one on the aisle. "If you've an explanation, I'd like to hear it."

He leaned an elbow on the back of his chair and looked at her. Then she couldn't meet his eyes. All she'd ever known from him had been kindness. The condemnation was too difficult to look at.

"Cowardice," she replied, staring at the fingers twisting in her lap. "Stupidity, selfishness. They all apply."

"What did you expect I would do to you," he asked, his voice eerily quiet, "for having had no control over who your father was?"

He'd phrased the question ironically, but she'd known the reality of living among people who *did* consider her somehow responsible.

"And have the grace to look at me when you answer," he added.

She steeled herself against what facing him would do to her. Then she raised her eyes and replied calmly, "Before you asked me to marry you, I thought the knowledge would lose me your friendship. I've lost friends before when they found out. After you asked me to marry you, I was afraid it would make you change your mind." Her throat tightened, but she forced the words out. "After we were married, I was afraid it would make you stop loving me."

Everything inside her seemed to dissolve when he seemed unaffected by her honesty. It was too late to try to explain. She stood to leave, unable to bear it a moment longer. "Apparently it was a fear that was justified."

His calm snapped then and he grabbed her wrist and yanked her down in the chair.

"A lot of things would be justified at this moment," he said, his voice rising a decibel. "Don't you know that I would have to be dead to stop loving you?"

For an instant, she didn't know what to make of that remark. A little flare of hope tried to form inside her but she stifled it quickly. That couldn't be what he meant. Particularly not in the tone of voice he'd used.

"Was there ever," he demanded, "in all our tender moments, one time when you considered me worthy of your trust?"

She frowned at him, horrified by the question. "Jack, it wasn't that I didn't trust you."

"Oh?" One of his eyebrows went up inquiringly. "What was it then? That you didn't consider me strong enough to learn that you weren't born of angels?" The eyebrow went down again. "My darling, I concluded that long ago."

She looked him in the eye, so important was it that he understand. "You needed a wife who would be a credit to your campaign. After all you'd been through to convince people that your past didn't affect who you were, I didn't—"

"You didn't think," he interrupted mercilessly, "that I could understand that that also applies to you?"

"No. I knew that I didn't have the courage to tell you and risk losing you, so I kept it to myself in the hope that it would all go away."

"Like magic?" he asked dryly.

A tear she could no longer control spilled over. "It didn't seem impossible. You'd brought such magic into my life already."

The tear and those words were almost Jack's undoing. But he held fast, still deeply hurt by her lack of faith in him. "So you laid the foundation," he said implacably, "for me to discover at an important function crowded with my friends and acquaintances that I didn't even know my wife's true identity."

That single tear was followed by another. "I'm sorry about your campaign."

"I don't give a damn about the campaign. My indignation isn't for myself as a candidate, but for myself as a man. Not only do I have to live with the knowledge that you didn't trust me, but with the knowledge that everyone in town knows it, too."

Tears were now streaming down her face. He hardened himself against weakening. "I'll grant you any right you seek, Charity, except the right to lie to me. And to think so little of my character to even consider that my love for you would be diminished by who your father was."

She rose to her feet again. "I can be gone in an hour."

He yanked her down again. "I would have you back here in even less time."

Charity stared at him. "I thought you would want me gone."

Her eyes, still moist with residual tears, were wide and heart-wrenchingly hopeful. Anger was slipping away from him, but he was still too hurt to let it go entirely. He looked at her evenly. "If you'll recall, we took vows before a priest only weeks ago. We promised before God to love and honor one another. I promised to cherish you, and you to obey me."

She sniffed, frowning. "But I haven't been honest with you. I believe you have some...some recourse under the laws of the church."

"Were you honest about loving me?" he asked. Even with all that had happened that night, it was the only fact that truly mattered to him.

Her eyes told him everything. They filled again and spilled over, full of guilt and regret and a desperation that mirrored what he felt. She loved him. He didn't understand why she hadn't trusted him, but that was something he could manage to put aside as long as she loved him.

"Jack," she whispered, putting a shaky hand to his cheek. "You know I do. I love you more than my own life."

He pulled her into his arms and held her close for a long moment. "Then I don't want to hear any more talk of your going away, because I love you and I don't think I could go on without you."

Charity sobbed against his shoulder for the generosity of his forgiveness and for the great chasm she still felt between them. He held her tightly and his words rang true. But she'd hurt him in a way she knew he wouldn't be able to forget even though he'd forgiven her.

"Come. Connor and Letty have sent his uncles home in a cab and are waiting to take us home in their carriage." Jack tried to stand, but she held his arms, her eyes pleading with him.

"Let me try to explain again," she said.

"It isn't necessary," he said. He forced a smile for her, hoping to reassure her. "I understand."

She looked into his eyes and said softly, "No, you don't."

"I understand why you wanted to start over."

"But not why I couldn't tell you about it."

"That doesn't matter," he insisted. "I told you I don't care."

She nodded, her lips determined despite their trembling. "I know. You're being noble. But neither of us will be happy in this marriage if we can't reestablish the rapport with which we began. Please let me try to help you see."

"Very well." He simply wanted to take her home and put the entire evening behind them. But she looked so desperate, he couldn't refuse her. And he knew she was right about their relationship. It had been so perfect. Anything less would be painful to accept.

He leaned back in his chair, arms folded, and propped a foot on the rung of the chair in front of him. "Go on."

Now that Charity had the opportunity, she felt sure she lacked the words. What collection of sounds could ever convey the humiliation she'd known growing up, the loneliness and hurt she'd felt when children whispered to one another while she stood alone in the schoolyard? How could she ever tell him how it felt to be roughly kissed by a man, then when she protested, be told she had no right to expect anything more because of who she was?

Was there any way to explain how she had felt tonight when Walter Johnson had ruthlessly exposed her before everyone?

Only the knowledge of what was at stake made her try. Slowly, she told him stories of her childhood. She told him about the farmer with the rude kisses, she told him about her mother who had thought she'd fallen in love with a rogue and found herself married to a criminal.

Jack listened patiently and thought he understood. It didn't melt the icy hurt at the center of his being, but he thought he understood.

Charity knew she hadn't bridged the distance between them, and dug a little deeper in her need to make him see. "When you literally leapt into my life right off the wharf," she said quietly, "I thought I was the luckiest woman in the world to have found a friend like you, and all the friends you shared with me—Letty and Jonathan and Rolf and everyone else at the Donovans."

He remembered his first sight of her that day, looking proper and a little stiff while trying to talk a bear into submission. Something softened inside him.

"Then I fell in love with you..." Tears pooled in her eyes again, but she sniffed and blinked them away, sitting a little straighter in her chair. "And—miracle of miracles—you fell in love with me."

He raised an eyebrow. "You mean you fell in love first? But you took such convincing."

A fractional smile played at the uncertain line of her lips. "That's the way the game is played, Jack."

"Ah. Continue."

"I knew nothing could come of our relationship," she went on gravely, her eyes lowering to her lap, but the pleat between her eyebrows showed him how difficult this was for her. He rested an arm along the back of her chair and a hand on her shoulder. "I knew that if my past was discovered, it would put an end to your career." She raised her eyes to him. They were filled with a combination of honesty and guilt. "Then you asked me to marry you, and everything I'd ever wanted all my life was dangled in front of me, and I wasn't strong enough to resist it. The young woman who'd had so little love and family was suddenly offered everything."

He moved his hand to cup her face, but she caught it and, twinning her fingers in it, pulled it down to her lap. She was beginning to lose her composure, and the breath she drew to try to hold it in held a sob. His touch would destroy her control.

"Try to imagine," she said, her mouth trembling, "that you are Jack McCarren, the young man. The man you were before you acquired the worldliness that's given you this wonderful acceptance of who and what you are. Imagine that you still feel out of place and insecure in a world that doesn't think your kind should be allowed to keep company with everyone else."

That was easy enough to recall, he thought. It hadn't been so long ago that he'd felt that way.

"Now imagine," she went on, her voice strained with emotion, "that you love a woman who doesn't know about your past. Who thinks you're someone special. And she wants to share her life with you."

Her fingernails were digging into the back of his hand.

"If you could see that she was fairly comfortable in the world that had shunned you, would you be able to tell her about your mother and Astor Street and be absolutely certain she would understand? Would you be able to risk losing her?"

And that was what dissolved the ice and swept away the pain. Reversing their positions and imagining himself in danger of losing Charity. He knew nothing would ever make him take that chance.

He would have protected himself as she had done.

He crushed her to him this time, real understanding and the love that had been bruised but not broken, alive in the grip that held her.

Charity felt the difference and sobbed into the collar of his elegant coat. Not only had he forgiven her, but now he understood.

He lifted her out of her chair and onto his lap, kissing her soundly, apologetically. "Charity, I'm sorry," he murmured against her lips.

"Oh, Jack." She rained little kisses all over his face. "No, I'm sorry. It was all my fault. It wasn't that I didn't trust you, it was that I didn't trust myself to be worth the risk to you."

He pulled her from him slightly and tilted her helplessly backward over his arm. "I'm going to beat you for that when we get home."

She didn't seem the least concerned. "Lily would come to my defense."

"Lily," he said menacingly, "is off tonight."

She smiled wickedly at him. "Then I'll just have to make you change your mind between here and home as to how you want to spend your time once we get there."

He righted her and set her on her feet, anxious to be put to the test.

Chapter Sixteen

"What are they doing now, Connor?" Letty teased in a loud voice as Connor guided the horses up the quiet street.

Connor glanced over his shoulder and gasped dramatically. "He appears to be swallowing her," he replied, reaching a hand out to tip Letty's face back when she would have peered into the second seat. "Much as a snake would a mongoose. Don't look. It's disgusting."

"Disgusting?" Jack freed Charity's lips, but couldn't move his eyes from the love and passion in hers. "You've been on the river too long, Con. You've forgotten what summer nights are for."

"No, I haven't," Con replied. "But I have the grace to confine my activities to somewhere other than a public street."

"There isn't a soul around."

"Someone could happen by at any moment."

"That's what I told you that afternoon in the park," Letty reminded Connor in a casual tone, "but still, you insisted that the blackberries provided sufficient cover and I returned home looking like I'd wrestled with a tiger."

He laughed throatily. "You had."

Giggling, Letty leaned over to kiss his cheek. "I don't think you're the one to set the standard for proper behavior, darling."

Connor pulled the horses to a stop in front of Jack's and Charity's home, then turned his head to take Letty's chaste kiss on the cheek on his mouth. When he finally freed her, he said wryly, "From the woman who danced on the bar in the Sunset Saloon."

"I did not dance on it, I marched down it, kicking over mugs of beer."

"It looked like the cancan," Jack said from the back. He leapt onto the street, reaching up for Charity. "Thank you, my friends, for the transportation and the excellent company. We're to expect you for dinner tomorrow night, then?"

Connor raised an eyebrow, indicating with a tilt of his head their tight embrace. "Do you think you'll be sufficiently separate by then for Charity to be giving orders in the kitchen while you ply us with brandy in the living room?"

Jack smiled. "If not, we'll have our brandy in the kitchen."

Charity smiled at Letty. Letty returned her smile, and in her eyes was the same sense of glorious good fortune Charity felt. Several short months ago they'd been two lonely women, their only prospects for the future being hard work and dedication to a cause.

Now Letty had Connor back, and Charity had found Jack.

Jack and Charity waved as Connor pulled away to proceed another block to his home.

Charity leaned blissfully against Jack as they followed the walk that led around the back to the kitchen. "Are you going to miss the excitement of a campaign?" She glanced at him. "You're certain you won't come to resent me for having destroyed your plans?"

He squeezed her to him. "You haven't destroyed anything. When the sheriff took Johnson away tonight after you ladies had left for Carnahan's Hall, I told my supporters I would withdraw and both parties could start fresh with new candidates. But they wouldn't hear of it. They were flatteringly insistent that I remain their candidate, and they made it clear that their support extends to you, as well." He kissed her temple as they walked between the roses growing on the trellis against the side of the house and the rhododendrons that separated their lot from the next one. "When we finally left, Johnson's supporters were scrambling to find another candidate."

"I can't believe it," she murmured. She felt filled with love and blessings. She wrapped both arms around Jack as they reached the back door. "I never imagined I would have all the things I'd dreamed of as a lonely little girl. I've found friends, a home . . . you." The last was said in a whisper heavy with emotion. "I'm not dreaming, am I?"

In reply, Jack combed his fingers into her complicated chignon and tilted her head. He kissed her possessively, passionately, promisingly. Then he raised his head and asked quietly, "Did that feel unreal?"

"No," she replied, her body beginning to tremble with the need for more. "But can real life truly be this wonderful?"

He shrugged and turned her toward the steps. "I imagine the next fifty years will give us our answer."

"I am afraid," a halting, silky voice said as a shadow materialized out of the bushes, "you will not have that long."

The voice struck a primitive reflex in Charity. It was like having a snake touch her skin. The shudder of revulsion ran deep. Ah Chun.

Jack stepped between the man and Charity.

Five men appeared to flank Ah Chun, enclosing Jack and Charity in a loose semicircle backed against the side of the house.

"I thought the sheriff would have been on his way to find you," Jack said. "Mrs. Johnson told many of your secrets tonight to a room filled with people."

Ah Chun nodded serenely. "He will find many empty buildings. You two have forced me to relocate my business." He crossed both hands over the red silk of his robe gleaming in the moonlight. "There will be no one around to verify her story." He paused and sighed, as though the night's turn of events was nothing more than a wearisome nuisance. "You will be dead," he said pleasantly, "and your scold of a wife will be on the *China Star* with me. I will test her . . . skills . . . personally, then sell her to the highest bidder."

Nausea rose in Charity's throat as a strange sense of fatalism replaced her fear. No one was going to hurt Jack.

She tried to step out from behind him.

Jack shot out an arm, blocking her path. "Charity," he said sharply, keeping his eyes on Ah Chun and his men, "stay out of the way and be quiet."

"I won't let them . . ." She tried to push his arm away, but it curled around her and pushed her behind him.

Ah Chun shook his head. "Do you not wish to be relieved of such an unmanageable woman?"

Jack's voice was dry. "I have a preference for annoyance and aggravation."

Ah Chun spread his hands in a gesture of reluctant helplessness. "Then you leave me little choice."

"Jack, no!" Charity tried to get around the other side of him but he yanked her against him again, this time removing a derringer from the inside pocket of his coat. He waved the pistol along the semicircle of men. They widened their distance just a little.

"Such a small weapon," Ah Chun challenged.

Jack smiled. "Between the eyes, that's all it takes. Now, move your men away from the gate because my wife is leaving."

"No," Charity said quietly from behind him. "I'm not."

Keeping her between him and the side of the house, Jack moved toward the gate. Ah Chun's men gave him room.

"You will do what I say," Jack insisted.

"I won't."

Charity knew his only concern was to get her to safety. But she also knew that once she was removed from the scene, he couldn't hold six men at bay with a gun that held two bullets.

Once they'd cleared the side of the house and Jack had room to maneuver, he pushed Charity toward the gate. "Go for Connor!" he ordered.

Charity remained stubbornly in place. "I will not leave you."

Jack was beside himself with frustration. He had a curiously out-of-place memory of arguing with her once before when she'd refused to leave him. That time he'd confronted a bear. She chose the damnedest times to be difficult.

"Charity McCarren," he said, keeping his eye on the two closest men, who had drawn knives and seemed to be considering taking advantage of the distraction Charity was providing to make a move toward him. He leveled the small gun at the closest man's forehead. The man stiffened to a stop. "Only weeks ago you promised to obey me."

"I also promised to stay with you until death do us part." She peeled off her gloves. "Well, if that's about to happen, you're not sending me to safety while you face this refuse pile all alone."

She squared off beside him, casting him a grin. "Besides. You taught me a few things, remember?"

He remembered only how light and fragile she'd felt every time he'd overpowered her. It occurred to him that if they survived this he was going to teach her a few more things—forcefully.

He sighed. "Perhaps you would put your nagging voice to good use and shout for a neighbor."

"No need." Connor, a rifle in hand, strode through the gate. He was followed by Rolf with a shotgun and Letty with a pistol. "We're already here. God, Jack. Must you cause a commotion wherever you go? I've had about enough for one evening."

With a groan of relief, Charity sagged against Jack. He put an arm around her as Rolf moved into the yard, gathering Ah Chun and his men together on the porch steps.

"Rolf spent the evening with Ming and Jonathan," Connor said, "and started home when Letty and I arrived. Fortunately he saw the goings-on in your yard before anyone saw him. He came back for us."

"The sheriff's looking for you gentlemen," Rolf said, prodding Ah Chun with the barrel of the shotgun when he resisted.

"He can prove nothing." Ah Chun sat on the bottom step.

"Not true," Rolf corrected. "Johnson kept a diary of all his transactions with you. It's very revealing. Added to the things Jack and I have learned about you in the past few weeks, you're either going to prison for a long, long time, or you're going home, where all the friends and families of the men and women you brought here and ruined will be waiting for you."

"Ming and Jonathan went for the sheriff," Connor said. "He should be along any moment. Letty, give Jack the pistol and take Charity inside. We're all going to need a brandy when this is over."

Ming stood in Jack's and Charity's doorway and watched the sheriff and a deputy lead away Ah Chun and his men. When they were out of sight, she slowly closed the door, then turned to Rolf, who stood behind her. Her beautiful almond eyes were filled with disbelief.

"He is gone," she said, her voice reflecting the same wonder.

"And he won't be back," Rolf confirmed. He turned toward Charity, who was seated in Jack's lap in a chair by the fireplace. Connor sat on the sofa between Letty and Jonathan, the boy asleep against him. "Excuse us, please," he said, catching Ming's hand. "We have things to talk about. We'll be out on the swing."

Letty stretched lazily in Connor's arm. "I'm so happy. I think that's going to work out. I was concerned for a while that the threat of Ah Chun was going to keep them apart forever." She grinned at Jack. "Of course, I didn't know you were at work on a solution at the time. Rolf told me while you were talking to the sheriff that you and he gathered enough documented evidence from a sea captain he'd cheated to call the federal officers.''

Jack nodded. ''What we collected is almost superfluous against what the Johnsons know. But I was just trying to help Rolf get Ah Chun out from the middle of his relationship with Ming. When he got rough with you and Charity, it became even more personal and more urgent.''

Charity kissed Jack's cheek. ''You're such a romantic.''

''No.'' He gave a long-suffering sigh. ''I've simply turned into one of those husbands who hates to see a free man when he himself has been trapped so completely.''

Charity sat up, the picture of indignation. ''Trapped?''

He pulled her down into his arms. ''Deliciously, of course.''

''It isn't at all distasteful once you get used to it,'' Connor put in helpfully. He explained in all apparent innocence, ''You have a charming companion at the breakfast and dinner table, you don't have to search around for someone to take to parties, they eventually give you a child . . .''

Jonathan, wearing a nightshirt tucked into a pair of pants, stirred in his father's arms. ''Sleepy, Papa,'' he said, then drifted off to sleep again.

Connor's expression was overtaken by tenderness as he soothed Jonathan. ''Then your life is never the same again.''

Letty placed a hand over the one he held to Jonathan's back. ''For better?'' she asked softly, seriously. ''Or for worse?''

He turned his face from Jonathan to her, his expression unreadable for a moment as his eyes went slowly over her face, feature by feature. ''Let's go home,'' he said finally, the answer visible in his eyes, "and I'll show you."

Jack and Charity waved goodbye from the porch as their guests began their short walk home. Connor carried Jonathan and wrapped his other arm around Letty. Rolf and Ming, arm in arm, followed.

Charity squeezed one of Jack's arms and leaned her cheek against it. "A fairy-tale ending for everyone," she sighed. "Isn't it wonderful?"

"Not quite yet," he said, pulling her inside and closing the door.

Charity looked into his stern expression with suprise. She had thought they had put the crisis that threatened to destroy their marriage behind them.

"Not that," Jack said, reading her eyes. "I'm talking about what happened with Ah Chun. It's time we had a serious discussion about your attitude."

He went about the room turning down the gas lamps until there was no light in the house but the one at the top of the stairs.

He pointed to it. "We'll talk upstairs."

She tried to reach for him. "Jack, I..."

"No," he said, turning her away from him and giving her a gentle shove toward the bottom stair. "You're not going to charm me out of this. Go."

She recognized this as a mood not conducive to argument. She climbed the stairs and turned in the direction of their room. It was dark and cool as she went to the lamp on the wall on her side of the bed and turned it on. The soft glow of gaslight spread its mellow warmth over the striped wallpaper, the little wicker chair, the large bed. She turned to face Jack, feeling just a little uncertain.

He still wore evening attire, though his jacket and vest and collar had been discarded somewhere downstairs when he'd poured brandy for everyone after the sheriff left. His tie had also been removed, and his stiffly starched white shirtfront stood open to the third button. The dark trousers moved smoothly against his long legs as he took several steps toward her and pointed to the bed.

"Sit down," he said.

She did, primly, on the edge of the bed. Her feet dangled inches off the carpet.

He came to stand over her, and she couldn't help a little shudder of apprehension. This mood was not quite the same as the hurt and anger of earlier that evening. This was determination with the vague suggestion of threat.

"I demand very little of you, Charity," he said quietly, his voice edged with the sternness in his eyes. "For the most part you are everything a man could ever hope to find in a woman."

"Jack," she whispered, rising to reach for him at the sound of what were obviously love words.

"But." He pointed her back in place. She subsided with a frown. "There are two attributes a man appreciates in a wife of which, it appears, you will have to be reminded."

She lowered her eyes, her conscience still stricken by the evening he'd had to endure. "One of them is honesty," she said.

He paced several steps away from her. "That's right. But we've discussed that, and I trust the issue is resolved."

"Yes." Just as she looked at him, he turned at the bedpost to fix her with a dark and steady gaze.

"Then we're free to talk about the problem you have with obedience." He paced to her.

She looked at him in confusion and disbelief. "Obedience, Jack? Do you mean that the man who talked tonight about leading Astoria into the twentieth century wants a subservient wife?"

He sat on the edge of the bed to face her, one long leg braced against the carpeted floor. "Not subservient," he said firmly. "Simply cooperative." His temper began to rise as he thought again about how she'd argued with him on the lawn. "Do you have any idea," he demanded, his voice also rising, "how close you came tonight to ending up in the hold of a ship on your way to God knows where? And all because you wouldn't do as I asked."

"You wanted me to leave you," she pointed out, stubbornly folding her arms.

"To go for help."

"To get me clear of danger," she corrected. "You know as well as I do that the fact Ah Chun wanted me unharmed was the only thing that kept his men from overpowering you."

"You think they would have found it that easy?"

"There were six of them, Jack. Seven with Ah Chun. And the moment I was out of the way, they'd have done just that."

He took a firm grip on her upper arm and gave her a little shake. "In a physically dangerous situation, the decision on how to react is mine to make." His fingers dug into her arm sufficiently to let her know how serious he was. She stiffened a little and her lips firmed, but she didn't struggle. "I grew up on the docks. I understand the ruthless and criminal turn of mind. You do not."

"Jack, I love you! I didn't want to—"

"Then if you love me," he said more quietly, "you will trust me to do what is best for both of us, and cooperate with me instead of further endangering us by arguing."

"You would have been killed!" she said stubbornly, tears of frustration filling her eyes.

"But you would have been safe," he insisted. "Had Connor and Rolf not arrived, you'd have died along with me."

She looked at him steadily. "Do you think I'd have wanted to go on without you?"

The words, and the absolute seriousness with which she spoke them, fringed what was left of his patience so that he pushed her back onto the fluffy coverlet with a growl.

He rose over her, pinning her wrists over her head. "Charity McCarren, you will promise me that from now on in matters concerning your personal safety, you will obey me without question."

She strained against him. "Jack McCarren, that is an absolutely feudal attitude."

"Comply with it," he said, "or suffer the consequences."

She narrowed her eyes. "What are they?"

He considered. She was too fearless to threaten with the stiff paddling that would have satisfied him enormously at that point. His nimble brain found another solution.

He freed her and pushed himself off the bed.

"Protecting you is an important part of my duties as your husband," he said, moving around the room, gathering robe, slippers, hairbrush. "If you resist it, then it's never been my way to perform halfway. All my other duties will be held in abeyance until such time..."

Charity followed him around the room as he collected what it looked like he would need to spend the night in another room.

"Jack!" she said, yanking him around to face her. "That isn't fair! You're using our lovemaking as a weapon to force me to obedience."

He gently removed her hand from his arm and walked around her to his bedside table. "Strong feelings require strong measures." He took his ring of factory keys and tossed them into one of the slippers balanced atop the pile of things in his arm.

She leaned a shoulder against the post at the foot of the bed and watched him walk around her. "You won't last a week."

"You underestimate me," he said, heading for the door. "I have considerable self-control when I choose to apply it."

Charity slipped between him and the door and flattened herself against it. "I will not come in search of you."

He did not appear upset. "After the past few days, a rest would be most welcome."

"You'll miss me," she warned softly.

"No doubt," he said without a change of expression. "Now will you let me pass?"

Charity looked into his steady dark eyes and accepted defeat. She wouldn't be able to stand one night without him, much less however long it would take to lower his stubborn defenses. He'd conceded much in the past twenty-four hours. She supposed she could compromise.

She pushed the teetering pile out of his arms, and everything fell to the floor.

He looked from the debris on the carpet to her eyes with a darkening purpose. "You know," he said, blocking her against the door with a hand on either side of her head, "you're begging for my second alternative to handling this disagreement—turning you over my knee and paddling you until you see it my way."

She sighed and leaned forward to wrap her arms around his waist. "Neither plan will be necessary," she said, reveling in the warm and solid feel of him against her. "Just what, specifically, must I concede?"

His hands left the door and came lightly around her. "You heard me, I'm certain."

Her small hand slid up his spinal column. He held on to his control. He wasn't losing this argument.

"Obedience," she said, planting her lips in the open V of his shirt. He held his control by clutching both fists. "In matters of my personal safety."

"*Unquestioned* obedience," he reminded.

She worked on the rest of his buttons. "So, what does this mean?" she asked, glancing tauntingly at him. "That I must consult you before I cross the street?"

Before she knew what had happened, she'd been swept up in his arms and was being carried to the bed.

"Very well," he said calmly. "If you refuse to take me seriously, I'll have to speak a little louder."

The words eliminated the possibility that he was carrying her to the bed to make love to her. She knew she was about to be subjected to his alternate plan.

"I was teasing!" she said quickly as he sat.

"Well, I am not," he replied, and pulled her toward him.

She resisted, falling back limply like a cranky two-year-old. "I concede," she said, breathless and disheveled.

Then added quickly, "You have my unquestioned obedience in matters of my personal safety."

She squealed as he yanked her up. She fell against the mattress, wrapped in his arms.

"That's better," he said, beginning to unfasten the many tiny buttons down the back of her gown. "Now that we've settled that, we can go on to more pleasing subjects."

"What, for instance?"

"Children," he said, kissing the back of her neck as he continued to unbutton. "We've never discussed them."

"Mmm. I love them."

"Good. I think an even distribution of boys and girls would be nice."

"True, but I don't believe it's that easily controlled."

He raised his head to look at her in mock surprise. His eyes were already growing languorous with passion.

"With your organization skills and my ability to produce? I think we should have six boys for another shift at the box factory for me, and six girls who will be able to vote in the presidential election of—" he winced as he calculated "—1924, I believe. Or thereabouts."

Her dress unbuttoned, Charity turned in his arms to wrap hers around his neck and bring him on top of her. She smiled into his eyes, overcome with love for him and the warmth and safety he made her feel.

"So you truly do believe that women should vote. That wasn't simply a political move tonight?"

He brushed a silky strand of hair from her cheek and felt weak with love. For all her talk of independence, he could see his mark of possession in her eyes. She was his, and she knew it. Of course, he accepted with cheerful fatalism, he was hers, as well. A happy arrangement, all in all.

"If they're all as brilliant and insightful as you are," he said, "they certainly should."

She kissed him noisily. "Well spoken, McCarren."

"But if they're all as impetuous and fearless as you are," he said, "I hope they all have patient, understanding husbands."

Bursting with happiness, she found it easy to agree. "Amen to that. Now, about our children. Which should we have first? A boy or a girl?"

He tugged at the neckline of her dress and nipped at the top of a breast. "I think we should give it our all," he said softly, "and try for one of each."

Another notion with which she could hardly disagree.

"Amen again, Jack," she whispered as she pushed at the sleeves of his shirt. "Amen."

* * * * *

Author's Note

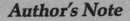

Oregon women were granted the vote in 1912.

Harlequin® Historical

FIRST IMPRESSIONS THAT ARE SURE TO ENDURE!

MARCH MADNESS

It's March Madness time again! Each year, Harlequin Historicals picks the best and brightest new stars in historical romance and brings them to you in one exciting month!

The Heart's Desire by Gayle Wilson—When the hunt for a spy pairs a cynical duke with a determined young woman, caution is thrown to the wind in one night of passion.

Rain Shadow by Cheryl St.John—A widower in need of a wife falls in love with the wrong woman, an Indian-raised sharp-shooter more suited to a Wild West show than to a farm.

My Lord Beaumont by Madris Dupree—Adventure abounds in this tale about a rakish nobleman who learns a lesson in love when he rescues a young stowaway.

Capture by Emily French—The story of a courageous woman who is captured by Algonquin Indians, and the warrior whose dreams foretell her part in an ancient prophecy.

Four exciting historicals by four promising new authors who are certain to become your favorites. Look for them wherever Harlequin Historicals are sold. Don't be left behind!

HHM94

Take 4 bestselling love stories FREE

Plus get a FREE surprise gift!

Special Limited-time Offer

Mail to Harlequin Reader Service®

3010 Walden Avenue
P.O. Box 1867
Buffalo, N.Y. 14269-1867

YES! Please send me 4 free Harlequin Historical™ novels and my free surprise gift. Then send me 4 brand-new novels every month, which I will receive before they appear in bookstores. Bill me at the low price of $3.19 each plus 25¢ delivery and applicable sales tax, if any.* That's the complete price and—compared to the cover prices of $3.99 each—quite a bargain! I understand that accepting the books and gift places me under no obligation ever to buy any books. I can always return a shipment and cancel at any time. Even if I never buy another book from Harlequin, the 4 free books and the surprise gift are mine to keep forever.

247 BPA ANRM

Name _____ (PLEASE PRINT)

Address _____ Apt. No. _____

City _____ State _____ Zip _____

This offer is limited to one order per household and not valid to present Harlequin Historical™ subscribers. *Terms and prices are subject to change without notice. Sales tax applicable in N.Y.

UHIS-94R

©1990 Harlequin Enterprises Limited

Harlequin® Historical

A SON OF BRITAIN, A DAUGHTER OF ROME. ENEMIES BY BIRTH, LOVERS BY DESTINY.

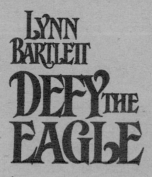

LYNN BARTLETT

DEFY THE EAGLE

From bestselling author Lynn Bartlett comes this tale of epic passion and ancient rebellion. Jilana, the daughter of a Roman merchant, and Caddaric, rebel warrior of Britain, are caught in the clash of two cultures amid one of the greatest eras in history.

Coming in February 1994
from Harlequin Historicals

Don't miss it! Available wherever Harlequin Books are sold.

HHB1G1

My Valentine 1994

Celebrate the most romantic day of the year with
MY VALENTINE 1994
a collection of original stories, written by
four of Harlequin's most popular authors...

MARGOT DALTON
MURIEL JENSEN
MARISA CARROLL
KAREN YOUNG

Available in February, wherever
Harlequin Books are sold.

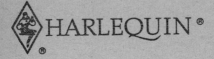

HARLEQUIN®

VAL94